PRAISE FOR THE NOVELS OF

#1 NEW YORK TIMES BESTSELLING AUTHOR BARBARA FREETHY

"Powerful and absorbing...sheer hold-your-breath suspense."

— *NYT Bestselling Author* ***Karen Robards*** *on Don't Say A Word*

"A fabulous, page-turning combination of romance and intrigue. Fans of Nora Roberts and Elizabeth Lowell will love this book." *NYT Bestselling Author Kristin Hannah on Golden Lies* "In the tradition of LaVyrle Spencer, gifted author Barbara Freethy creates an irresistible tale of family secrets, riveting adventure and heart-touching romance."

— *NYT Bestselling Author* ***Susan Wiggs*** *on Summer Secrets*

"This book has it all: heart, community, and characters who will remain with you long after the book has ended. A wonderful story."

— *NYT Bestselling Author* ***Debbie Macomber*** *on Suddenly One Summer* "

"Freethy has a gift for creating complex characters."

— ***Library Journal***

"Barbara Freethy is a master storyteller with a gift for spinning tales about ordinary people in extraordinary situations and drawing readers into their lives." -- *Romance Reviews Today* "Freethy's skillful plotting and gift for creating sympathetic characters will ensure that few dry eyes will be left at the end of the story."

— ***Publishers Weekly*** *on The Way Back Home*

"Freethy skillfully keeps the reader on the hook, and her tantalizing and believable tale has it all– romance, adventure, and mystery."

— ***Booklist*** *on Summer Secrets*

"A page-turner that engages your mind while it tugs at your heartstrings...Don't Say A Word has made me a Barbara Freethy fan for life!"

— *NYT Bestselling Author* ***Diane Chamberlain*** *on Don't Say a Word*

"I love *The Callaways*! Heartwarming romance, intriguing suspense and sexy alpha heroes. What more could you want?"

— *NYT Bestselling Author* ***Bella Andre***

"If you love nail-biting suspense and heartbreaking emotion, Silent Run belongs on the top of your to-be-bought list. I could not turn the pages fast enough."

NYT Bestselling Author ***Mariah Stewart*** *on Silent Run*

"Hooked me from the start and kept me turning pages throughout all the twists and turns. Silent Run is powerful romantic intrigue at its best."

— *NYT Bestselling Author* ***JoAnn Ross*** *on Silent Run*

"An absorbing story of two people determined to unravel the secrets, betrayals, and questions about their past. The story builds to an explosive conclusion that will leave readers eagerly awaiting Barbara Freethy's next book."

— *NYT Bestselling Author* ***Carla Neggars*** *on Don't Say A Word*

"Freethy is at the top of her form. Fans of Nora Roberts will find a similar tone here, framed in Freethy's own spare, elegant style."

— ***Contra Costa Times*** *on Summer Secrets*

"In the tradition of Lavyrle Spencer, gifted author Barbara Freethy creates an irresistible tale of family secrets, riveting adventure and heart-touching romance."

— *NYT Bestselling Author* ***Susan Wiggs*** *on Summer Secrets*

PERILOUS TRUST

Off The Grid: FBI Series

BARBARA FREETHY

HYDE STREET PRESS
Published by Hyde Street Press
1325 Howard Avenue, #321, Burlingame, California 94010

© Copyright 2017 by Hyde Street Press

Perilous Trust is a work of fiction. All incidents, dialogue and all characters are products of the author's imagination and are not to be construed as real. Any resemblance to persons living or dead is entirely coincidental.

All rights reserved. In accordance with the U.S. Copyright Act of 1976, the scanning, uploading, and electronic sharing of any part of this book without the permission of the publisher is unlawful piracy and theft of the author's intellectual property. No part of this book may be used or reproduced in any manner whatsoever without written permission except in the case of brief quotations embodied in critical articles and reviews.

Printed in the United States of America

Cover design by Damonza.com

ISBN: 978-1-94441732-1

Prologue

"Sophie, I'm sorry." It wasn't the best start to the worst message he would ever have to leave, but it had to be done. He'd spent the last six hours creating a trail that would hopefully lead away from his daughter. He'd left New York City hours ago and was now driving along lonely, rural, winding roads in northern New Jersey, the beautiful scenery barely registering in his brain as he escaped from his life.

His left hand tightened on the steering wheel as he cleared his throat and tried to find the right words. "I've made a mistake—more than one. I thought I could stay out of the mud, but it turns out that I'm covered in it. I don't have time to explain, but—" He stopped abruptly as the beep from her voicemail cut him off.

He punched in her number again, knowing she wouldn't answer. It was two o'clock on a Wednesday, and she'd be teaching a class in archaeology at NYU, probably getting her students ready to go on one of the summer digs starting next month. Ever since she was a little girl, Sophie had been fascinated with history, with the past, with finding answers to century-old questions. Now she taught during the school year and went on digs in the summer—the perfect combination.

It had been worth it—giving Sophie everything she

wanted. Hadn't it?

He glanced back at the phone. With Sophie's schedule, he doubted she'd get the messages for a few more hours. Maybe by then he'd be somewhere safe and they could actually talk. But if that didn't happen...he had to tell her what to do. He couldn't wait another second. He couldn't keep pretending everything would be all right. He'd been preparing for weeks...just in case. He now had to execute the plan.

Her voicemail encouraged him to leave another message.

"Remember how much your mom loved spring cleaning and how we hated to get rid of the things we loved—like my beer bottle collection? Remember our secret stash? Well, I've left you something there. But in order to get it, you'll need to find the key that's hidden away at your favorite place in the world."

He was being cryptic, but he couldn't risk the information being heard by the wrong person. Hopefully, only Sophie would be able to figure out what he was talking about. While she might wonder why he was sending her so far away, he needed to get her out of town as quickly as possible. That would buy her time.

"Get the key and follow my instructions," he continued. "I know you'll have a million questions about this message. You'll try to call me, and I won't answer. You'll wonder why I didn't talk to you before now. You'll think twice about doing what I'm asking you to do, but you can't do that, Sophie. Above all, you have to be safe. You have to live a long life. It may not be the life you planned, but it can still be happy. So, no questions, no second thoughts, no wondering if there is another way. You can't trust anyone. Not the police and definitely not the Bureau—no one. Whoever you think might be my friend or yours—*isn't*." The phone cut off again.

"Dammit," he swore, seeing a vehicle appear on the road behind him. It could be just another motorist, but as the car picked up speed, he realized that his sins were gaining on him fast. He hadn't been smart enough. He hadn't done enough to make a clean exit.

He pressed his foot down on the gas pedal, his small sedan almost trembling with the speed required to get away. He'd once been an incredible driver, able to avoid almost any tail, but so many of his skills had broken down in recent years, he could barely remember the person he used to be. He had many regrets, but if he lost his life on this road, maybe no one would ever really know why. *Maybe that was a good thing.*

He called Sophie again. "If I can find a way out of this, I will. In the meantime, do exactly what I told you. I want you to know how proud I am," he said, his voice choking with emotion. "Everything I did—the choices I made—were to make our lives better, especially your life. I feel sick at the heartache you may have to go through. The last thing I ever wanted to do was hurt you. You have always been my everything. If something happens to me, don't try to find out who is responsible. Don't go to my house. Don't go to your apartment. Don't trust anyone, especially not those you think are my friends."

He should give her a name, but then she might think that was the only person to avoid, and there were more…more than he knew…

"Just run," he continued. "Get rid of your phone as soon as you finish listening to these messages, so they can't track you. I'm sorry again, Sophie. I hope you can make a new life for yourself, and I pray one day you'll be able to forgive—"

The phone flew out of his hand as his car was rammed from behind. He pushed the pedal all the way to the floor, but the vehicle behind him had more power. He swerved around another turn, down a straightaway, to a harder curve. He saw the narrow bridge ahead as his car took another hit.

He yanked the wheel, trying to regain control, but the car skidded across the concrete. He was headed straight for the guardrail. He had some impossible hope he might clear the water and land on the other side of the pond, but that would take a miracle.

The last thing he deserved was a miracle.

One

Her second-year university students were restless and as eager as she was for the academic year to be over. It was the first of June, and with the unusually hot weather, Sophie Parker could see their gazes straying to the windows as she spoke, the lure of summer interesting them far more than the study questions for the final exam they would take next week. She couldn't blame them.

Six weeks from now, she'd be out of the classroom, too, taking eight of these students on an archaeological dig in Egypt. They would finally get a chance not just to read about history but to experience it, to feel the heavy, haunting atmosphere at a century-old site, to dig for something real, something from the past, something that could change what they knew of history.

Discovery was an addicting thrill—one she'd never been able to shake. Unfortunately, she had to limit the thrilling moments to the summer months. The rest of the year, she was a professor at NYU, where she shared her passion with her college students.

Glancing over at the clock, she realized it was one minute to four. *Time to free them for the weekend.*

"That's it," she said. "I'll see you for our final exam next

Wednesday. If you have questions, you can email me, or come by my office hours on Monday from ten to noon. Good luck with your studying."

As the class ended, she answered a few questions about the exam, then gathered her things together. She was about to leave when a man in a dark suit entered the room. He was in his fifties and had short, pepper-gray hair and dark eyes. He walked toward her with a deliberate, purposeful step, the expression on his face intensely serious.

Peter Hunt was an FBI agent, and one of her father's best friends. He'd gone to Yale with her dad. He'd been in her parents' wedding. He'd been Uncle Peter to her for as long as she could remember. And he had never, *ever*, visited her at work.

A chill ran through her.

Something was wrong—terribly wrong.

Following Peter into the classroom was Karen Leigh—a tall, stylish blonde in her late-thirties, wearing a navy-blue pencil skirt and cream-colored silky blouse. Despite the hot weather, Karen looked impeccably cool.

She'd met Karen once when she'd stopped in at her dad's office. He'd told her how much he respected Karen's instincts, which was why he'd made her assistant special agent in charge of the organized crime division, of which he was the head. The fact that both Peter and Karen had come to see her did not bode well.

She tried to stay calm, not jump to conclusions, breathe, but her chest was tight, and she couldn't get any air into her lungs.

"Sophie," Peter said, his dark eyes somber. "I'm afraid we have terrible news."

"I'm sorry, Sophie," Karen added, compassion in her gaze.

"Sorry about what?" She didn't really want an answer, because she knew that whatever they were going to say would not be good. "Where's my dad? Has something happened to him?"

"He was in an accident," Peter said gently. "A car accident. He didn't make it, Sophie."

"What?" she gasped, putting a hand to her heart. "What do you mean—he didn't make it?"

"Your father drove through a guardrail and flipped his car into a pond. He died at the scene." Peter delivered the statement in a slow, purposeful manner. "I'm truly sorry, Sophie. This is not the kind of news I ever wanted to give you."

She immediately started shaking her head in denial. "There must be some mistake. My father is not dead. He can't be dead. He's healthy. He runs every day. He's going to barbecue ribs for me this weekend—his famous pork ribs. We're getting together on Sunday to watch the Yankees. We're going to talk about my trip to Egypt next month." She blew out a breath. "Oh, God!" Her legs felt suddenly weak as she realized none of those things were going to happen.

Peter grabbed her arm and led her to the chair by her desk.

She practically fell into her seat.

He squatted down in front of her and looked into her eyes. "Breathe, Sophie."

"Tell me it's not true." She silently implored him to say it was some awful joke, but she could see the pain in his gaze.

"I wish I could. I really do. Alan was a good friend. I can't believe he's gone, and I know how difficult this is going to be for you. The two of you became so close after your mom died."

Burning tears pressed at her eyes. She put a hand to her mouth, feeling like she was going to throw up. His words reminded her of the last time she'd heard horrible news. But her mom had been sick for years. They'd said their good-byes more than once. She'd known the end was coming, and it had been a blessing, because her mom had been suffering.

But this? This sudden end to her dad's vibrant life was impossible to accept. It had been him and her against the world since she was sixteen.

"Where did it happen? The accident? Was it here in the city?" she asked.

"No, it was a few hours away—in northern New Jersey," he replied, as he stood up.

"What? What was he doing way over there?" she asked, even more confused. "Did it have to do with a case?"

"To be honest, we're not sure why he was in that location," Karen interjected. "We're trying to figure that out. When did you last speak to your dad?"

She had to think for a minute. "Two days ago—Monday night. We haven't seen each other in a few weeks, and he asked me to come by on Sunday. I didn't actually commit to going to his barbecue, because I have finals next week, and I need to finish writing the test this weekend." She drew in another tight breath. "You're sure there's not a mistake?"

"I'm sure," Peter said. "There's no mistake."

"Was there another car involved? Were other people hurt?"

"We're not sure if another vehicle was involved."

His answer confused her more. "My father just drove off the side of the road? That doesn't make sense."

"It appears he was driving at a high rate of speed."

"What time did it happen?"

"Around two o'clock this afternoon."

Two hours ago. Her dad had died two hours ago, and she hadn't known, hadn't felt anything change. How could that be?

"Where is my father now? I want to see him."

"He's at the medical examiner's office in New Jersey, and you can't see him yet, Sophie," Peter said. "Not until they're done with the examination."

She looked at him in confusion. "They're doing an autopsy?"

"Yes. We need to know if Alan had a medical emergency, or if there were any substances impairing his judgment," Peter replied.

"My father did not take drugs. He was in great health. He

barely drank. You know that." Anger ran through her. How could Peter speak so clinically about her father?

"It's protocol," he said. "We're also working with the New Jersey police to determine whether another vehicle might have caused the incident and left the scene."

"Who found him?"

"There was a 911 call from a hiker. He saw the accident from a good distance away, so he couldn't render aid, but the police arrived within minutes. It appears that Alan was killed on impact, Sophie. He didn't suffer."

"But you don't know that for sure, because no one was there for at least a few minutes." The thought of her father knowing he was trapped and dying made her sick to her stomach.

"Sophie," Karen said, bringing her focus back to the conversation. "I know you're devastated by this news. We all are. But I need to ask you a few questions."

"Like what?"

"Did your father tell you about any problems in his life, at work, with friends or coworkers?"

"No, but he rarely spoke about his job with me. He always said there was so much he couldn't talk about that it was easier just to avoid everything."

"What about a woman? Was there someone in his life?" Karen continued.

"I don't know. He went out to dinner sometimes. He had female friends. He didn't discuss them, and I didn't ask."

"When you spoke to your father on Monday, did he say anything about any meetings or plans he had this week?" Karen continued.

"I don't think so. We mostly talked about me and the archaeological dig I'm organizing." She felt guilty now that she hadn't asked her dad more about how he was doing and what was going on in his life. Perhaps she'd missed some important clue or sign of what was to come.

"What about Harrison Delano?" Karen asked. "Your father had a dinner on his calendar with Mr. Delano scheduled for tonight. I understand from Peter that Mr. Delano was a friend from Yale."

"Yes. They kept in touch." She glanced at Peter. "You know Harrison. Why don't you just ask him?"

"We will; we haven't had a chance yet," Peter replied. "We wanted to speak to you first."

"Why are you asking me these questions? What do my dad's dinner plans have to do with his death?"

"Karen has been going through Alan's calendar to see if we can find any clues," Peter said.

"I'm trying to piece together a timeline for the week," Karen added. "Your dad was in the office yesterday and left before three, which is early for him. He didn't come in this morning, and he didn't call in sick. I tried to reach him on the phone several times, but he didn't pick up or return my calls. I was concerned because we have several important cases that require his attention, so I went to his house, but he didn't answer. As far as I can ascertain, the last person to speak to him was the security guard in our office building when he left yesterday afternoon. I would love to find someone else."

"Well, it wasn't me." She licked her lips, realizing the truth behind the questions. "You don't think it was an accident, do you? Because FBI agents don't just drive their cars off mountain roads."

"We're not discounting any possibility, Sophie," Peter said. "Figuring out what happened to your father is our top priority."

"We will get answers," Karen promised, determination in her eyes. "Your father was loved and respected by many people in the New York field office and all over the country. We will do right by him."

"I hope so." At the mention of her father's extended network of friends, she realized that she needed to start making calls, think about planning a funeral, talk to her father's estate attorney, go to his house and get the big notebook from the drawer in his desk that he'd told her had all the information she would need if anything ever happened to him.

She'd never wanted to look at that book or open that drawer, even though he'd reminded her every time he'd updated it. After her mother had died, he'd realized how difficult it was to find passwords, and he'd vowed he'd never leave her with messy problems to clean up. She'd told him she didn't want to think about him being gone. They had years—decades—to get organized.

Another tear slipped out of her eye, and she brushed it away with her fingers. There would be time for crying later. "I need to start making calls."

"I'm happy to help with arrangements, Sophie," Peter said, pain in his gaze now that they'd gotten past the questions. "There's no need to rush into anything. You can take your time."

"I can't even begin to think of everything I need to do," she murmured. "All the people I need to tell."

"I can take care of the Yale group," he offered. "Harrison Delano, Michael Brennan, Senator Raleigh, Diane Lewis and anyone else I can think of. I need to interview each of them anyway to find out when they last spoke to your father."

"That would be good."

"And, of course, everyone at the Bureau—in the New York field office—and around the world will be notified," Karen put in. "Your father mentored a great many agents when he was an instructor at Quantico." She paused. "I've had the opportunity to experience his generosity and brilliance firsthand. Alan made me the agent that I am, so I can assure you that we will find out what happened to him. We will do him proud."

"Thank you. I appreciate that."

"Why don't we take you home now?" Peter suggested. "We can continue this conversation at your apartment. As much as I wish we could just discuss funeral plans, we have quite a few more questions to ask you, and I think doing that at your place would be the best idea. You'll be more comfortable there."

She doubted she'd be comfortable anywhere, and the last thing she wanted to do right now was answer questions. "I need a little time," she said, their expectant gazes and determination to jump right into crime solving a bit overwhelming. "Thank you for the offer of a ride, but I only live a few blocks away, and I could use some air."

"We'll walk with you then," Karen said.

She frowned. "I—I don't want to be rude, but I really need some time to myself."

"You're right. Look, why don't you go home and regroup?" Peter suggested. "We'll meet you at your place in two hours—say around six thirty? We'll bring Indian food. As I recall, it's your favorite."

"I'm not hungry." She couldn't imagine eating ever again.

"I'll still bring something," he said. "It's important that we talk sooner rather than later, Sophie. We don't want to let the trail go cold."

"But I don't know anything about my dad's activities."

"You might know more than you realize."

"All right," she said, getting to her feet. She didn't want to argue; she just wanted to be alone.

"Good. And please don't speak to any reporters before we speak again," he added.

His statement made her realize that her father's death was going to be publicized. She would need to make her calls fast. She grabbed her bag and led the way out of her classroom.

They parted company at the stairwell, and she went up to her third-floor office alone.

She sat down at her desk and stared at the framed photo taken of her and her father at her college graduation. He'd gotten her a lei from Hawaii, and the beautiful pink flowers added color to her white gown. Hawaii had been one of their favorite vacation spots. Her parents had gone there on their honeymoon, and every year after that, they'd made a trip to the islands. They'd even thrown her mother's ashes in the sea off Oahu in a beautiful twilight ceremony. It was what her mom had wanted.

Where would her dad want to be buried? She had no idea. She would have to go to his house and check the book—the *damned* book.

How could she do this again? She was twenty-eight years old and she was going to have to bury a second parent. It wasn't fair.

She breathed through the pain, knowing she was barely holding it together, but she had to think about what to do next. First, she had to get up. She had to go home, make calls, tell people what had happened. The only relative she had left was her Aunt Valerie, her mother's sister, who lived in Australia with her husband and children. She hadn't seen them since her mom had died twelve years ago. But before that, her aunt had been a mother to her while her mom was sick. She definitely needed to call her aunt.

She reached into her bag and pulled out her phone. She kept it on silent during the day, and she'd had back-to-back classes since noon, so she hadn't checked it in hours.

Now, she saw four voicemails from the same number—it wasn't a number she recognized.

Telemarketers didn't usually call that many times or leave messages.

Her dad's voice came across the speaker, stabbing her in the heart.

For a moment, she thought that Peter and Karen were wrong, that her dad was alive, that there was some mistake, but as she listened to the messages, she heard emotions in her father's voice she'd never heard before. He sounded frantic, worried, terrified, and his words were rambling and not making sense.

The first message ended abruptly, and as she moved through the rest of the voicemails, her bewilderment grew. Her dad was talking in riddles. Setting up clues to hunt for, offering apologies, telling her to be careful, not to trust anyone, but never saying exactly what was going on, why he was calling, where he was, what he was doing.

The last message cut off in mid-word. She heard a

horrible crash and then nothing.

Her stomach turned over.

Had she just heard the moment when her father had driven through the guardrail?

Had he died because he wasn't paying attention to the road, because he was talking on the phone?

Or had he died because whatever danger he was running from had caught up to him?

She called the number back, but there was no connection, no service, nothing.

As she stared at the number, she wondered why her dad had called her from a phone other than the one he normally used. Not that it was that unusual for him to have more than one phone. He'd always had a separate phone for his work as an FBI agent and one for personal use. But he hadn't used either of those, and she wondered why.

He was obviously in trouble. He'd talked about trust and making bad choices. What were those choices? What had he done? And why hadn't he called someone for help—someone like Peter or Karen? Surely, he trusted Peter. They'd been friends forever.

But he hadn't called Peter; he'd called her. He'd told her what he needed her to do, and she would do it.

Jerking to her feet, she threw her phone into her bag and left the office.

She walked as quickly as she could to the edge of campus, then joined the streams of people on the crowded streets of New York. Everything felt surreal. Life was going on normally for everyone else, but not for her.

Sweat beaded her brow as the summer heat beat down on her head, but she couldn't let the weather slow her down. She suddenly felt as if time was not on her side. Peter and Karen were coming by her apartment at six thirty.

She needed to be gone by then. She'd change her clothes, pack a quick bag, and get in her car.

But those plans came to a crashing halt when she turned the corner and saw two men get out of a dark SUV and head into her building. They wore slacks and button-down shirts, and while they didn't look dangerous, there was something about them that made her pause.

Through the windows in her building stairwell, she could see the men going up to the upper floors. Her gut told her they were on their way to her apartment.

Her dad's words rang through her head: *Don't trust anyone, especially not anyone from the police department or the FBI. Get rid of your phone as soon as you finish listening to these messages, so they can't track you.*

She took her phone out of her bag and stared at it for an indecisive minute. He'd told her to throw it away, but if she did that, she'd never hear his voice again.

She couldn't do it—*not yet.*

She'd hold on to it for a while longer.

But she would do what else he'd asked. Turning on her heels, she walked in the other direction. She had to find a place to hide, to listen to the messages again, and figure out what to do next.

As she tried to blend into the crowd, she felt more alone than she ever had before. *Was there anyone who could help her?*

She had friends, but how could she bring them into this situation? How could she put them in danger? Especially when she didn't know what the danger was exactly.

She had to follow her dad's instructions, as cryptic as they were. He'd made it clear she was in danger, and since he was dead, she had to believe him. She had to find a way to save herself.

She pulled out her phone again and let the voicemails play through her ear as she walked away from her life.

Two

Special Agent Damon Wolfe hated summer, especially the kind of hot, sticky, New York City heat that made him sweat at six o'clock at night. In his life, everything bad that had ever happened had occurred during some kind of intense heat wave. Coincidence, maybe, but that possibility didn't make the season any more appealing, and it was only June.

He should have thought about the humid summer heat when he'd agreed to come to New York and work for his mentor, Alan Parker, who ran the organized crime division out of the FBI's New York field office. But when Alan had called with a job offer three weeks ago, he'd had no choice but to say yes. Alan had been his instructor at the FBI Academy in Quantico, and he'd mentored him after graduation as well. He had always wanted to work for the best, and Alan was the best.

But since Damon had arrived in town a week ago, he'd been finishing reports on a case he'd been working for the past two years, so he hadn't seen much of Alan yet. Alan had also been in and out of the building and had told him he would speak to him soon about his new assignment. He was hoping that assignment would involve Wyatt Tanner, the friend and agent who had him now headed to a park by the

East River instead of to a bar for a cold beer.

Wyatt had sent him a cryptic SOS in a private chat room they'd set up for emergencies four years ago while they were at the academy. Six people knew about the chat room, but he'd been the only one to respond. He had no idea if the others were still watching the forum, since it was rare that anyone used it these days, but he still made it a point to check in every day.

Wyatt was working undercover with a crime organization, and any contact outside his handler—which was Alan Parker—could jeopardize his cover. Which meant Wyatt was in trouble.

As Damon neared the park, his gaze swept the surrounding area. There was a basketball court with two hoops and groups of teenagers making use of both. A nearby playground area was filled with families. Everything looked very normal, innocent—a relaxing summer evening in a tiny space of green, in a city filled with high-energy people, endless concrete, frustrating traffic jams, and very tall buildings.

A furtive movement in a cluster of trees by the river caught his eye. It was Wyatt—or at least a shadowy version of him.

Wyatt hadn't just lost a few pounds; he'd dropped at least twenty, his ripped, faded jeans hanging low on his hips. His brown hair was longer than Damon had ever seen it. Wyatt also had a full beard going, and as Damon drew closer he saw an abundance of tattoos on Wyatt's arms and a multitude of bruises on his face, as well as a nasty gash on his forehead. His left eye was almost swollen shut.

"What the hell happened to you?" he asked.

"Got jumped," Wyatt replied.

"Are you all right?" He was disturbed by the bright lights in Wyatt's eyes, the jerky way his gaze darted in every direction, as he nervously rocked back and forth on his heels.

"Anyone follow you?" Wyatt demanded.

"No. What's going on? Are you made?"

"Not sure. Probably. Yes."

Wyatt's clipped responses deepened his worry.

"Are you on something?"

"No. Don't think so. Not sure. Haven't slept in two days." Wyatt took his hands out of his pockets and slapped his cheeks, as if to keep himself awake.

"You need to go to a hospital, Wyatt. You're messed up."

"Not safe. Someone tried to kill me, Damon."

"Who?"

"Don't know. Couldn't see. Too dark. Barely got away."

"Did you contact Alan?"

"I was supposed to meet Alan where it happened. I think he set me up."

"No way," he said emphatically, shocked by Wyatt's unexpected words.

"Then why hasn't he answered my messages? I've been trying to talk to him for two days. I get nothing back."

Frowning, he couldn't answer that question. "He hasn't been in the office much this week. In fact, I've barely seen him since he asked me to join his team."

"He told me he was bringing you in a few weeks ago. I thought it was a good thing. He's off his game. I've been feeling it for months." Wyatt paused, his lips tightening. "Or maybe he's not off his game. Maybe he knows exactly what he's doing."

He had no idea what Wyatt was talking about, but it was clear he needed help. "Look, I don't know what's going on, but you need medical attention. You're in bad shape."

"You think I don't know that?" Wyatt asked angrily. "But if I come out of the shadows, I'm dead."

"Then we'll keep you in the shadows. There has to be a doctor in the city the Bureau uses. There was one in DC."

"Can't trust anyone at the Bureau. Someone is a traitor. Maybe Alan. Maybe someone else."

"Well, you can trust me." As he finished speaking, his phone buzzed.

At the sound, Wyatt jumped like he'd been shot, backing

up a few feet, his dark eyes blazing with fear and fury. "Did you tell someone you were coming to meet me?"

"No, I didn't. This is from Bree." He turned his phone around so Wyatt could see the message. "She's getting back into town tomorrow. She just finished up a case in Michigan and wants to have lunch and catch up. I haven't seen her since I moved here."

For a brief moment, Wyatt's expression softened and his gaze cleared, as if he were remembering the days when he and Bree and Wyatt had first become friends. They'd met at Quantico on the first day of training, eager to become agents, to make their mark on the world. Hard to believe that was four years ago. So much had happened since then.

His explanation seemed to ease the stress in Wyatt's eyes, but then a car came speeding around the corner.

Wyatt grabbed Damon's arm and pulled him into the thicket of trees as the black SUV stopped in the street next to the basketball court, its engine idling.

"What did you do?" Wyatt demanded, fear as well as anger in his eyes now. "What the hell did you do, Damon?"

"Nothing. I didn't do anything. I have no idea who is in that car."

"You're lying."

He was further shocked to feel the hard nuzzle of a gun against his side, and with Wyatt in the condition he was in, he wasn't at all sure Wyatt wouldn't shoot him. "I'm not lying, Wyatt. I didn't tell anyone you contacted me. I'm on your side."

"Or pretending to be. Just like Alan."

"Alan would never give you up, Wyatt. He wouldn't do that."

"I'm no longer surprised by what people will do, given enough motivation," Wyatt said cynically.

"You're exhausted. You're not thinking straight. You need to sleep and eat. Come to my apartment. Once you're rested, we can talk. We'll figure things out."

Wyatt looked like he was considering the offer, then he

stiffened as the doors on the double-parked vehicle suddenly opened. As a jean-clad leg came out of the car, Wyatt said, "Gotta go," and took off through the trees.

Damon was torn between going after him and seeing who was in the vehicle.

A second later, three male teenagers, one with a basketball in his hands, exited the SUV. They headed straight for the court. They weren't trouble, and if Wyatt had been operating on normal brain cells, he would have seen that.

He moved toward the river in the direction that Wyatt had gone, but his friend had vanished. He spent ten more minutes looking for him, then gave up. Wyatt was better than anyone at disappearing.

As he thought about their disjointed conversation, he couldn't believe Alan had set Wyatt up. But if Wyatt's cover was blown—and judging by his appearance, someone had tried to kill him—then Wyatt was clearly in danger. And he wasn't going to keep himself alive as jumpy and paranoid as he now was. Wyatt had always been sharply intuitive and a chameleon, easily able to blend into any group, which made him perfect for undercover work, but that guy didn't exist anymore.

He debated what to do. Pulling out his phone, he punched in Alan's personal number. He wouldn't tell him he'd met up with Wyatt yet, but he'd feel him out, see what Alan had to say.

Unfortunately, Alan's phone went to voicemail.

He debated for another second, then tried his work number. To his surprise, it wasn't Alan who picked up the call; it was a woman.

"Agent Leigh," she said crisply. "Who's calling?"

He was surprised to hear her voice. Karen was the assistant special agent in charge of the organized crime division, but she didn't answer Alan's phone.

Something was wrong.

"Karen, it's Damon. I'm looking for Alan."

"I had his calls transferred to me."

"Why?"

"You don't know?"

"Know what?" A bad feeling crept down the back of his spine.

"Alan is dead, Damon. He died this afternoon."

"What?" His hand tightened around the phone. "What are you talking about?"

"He was killed in a single vehicle accident in a rural area in northern New Jersey."

"My God. That's…" He had no words.

"I know. It's tragic," she said.

For the first time, he heard a tremor in her voice.

"And it doesn't look like it was an accident," she continued. "He was traveling at a high rate of speed and there were no skid marks, no evidence that he attempted to brake before crashing into a pond."

"Any witnesses?"

"A hiker—from almost a mile away. He didn't see much."

"Other vehicles?"

"The witness thought he saw another car on the road, but he was so stunned by the accident scene that he wasn't certain. He did call 911 and the police got there quickly, but it was too late."

"I can't believe this," he muttered, his pulse racing, his head hammering with questions and a deep-rooted pain that was starting to take hold.

Alan was dead? How was that possible?

"None of us can believe it," Karen said. "Did he tell you where he was going today—why he was in New Jersey? He didn't show up for work, and he didn't call in sick."

"I haven't spoken to him since Monday. He said he had some things going on, and since I was finishing up my case on MDT, we agreed to speak next week." He paused, wondering if Alan's death had any connection to the attempt made on Wyatt's life. Wyatt thought Alan had set him up, but maybe someone had set them both up. He wanted to ask

Karen, but after Wyatt's paranoia and now Alan's death, he didn't want to say too much without thinking everything through.

"I have to go," Karen said. "There's a lot going on."

"What can I do to help?"

"We're going to be working all night to see if we can identify anyone who might have posed a threat to Alan, but with the number of cases he's worked on the last twenty-plus years, it's going to be a long list."

"I'll be in shortly." He cleared his throat. "What about Alan's daughter? Has she been notified?" His stomach twisted again at the thought of Sophie receiving the horrific news.

"Peter and I spoke to her several hours ago. She was—shattered."

His heart split apart at the thought of the beautiful blonde with the warm, gold-flecked, brown eyes, irresistible smile, and soft, sexy, kissable lips. He hadn't seen her in four years, not since the one night they'd spent together—a night that never should have happened.

Since then, he'd tried *not* to hear about Sophie. When Alan had brought her up on the odd occasion, he'd quickly changed the subject. She was a part of his past, and that's where he'd been determined to leave her.

But now...

He could only imagine the pain she was in. He felt like someone had just torn off his right arm, and Alan was only his mentor, not his father. Sophie had to be dying inside.

"How—how is she doing?" he asked, feeling as if the question was completely ridiculous, because of course she wasn't doing well.

"I don't know. Peter and I spoke to her around four. We told her we'd meet her at her apartment around six thirty. She wanted some time to catch her breath and regroup. When we got here, we found her door open, and her apartment trashed."

"You're at Sophie's apartment now?" he asked, his pulse quickening.

"Yes."

"And Sophie?"

"No sign of her. We're trying to trace her phone. Hopefully, she's just taking a walk or went to see a friend. Do you know any of her friends? You and Alan have been close for a long time. Do you know Sophie as well?"

"No," he bit out. "I have no idea who her friends are."

"All right. So, why were you calling Alan? Is it something I can help you with?"

He hesitated, then said, "It doesn't matter now. I'll see you back at the office."

He put the phone in his pocket and let out a breath. Since he'd arrived at the park, his entire world had shifted. First, Wyatt acting paranoid, hyped up, and completely off-balance. Then Alan…

He couldn't believe Alan Parker was dead. The man wasn't even sixty years old yet. He was healthy, fit, and energized—a natural leader, an intelligent boss, a good friend.

He should be used to people vanishing from his life. It had certainly happened often enough, but he never seemed to be ready for it. Not that those people had died; most had just walked away from him.

But this wasn't about him. This was about Alan…and Sophie.

With a quick glance around, his nerves now on edge, he left the shadow of the trees and walked through the park, his thoughts turning to the woman who'd made a huge impression on his life, an impact so big he'd run away from her as fast as he could.

He'd met her at a very, very low moment in his life—and also in hers. They'd both been mourning the loss of a good friend—Jamie Rowland. Jamie and he had been Army buddies for ten years before switching careers to join the FBI. Sophie had known Jamie in her childhood, her father Alan and Jamie's father Vincent having worked together at the Bureau.

He'd met Sophie at Jamie's wake. He hadn't known who

she was beyond the fact that she was a gorgeous blonde, who was hurting as much as he was. Her eyes had held a haunting pain, and her sweet mouth seemed to tremble between gulps of wine and champagne as she came to terms with her grief.

They'd had an instant, intense physical attraction to each other, a desire to lose themselves in a happier place, and for two strangers—a surprisingly deep understanding of what they'd each needed that night.

It was only later—when he'd realized who she was—who her father was—that he'd realized how stupid he'd been to sleep with the daughter of someone who had the power to kick him out of the academy from which he was so close to graduating.

But apparently Sophie had never shared their one-night stand with her father, because Alan had not said a word. And he'd certainly never spoken about it to anyone, especially not to Alan, a man who had helped him shape his new career in the FBI.

Now Alan was dead.

Sophie must be going out of her mind—*wherever she was.*

Was she just crying away her grief in a bar somewhere? Or had someone taken her? The same someone who had forced Alan off the road?

God, he hoped she wasn't in danger, too. But the fact that her apartment had been broken into did not bode well.

He stepped off the curb and raised his hand to hail a cab. A moment later, he was on his way back to the office. While the cab made its way slowly through the city traffic, he pulled out his phone. First, he sent a text to Bree that lunch was on for the next day and that he wanted to talk some baseball with her.

After that, he went on the Internet to visit the same baseball chat room where Wyatt had left him the message. They spoke in coded baseball lingo, each of them using the name of a player from the 1986 World Series Mets team. They'd started the private forum while at Quantico, during missions where they needed an outside way to communicate. They'd always referred to Alan as Coach when they were on academy assignments. Wyatt had been Fernandez, after the lefty All-Star pitcher. He didn't know if Wyatt would check the forum again, but it was his best chance at getting him a message.

He thought for a moment, then typed in: *Coach is dead. Fernandez in trouble. Need the starters back on the field. Who's available?*

Three

Sophie had almost used her credit card to rent a car, but then she'd thought about all the ways her card could be tracked. She didn't know who she was running from, but her father had told her to be careful, especially where law enforcement was concerned, so she'd found an ATM and withdrawn seven hundred dollars in cash, the maximum amount she could take out of her account in one day. Then she'd grabbed a cab to a rental car office and booked the cheapest car she could find.

Her father had told her to go to her happy place and that was five hours away—a lakeshore cabin in the northern Adirondacks. She had no idea why he would send her there to start her on this crazy, sad, frustrating scavenger hunt. Nor did she know why he had spoken so cryptically about protecting herself when he hadn't told her who she needed to protect herself from. A name would have been nice.

Unless, he hadn't known exactly who was dangerous?

Or perhaps he'd run out of time...

How she wished she'd picked up the phone when he'd called, but he probably hadn't expected her to do that. He knew she kept the phone off when she was teaching. *Why hadn't he called her in the morning before she'd gone to work when they could have actually spoken to each other?*

She had so many questions and no answers.

It was still difficult—make that *impossible*—to believe he was dead. It felt like a dream—a very bad dream. If only she could wake up!

Her phone vibrated again, and she knew she had to get rid of it. It had been buzzing off and on for the last thirty minutes.

She picked it up off the console and clicked to hear the new voicemails. It made her angry that there were other voices covering up her dad's voice now. She needed to ditch the phone as he'd asked, but she didn't want to let go of her last connection to him.

The first call was from Peter Hunt. *"Sophie, we're at your apartment, and you're not here. It looks like your place was broken into. I'm concerned about you. Where are you? Please call me back as soon as possible."*

Her apartment had been broken into? Maybe by the two guys she'd seen going into it.

The next call was from her friend, Kathleen, a fellow professor at the university. "*Oh, my God, Sophie. I was just watching the news and heard about your dad's accident. I am so, so sorry. I want to help. Please call me back or come over. I can't believe this has happened. I know how close the two of you were. I want to be there for you. Call me back."*

Maybe she would call Kathleen back—but not now, not yet.

She clicked through to the next voicemail from her friend and neighbor. *"This is Becky, Sophie. I just heard the news. I'm really sorry. But right now, I'm more worried about you. Where are you? There are police in your apartment, and the landlord said your place was broken into, and no one knows where you are. There's a news crew out front, and guys in dark suits knocking on everyone's door asking if they saw anything or heard anyone. I just got home a few minutes ago so I don't know what happened. If you're in trouble, I want to help."*

She was happy now that she hadn't gone into her

building, that she'd followed her instincts and run. Whatever her father had been trying to warn her about was already happening.

She had to follow his directions, however crazy they might seem. She had to be smart and stay safe until she could figure out what was going on.

An exit sign called her attention, and she impulsively moved to the right, getting on a highway going away from her destination. She stayed on the road for ten miles, and then she pulled off to the side, her engine still running.

She picked up her phone and played her dad's messages one last time, trying to burn the words and the sound of his voice into her head. She searched for clues in every sentence, wondering if she was missing something, but she was as confused as ever when she was done, and huge, rolling waves of pain ripped through her, threatening to take her under and drown her in sadness. She couldn't let that happen. She had things she had to do.

"Good-bye, Dad," she whispered.

She got out of the car, put the phone in front of her front tire, then got back behind the wheel and drove over it. She got out once more to check that the phone was shattered. Satisfied, she kicked the pieces into the nearby brush. Once that was done, she returned to the car and pulled back onto the highway. She drove another five miles, then took the next exit and doubled back the way she'd come.

If they traced her phone to this area, hopefully they wouldn't know where she was going next, or at least not right away. She had no doubt that the FBI could find her with all their resources. In fact, all they had to do was talk to Vincent Rowland.

Vincent and her dad had come up together in the FBI and had bought cabins next to each other at the lake over twenty years ago. They had been the best of friends and felt that they needed a place to go where they and their families could be safe. They'd set up layers of secrecy regarding the ownership of the cabins, and when they were there, they used fake names. Her family had been the Framinghams; and the Rowlands were the Baldwins.

It had been a fun game when she was a kid, and on the summer trips to the lake, she'd become good friends with Vincent's son Jamie and his daughter Cassie. Unfortunately, after her mother got sick, trips to the lake had become less frequent. After high school, her dad hadn't wanted to go there anymore; the cabin held too many memories. She'd occasionally gone up with Jamie or Cassie for a weekend, but those outings had also dwindled as their lives moved in different directions.

Jamie had gone into the military. Cassie had moved to California. Vincent had divorced Jamie and Cassie's mother and quit the FBI to travel and play golf, while her father had gone to Quantico for a while to run the academy.

Maybe her father hadn't considered Vincent in his rush to keep her safe from some unnamed danger. Or maybe Vincent was the one person her dad trusted not to betray him.

She frowned, thinking back to the voicemails she'd just listened to. Her father had told her to avoid the FBI, which included his best friend Peter and his number two, Karen Leigh.

Their questions to her now took on different overtones. Had they been interrogating her because they wanted to solve her father's murder, or because they wanted to know what she knew? Hopefully, there would be more clues at the cabin.

Pressing her foot down on the gas, she sped up, careful to stay close to the speed limit; she couldn't risk a traffic stop.

As the hours passed, and her adrenaline rush began to fade, she took a chance and stopped at a drive-through coffee stand so she could make it through the mountains without falling asleep.

She turned on the radio for a distraction, and the music helped for a while until she got to one of Jamie's favorite songs—a song his sister Cassie had played at the wake she'd held for Jamie. The wake had just been for Jamie's friends; the family had had a more formal service a day earlier with an official burial, but Cassie had wanted to toast her brother in a place he'd loved very much, and Sophie had been more than happy to go along.

The last time she'd been on this road had been the weekend of that wake.

While it had been cathartic to be with other people who loved Jamie as much as she had, it had also been incredibly sad. Jamie had been one of her confidants, even more than his sister, because for all his carefree charm and jokes, he was also a deep thinker, and they'd had a lot of really good conversations over the years.

Many of the people at the wake had been coupled-up, including Cassie, who'd brought her boyfriend of the moment.

But she'd been alone—and so had a very attractive, dark-haired man with piercing blue eyes and a gaze that had scorched her soul the first time he'd looked at her.

She'd never felt such a strong, visceral reaction to a man—almost like a punch in the stomach—something so hard it took the air out of your lungs, weakened your legs, made you feel like you could fall if you weren't careful.

Of course, she hadn't been careful.

She'd accepted a glass of wine from him and then another and another. They'd sat by the fire on the beach and talked about Jamie and then the music had started and she'd had the crazy idea to dance. Somehow, they'd ended up far from the beach…

She swallowed a sudden knot in her throat.

Damon Wolfe had come into her life at the absolutely worst possible moment.

She hadn't known anything beyond his first name that night. She hadn't wanted to know. All she'd wanted was him. The pull between them was impossible to resist. She'd never felt such an intense connection, and she didn't want to question it. She just wanted to let herself feel it, and it had truly been amazing.

But when the sun came up, she was alone.

She'd found out later that Damon was training to be an

FBI agent at Quantico and that her father was one of his instructors.

She didn't know if her dad was the reason that Damon had never followed up with her, but it hadn't really mattered. She'd known from the first second she'd met Damon that he wasn't a man she could keep for more than a night. And perhaps it was better that way.

Damon was pursuing his life as an FBI agent, and she was doing the same, following her dreams to be an archaeologist.

She supposed she should be glad now that her father had seen her get her doctorate, had heard about her first discovery, had watched her teach a class, but all she could think about was all the things he wouldn't see…her wedding, her children, the rest of her life...

The pain felt overwhelming, made worse by the fact that she couldn't talk to anyone, couldn't go to her friends for a hug, couldn't share her sorrow with people who had known her father, who knew her. But her dad had told her what she needed to do, and she would do it. Hopefully, one day it would all make sense.

When Damon got into the office, there were a dozen agents gathered around the long table in the conference room adjacent to Peter Hunt's office. Peter Hunt was the special agent in charge of the New York field office, serving just under Walter Holmes, the assistant director in charge. They oversaw a dozen specialized divisions and task forces, one of which was the organized crime division run by Alan Parker.

Karen Leigh, who had been second in charge of Alan's division, stood at the front of the room, giving her thoughts on what organizations might be involved in Alan's death—if his accident had been instigated by one of the crime families or syndicates under his watch.

"We believe these three organizations require the most

scrutiny," Karen said. She pointed to a whiteboard where three names were listed. "The Rasulov group, a Russian crime syndicate operating out of Brighton Beach, led by Sergei Rasulov; the Venturi family, a longtime Italian Mafia family run by brothers, Stefan and Lorenzo Venturi; and lastly, an offshoot of the Japanese Yakuza gang run by a new player Toshi Akita," she said. "Our department will be focusing our investigation on these players, but any other information is vital and welcome."

Karen stepped back, giving the room to Peter Hunt.

"Our top priority, and the directive from Director Holmes, is finding Alan's daughter," Peter said, drawing Damon's attention to the large wall monitor where Sophie's image appeared.

His gut clenched at the sight of her. She'd lived in his head for the past four years, but he'd always tried to blur her features. Now she was staring right at him with her gold-flecked brown eyes, framed by long, black lashes. Her blonde hair fell in thick waves around her shoulders. Her skin was perfect with just a touch of pink on her cheekbones. She had three freckles above her right eyebrow that weren't really noticeable in the photo, but he knew they were there. He also knew there were more on her shoulders and her breasts...

He shook that image out of his head as Peter continued his recap of the night's events.

"Sophie walked out of her office building at NYU shortly before five, as evidenced by the campus security cameras," Peter said. "We're tapping into other cameras along her route home, but don't have that information yet. We're also getting a trace on her phone. We're hopeful that she went to a friend's house and that she wasn't at home when her apartment was broken into, but we need to find her to confirm that. You all know that Alan's daughter was the light of his life. Let's do our best work in not only locating Sophie but also in finding out who killed Alan. Everything else on your list that doesn't require immediate attention takes a backseat."

As Peter ended the meeting, the agents got up to go back

to their cubicles and offices. A few of the women were crying. Others fell into conversation with each other as they mourned Alan's unexpected death.

Damon felt very much alone as he left the conference room. He probably knew Alan as well as anyone in the building, but he'd only been in the office a week, and in this group, he was very much an outsider.

"Damon."

He stopped and turned as Peter came toward him.

"Let's talk in my office," Peter said.

"Sure." He didn't know Peter at all. He had had only one brief conversation with him when Alan had introduced him on his first day of work.

As he followed Peter into his office, Peter motioned for him to close the door behind him.

He did so, then took a chair in front of Peter's desk, noting the pale, tense expression on his face, and sudden drop in energy from what he'd displayed to the group a few moments earlier.

"What can I do for you?" he asked.

"I know Alan asked you to come to New York to work on his team, but Karen said you haven't been assigned to a case yet, which seemed odd to me."

"I've been finishing up some loose ends on a previous case."

"With MDT," Peter said with a nod. "I followed that. You did good work, Damon."

"Thank you. I have to admit I had some civilian help."

"The Monroe family—yes, they turned out to be quite helpful."

"They did," he agreed.

"I'm curious as to why you left DC?"

And he was curious as to why Peter had so many personal questions, but he kept that to himself. "I've always wanted to work for Alan. He's the best—was the best," he amended, feeling another rush of anger and disbelief that Alan's life had been taken. He was going to find out why and do his best to put whoever was responsible behind bars.

"Alan was one of the best agents I've ever worked with," Peter said. "He actually got me into the FBI."

"I didn't realize that."

"Yes. We went to Yale together. I was the cyber nerd of our group. After college, I got involved in computer security systems, and about ten years later, Alan recruited me to work for the Bureau. He changed my life." Peter paused. "He had that impact on a lot of people."

"He was very charismatic," Damon agreed.

"And he could assess talent better than anyone. He knew how to get the best from his people. That's why he did so well at Quantico. He could spot the future heroes from day one."

Damon listened to Peter ramble and had a feeling that they were moving closer to some point, but it was taking a hell of a long time to get there. When Peter finally paused, he said, "What do you really want to ask me?"

Peter straightened, as if realizing he'd gotten lost in his memories. "Alan respected you, Damon. I believe he called you to New York for a specific reason, a problem that he wasn't willing to share with anyone else. And I think that problem got him killed."

Peter's gaze met his, a challenge in his eyes, a dare to refute his words.

"Alan told me that he wanted to talk about my next assignment this week, but we never got a chance to do that. If he had a secret, he didn't share it with me."

"That's a shame. I was hoping you could be more helpful."

"I would like to be helpful, but I think Karen Leigh would know everything that Alan was involved in."

"They were very close, but she told me that he's been acting oddly the past few weeks. He's been secretive, sometimes unreachable. She thought something was going on in his personal life. Now, she's wondering if it was work related."

"I wish I could say I knew."

"So do I," Peter said with a sigh. "We need to find Sophie. I can't bring Alan back, but I can sure as hell try to save his daughter. I assume since you were good friends with Alan that you know Sophie?"

"I met her once years ago."

"You don't know who she might have sought out or where she might have gone if she wanted to get away from everything?"

"Given your history with her dad, I would have thought she'd run to you."

"Yes, I would have thought so, too," Peter said heavily. "Which leads me to believe she didn't go willingly."

His stomach turned at the thought of Sophie being someone's captive. "I hope that's not the case."

"Me, too. Thanks. You can go."

As he headed for the door, Alan's phone buzzed.

"Senator," Peter said. "I know. I can't believe it. A tragic loss."

As Damon closed the door to Peter's office, he wondered which senator had called to offer condolences. He didn't envy Peter having to tell Alan's friends he was dead.

He'd seen a lot of people die—both as a soldier and as an FBI agent—and notifying family and friends was never easy.

He walked back down the hall and took the elevator to his floor. When he got to the cubicle he had yet to feel at home in, he was faced with another surprise—this time a happier one.

The pretty brunette with the light-blue eyes made him feel like he finally had a friend in the building.

"Bree," he said. "I'm glad to see you."

She gave him a hug. "I can't believe Alan is dead. I heard the news when I got off the plane. I thought it had to be a mistake."

"I wish it was." He sat down at his desk as she took the adjacent chair.

"From the number of people in the building at this time of night, I'm assuming it's not an accident," she said.

"No, and worse, Alan's daughter is missing. No one is sure if she ran or if someone got to her."

Bree's gaze clouded with concern. "That's disturbing."

"Her apartment was trashed, searched thoroughly, sofa cushions ripped apart, drawers broken."

"They think she has something."

"Or knows something, but I can't see Alan reading her in on anything to do with his work. He kept her away from his job. He told me once he didn't want her to be part of this world."

"Whoever searched her apartment may not know that. Are there any leads?"

"Not that anyone has shared with me, but I don't know too many people here. Maybe you can get a little more insight."

Bree had been in the New York field office for three months, and while she didn't work in Alan's division and was often out of the building tracking down kidnappers and missing children, she still had more contacts than he did. And he could trust Bree. She was another person from their academy group that Alan had recruited to come to New York. Now that Alan was dead, he couldn't help wondering if there had been some reason Alan had wanted so many of them in New York.

"I'll certainly try to get some information." Bree cast a quick look over her shoulder to make sure no one was in earshot. "We need to talk some baseball."

"Let's take a walk outside."

They didn't speak again until they were out on the sidewalk, a few hundred yards away from the federal building.

"Did you speak to Wyatt?" Bree asked.

"Yes, I met him at a park by the East River earlier tonight. He looked like shit, Bree. He said someone tried to kill him, and it appeared that that person had beaten the crap out of him. He was also hyper and paranoid, giving me short, one-word responses. I thought he could have been on something or else he hasn't slept in a week."

Her brows furrowed together in concern. "That doesn't sound like Wyatt."

"He was like a stranger, Bree. He told me Alan set him up."

"That's crazy. Alan would never do that."

"That's what I said. Wyatt wasn't convinced. He told me Alan set the meet with him, but he didn't show up, and Wyatt was ambushed. If it wasn't Alan who set him up, then it might have been someone else at the Bureau, because they were operating under strict protocols."

Her gaze grew troubled. "Alan would never sell out an agent under his command."

"Well, the bottom line is Wyatt is compromised and in danger. I tried to get him to go home with me, but he flipped out when a car pulled up by the park. It was nobody—just a bunch of teenagers—but he obviously didn't feel like he could wait around to see who was in the car. I need to know what case Wyatt is working on."

"You don't know?" she asked in surprise. "He didn't tell you?"

"No, he didn't get a chance or he thought I already knew."

"But you're on the same team."

"Alan hasn't read me in on any of the current operations yet. Now that he's dead, I'm wondering if Wyatt's attack and his accident are tied together."

"You need to talk to Karen Leigh."

"I know, but can I trust her? What do you think? Do you know her?"

Bree hesitated. "Not well enough to say."

"What does your gut tell you?"

"I'm not sure," she said slowly. "She's smart, ambitious, driven, very dedicated, works long hours. She and Alan seemed extremely close, very much in sync. I did have a moment when I wondered if they had a more personal relationship, because I saw them together having a late dinner one night, but that could have just been a working dinner."

"Interesting."

"What are we going to do about Wyatt? I saw your message about Alan to him, but he didn't respond—nor did anyone else."

"I think Parisa and Diego may be out of the country. They may not have access to the forum. This is on us, Bree."

"Hopefully, Wyatt gets back in touch and sets up another meet."

She pushed a strand of hair off her cheek, and he saw the dark shadows under her eyes. "You look tired."

"I haven't slept much this week, but it was worth it. I got to reunite a mother and daughter. It doesn't happen that often, so I don’t care how exhausted I am."

He smiled, knowing how important it was to her to bring families back together. "Congratulations."

"Thanks."

"Should we go back to the office?"

Guilt flashed through her eyes. "I feel bad, Damon, but I really need to sleep for a few hours so I can get my brain working again."

"No need to feel bad. There are a lot of people working on Alan's case."

"I'll dive in tomorrow morning. But if you need something before then…"

"I'll be in touch."

"I'm glad you're in New York, Damon. Even though we won't be working directly together—it will be nice to have you in the office."

"To be honest, I don’t know what I'm going to be doing now that Alan is dead, but one step at a time. We've got to get Wyatt out of trouble."

"We will," she promised, as she turned and walked away.

And Sophie, too, he silently muttered, as he headed back to the office.

Four

Wyatt Tanner moved through the crowded streets of New York like a wary cat, keeping in the shadows, choosing alleys whenever possible, staying away from the lights. He probably should have taken Damon up on his earlier offer of help. He'd always trusted Damon, but then he'd always trusted Alan, too, and now…now he didn't know what to think.

He didn't want to believe that the man who had had his life in his hands the past ten months had sold him out, but he couldn't come up with a better answer no matter how hard he tried. And if it wasn't Alan, it was someone else at the Bureau, someone who knew where he was, what he was doing, and that boiled down to a very small group of people.

Alan had brought him into the New York field office ten months ago for the express purpose of planting him with the Venturi family, an Italian Mafia family that had been decimated in the eighties, only to spring back into business after 9/11 when the government's interest turned to Islamic terrorist groups. The Venturis had also resurged because the old man Giancarlo Venturi had died in prison a year ago, and his two sons had decided to bring back the family business.

Lorenzo and Stefan Venturi had been laundering money for quite some time, but they'd moved beyond cleaning dirty money through real-estate development, wholesale diamonds and gambling to dealing drugs that were fueling the opioid crisis in the Northeast.

He'd found his way into the organization through his construction skills, the same skills he'd learned from his very respectable, very upstanding contractor father. He was sure his dad had never imagined he'd use what he'd been taught on numerous job sites to infiltrate a crime family, but that's exactly what had happened.

He'd gone slow at first, getting close to one of the construction supervisors, who'd taken him to a poker game, where he'd used his card counting skills and reckless gambling attitude to get invited to the high roller's game. Eventually, and as planned, he'd found himself in debt to the youngest Venturi brother—Lorenzo.

With a desperate need to pay off debts to the family, he was able to pick up side jobs, starting with small things like making cash deposits at different banks into different accounts, and then when he'd proved himself trustworthy, he'd been brought into other deals, delivering drugs, weapons, and diamonds.

He'd been building a damn good case against the Venturis until something had changed a few weeks earlier.

There was a new player in the game. The Venturi brothers were having secret meetings and rumors of joining forces with a larger syndicate had rumbled around the organization.

Alan had set up a meet with him two days ago, saying he had important information to discuss, which had been unusual, because in the past Alan had always let him initiate contact. Alan hadn't shown up at that meeting, and he'd come close to losing his life, so it sure as hell felt like a set-up.

He'd thought for a while that the Venturis had someone inside at the FBI. It was difficult to believe that Alan might have been that mole, but he looked damned guilty at the moment.

He had to figure out a way to keep himself alive and get

to the truth. He shouldn't have panicked at the park, but he'd had the sudden thought that if Alan was a mole and he'd personally picked Damon to work for him, then maybe Damon was dirty, too. But that was wrong. Damon was a good guy. He knew that. He just wasn't thinking straight. He was exhausted, running on fumes, and every bone in his body hurt. His head was throbbing, his vision was blurry, and he was almost out of cash and options.

He hated to ask for help, but Damon was his best bet. Hopefully, he'd be willing to talk to him again. He just needed to get on the Internet, which was what was driving him toward an Internet café shortly before midnight. The café was occupied by a clerk and one older teenage boy.

He used the last few dollars he had to buy ten minutes on a computer and then logged in to the baseball forum. His nerves jangled as he opened the private chat room and saw a message from Damon.

The breath left his lungs as he read Damon's post. *Coach is dead. Fernandez in trouble. Need the starters back on the field. Who's available?*

The coach was Alan. He was Fernandez, and Damon was calling anyone else who could make themselves available to help. But no one else had answered yet.

He sat back in his chair and stared at the screen.

Alan was dead?

Maybe he wasn't dirty after all.

Or Alan had failed at doing what he was supposed to do—which was to take him out. Not that it was Alan who had attacked him, but he could have easily hired the muscle.

But that didn't matter anymore. Alan was dead and it couldn't be an accident. So, who had killed him? Someone from the FBI? Someone from the Venturi family? The new player in town?

He tapped his fingers lightly on the keyboard, thinking that Damon might be in as much trouble as he was, because he was Alan's latest recruit.

He typed in a note for Damon, who'd chosen the All-Star

catcher Gary Carter as his moniker on the site…

Carter never should have signed with a new coach. Might want to go back to the minors. Better players there. Let's meet for batting practice at the cages tomorrow night at nine. Need some tips on my swing.

Damon would know he was referring to the 8th Street arcade where they'd had a few meets in the past. It was a good, crowded location, with a lot of people around.

He hit Send, hoping he wasn't making a mistake.

Even if Damon could be trusted, if he talked to the wrong person at the FBI about any of this, he could be risking both their lives…

Damon didn't sleep all night, tossing and turning in his ridiculously hot apartment that was barely livable with all the windows open and two fans blowing. He was supposed to have air conditioning, but it wasn't working. He'd grabbed the apartment fast because it was close to his new job, but he was definitely going to have to rethink his living situation.

During the restless and interminably long hours, he thought about where Sophie might have gone if she was in danger. He kept coming back to the place where they'd met, the last time he'd seen her—in a small lakeshore cabin in the Adirondacks.

He didn't know if Sophie's family had a place there or if she'd just gone there with the Rowlands—with Cassie and Jamie. But he did know that she'd spoken fondly of summers at the lake. The Adirondacks were a good five hours north of the city. Maybe it was a place where she'd feel safe.

But would she be safe there?

He kept coming back to one puzzling question. Sophie had grown up with the FBI as her second family. If she was in trouble, why would she run away from her father's friends? She had to have had a really good reason.

Tired of his thoughts running endlessly around in a

circle, he rolled out of bed around four, showered, dressed in jeans and a T-shirt, and checked the baseball forum.

He was thrilled to see a message from Wyatt. His friend was still alive and had set up a time to meet that night.

Checking his watch, he calculated the time it would take to look for Sophie at the lake and get back to meet Wyatt. He decided he could do both. He hopped into his car, made a quick stop to grab coffee and a breakfast burrito and then it was onto the interstate. He could be taking a five-hour drive for nothing, but he could be at the lake by ten and back in the city by early evening.

Sophie might not be at the lake. She might not have run at all. She could have been kidnapped. *She might not even still be alive.* His stomach rolled with nausea at that horrific thought. But he couldn't dwell on it. He could only do what he could do, and that was to check out the cabin. He wasn't going to accomplish much at the office. Alan's team hadn't exactly shut him out, but they definitely hadn't felt compelled to share information with him. Apparently, they didn't trust him any more than he trusted them.

Maybe Bree would get him some information. She might not be on Alan's team, but she had friends who were. Which reminded him—he was supposed to meet her for lunch. He'd text her later and cancel. She wouldn't be awake this early.

As the miles passed, it felt good to be in his car with the air conditioning blowing in his face. He'd been stressed out and overworked since he'd joined the Bureau four years ago. Most days he liked the hectic pace. He wasn't good with downtime—too much opportunity to think. He preferred to be busy, moving forward, making things happen. But now seemed like a good time to take stock in his situation.

His mentor and the man he'd come to work for was dead. Where did that leave him? He wasn't sure he wanted to work for Karen Leigh, if she got moved up. On the other hand, the FBI could bring someone new in to replace Alan. But nothing would happen too fast. He could easily be in limbo for a while, but that might be a good thing. He'd have more time to help Wyatt and to look for Sophie.

His jaw tightened as he thought about the last time he'd been on this road, when he'd made the trip to the lake for Jamie's wake.

He could still remember the first time he'd seen her. The room had been packed with people, and he'd actually been looking for Cassie, but when his gaze had connected with Sophie's, everyone else in the room had faded away. He'd felt a compelling need to get closer, and that's exactly what he'd done. In fact, he didn't think he'd spoken to anyone else there.

He'd listened to stories of Jamie shared by various people, but he hadn't told any of his stories. It was just too painful to talk about someone who shouldn't have died so young.

His chest tightened. *Damn!* It still hurt to think about that day.

He'd almost quit Quantico after Jamie's death. But it was Alan who had convinced him to keep going. He was so close to graduation, to a new career, and it's what Jamie would have wanted him to do, so he'd done it.

But first he'd spent one incredible night with a beautiful woman, whose attraction had terrified him so much that he'd left before she woke up, before she could smile at him, beckon him with her eyes, tempt him with her body, make him forget all his plans, all his goals.

Maybe if he'd met her at another time, in a different place, things would have been different…or not.

He didn't believe in love, and Sophie had that love-ever-after vibe about her. Stay or go—he would have ended up disappointing her with either choice, so he'd left, and deep down inside, he'd always been a little afraid to see her again.

He was going to have to get over that…and fast.

He owed Alan Parker a lot, and if he could help Sophie, he would.

Then he'd leave her—*again.* Hopefully, it would be easier the second time around.

Sophie couldn't find the damn key, and every passing minute reminded her how fast time was flying. It was nine-thirty on Thursday morning, and the sun was rising higher in the sky.

The cabin was set back from the shoreline and tucked between tall, thick trees that separated the structure from neighboring buildings by a good twenty-five yards. The nearest cabin belonged to the Rowlands, but she couldn't see it from here. From the front windows, she had a partial view of the water, and in the past several minutes, she'd seen a few dog walkers and kids heading down to the lake. The town was waking up, and she needed to be gone before anyone realized she was there.

She'd tried to look for the key when she'd arrived around midnight, but when she'd finally gotten to the cabin after hiding her car behind a boathouse a mile away, she'd realized the electricity was off. No one had used the place in forever, and a caretaker only came by a few times a year in the daylight to dust away the cobwebs and make sure the property was intact.

She'd tried looking for candles but without even a cell phone flashlight, she'd gotten nowhere fast. Finally, she'd laid down on the couch and fallen into an exhausted sleep.

She'd been surprised she could sleep at all, but her brain and her heart had obviously needed a time-out from the pain and the worry. She'd woken up an hour and a half ago and had started her search, but she'd found nothing.

It was ridiculous. The place wasn't that big. There were two bedrooms, one bath, a living room, and a small kitchen. There was a hall closet that was still filled with beach supplies, chairs, paddles for the two kayaks that sat in the garage, beach towels and other random items that she had already looked through. She'd also gotten into the attic space and searched through old boxes that had gotten stashed up there at some point.

That venture had taken her down a very sad memory lane, and she'd had to push back more tears as she'd seen old, loose photographs taken of her and her family during various summer vacations.

So, what next? She'd looked through her dad's bedroom and the dresser that held only musty linens. The bathroom was empty. She'd dug through the kitchen drawers, tossing the loose items onto the counters, and she had come up with a couple of keys, but they were all for the front or back door of the cabin, or a boat that had been sold long ago.

She moved back to the doorway of the second bedroom, the one she'd always used. There was a queen-sized bed; she'd already pulled off the quilt and checked under the pillows, which hadn't been easy since the bed had reminded her of Damon and the night they'd spent together.

She hadn't been in the cabin since that night. Like her dad, this lake house held too many memories, both good and bad, and while she loved to dig into the pasts of people from centuries ago, she tended to leave her own past alone.

Turning away, she walked into the middle of the living room.

What was she missing?

Had she made a mistake in coming here? Had she thought her dad meant this cabin, when in fact he'd been talking about some other happy place?

But nothing else jumped into her head. Although, she did wonder why he would have sent her so far away to get a key. Why not leave it somewhere in New York City? If not her house, or his, why not somewhere closer, easier to find?

He had to have had a reason. Maybe he'd just wanted to get her out of town quickly. Or he'd left the key here a long time ago and had never come back to retrieve it. She certainly couldn't remember him talking about any trips to the lake in recent years, but then she knew little about what he did on the weekends. They were close, but they were also busy, and while they talked or texted often, they didn't see each other in person more than a few times a month.

As her gaze swept the room, an old memory poked at her brain, telling her to pay attention.

She'd been about ten or eleven. Her mom was making cookies in the kitchen. She'd left the kitchen and come into the living room to ask her father to take her out on the boat.

"What are you doing, Daddy?" she'd asked, as her father carefully pulled a brick out of the wall above the fireplace, revealing a small space.

"Making a hiding place," he replied, the tension in his eyes warring with the smile on his face.

"For what?"

"Whatever we need. It will be our secret place, just like this is our secret house. You can keep a secret, can't you, Sophie?"

"I won't tell anyone," she promised.

"You're a good girl. I hope you always know how much I love you."

The last words of her memory stung, but she walked quickly across the room, running her fingers over the rough-edged bricks, trying to remember which one was loose. He'd said something about her age marking the spot—*eleven.*

She counted eleven up from the bottom and pushed at the brick. It wobbled, and she grabbed it more firmly, pulling it out of the wall.

Her heart leapt against her chest as her gaze fell on a silver key.

She'd found it.

But the key wasn't the only item in the hiding place. Next to it was a small 9 mm gun, similar to the one she'd seen her father carry.

Her breath came short and quick. She wasn't a stranger to guns. Her dad had taught her to shoot when she was a teenager. But the gun and the key made her think about the person or people who had taken her father's life.

She took out the key and put it in her pocket, then retrieved the gun.

She'd no sooner done that when she heard heavy

footsteps on the porch.

Someone was coming!

Was it a neighbor, a friend, or an enemy?

Through the window, she saw the shadow of a man.

He knocked.

She didn't answer.

Maybe he'd go away.

He didn't.

He knocked again, and then he kicked open the door.

She raised the gun and pointed it at him. "Stop right there. Hands up."

Five

"I didn't expect you'd be happy to see me again, Sophie, but I didn't think you'd want to shoot me," Damon said, putting up his hands.

"Damon," she said in shock.

He was the last person she'd expected to see. Four years had passed since their gazes had last met. She wished he'd gone bald or gray or gotten fat, but that hadn't happened. He looked just as mouthwateringly delicious as he had the first time she'd seen him.

His dark-brown hair was still thick and wavy, perfect for running her fingers through. His blue eyes were as mysterious and enticing as the sea, changing colors with his mood, with his passion. His full-lipped mouth was still oh-so-sexy, and his broad shoulders, lean hips, and long legs made shivers run down her spine that had nothing to do with the danger lurking in the shadows, and everything to do with him, and a ridiculous attraction that, apparently, she still hadn't gotten over.

"Want to lower that gun?" he asked, his voice quiet but purposeful.

She started, realizing she'd already gotten lost in him, and that couldn't happen—not this time. "What are you doing here? Why did you kick down the door?"

"I was looking for you, and when you didn't answer, I decided to make sure you weren't hurt—or something."

"Or something? You heard about my father, didn't you?"

"I did. I'm really sorry, Sophie. I mean that."

He probably did mean it. He'd been one of her dad's star pupils and someone her father had kept in touch with over the years.

It was ironic that Damon was probably the one man she could have introduced to her father who he would have liked.

Or maybe not.

Her dad had never encouraged her to get involved with anyone from the FBI. In fact, he'd made a point of keeping his work relationships away from her. That had made it easy for her to never see Damon again.

"We need to talk," Damon continued. "I'd like to do that without a gun in my face."

"How did you know I was here?"

"I had a hunch. When we were at the wake, you said this place meant a lot to you and to Jamie."

Her gut clenched as she thought about Jamie again. Just about everyone she'd ever loved was dead. "Did you tell anyone else you were coming here—anyone from the Bureau?"

Damon gave her a steady, measuring look. "No, I came alone. But a lot of people are looking for you. Did you know that your apartment was broken into?"

"Yes. A friend of mine left me a message. But I couldn't call her back."

"Why? Because you lost your phone hundreds of miles away from here?"

So, they'd traced her phone signal. She'd figured they would.

"It was a good move," he said. "To throw people off the track."

"Well, it didn't work. You're here."

"I wasn't going off your phone signal." He paused. "I'm

closing the door. Don't shoot me."

She didn't know if she *could* shoot him, and he didn't seem to be too worried, but she kept the gun pointed at him anyway, just because it made her feel like she had a little more control over the situation.

He closed the door, but it didn't latch, not after he'd broken the lock.

"You'll have to get that fixed," he said. "Not that it was doing much for you anyway."

"You need to go, Damon."

"Let's talk first. Why did you run away from your apartment, your friends, your father's coworkers? Why did you just disappear, Sophie?"

"Because someone killed my dad."

"It's possible it was an accident."

"You don't believe that any more than I do," she said sharply.

"Maybe not, but I think something specific spooked you."

"You mean like the two men I saw going into my apartment building?"

"You saw the men who broke into your apartment?" he asked in surprise.

"I don't know if they were the ones, but they could have been."

"What did they look like?"

"Law enforcement, maybe—I don't know."

Damon stared back at her, and she could see him running through her words in his head. "Why would you be afraid of law enforcement when your father is FBI?"

"Gut instinct," she lied, knowing she wouldn't have been afraid at all if her father hadn't told her to be. "And it looks like I was right to run. If I'd gone to my apartment, who knows what would have happened?"

His lips drew into a hard line. "Look, Sophie, I want to help you."

"Why? Why on earth would you want to help me?"

His gaze darkened, and the air sizzled between them as they found themselves back in a place probably neither of them wanted to revisit, but they were there all the same.

"We're not friends," she said quickly, needing to break the tension. "We're not anything. We haven't seen each other in four years. Why do you care where I am, what I'm doing? Is it because of loyalty to my dad? That has to be it, right? Nothing else could have made you drive all the way up here."

"I should have called you after that night," he said.

"I'm not looking for an apology."

"Aren't you?"

"No. Maybe. No," she said, hating to sound so uncertain. "None of that is important. I have bigger problems."

"Then let's talk about now," he said, relief in his eyes as he changed the subject. "I respected your father. He was a mentor to me. I owe him for that, and I know that he would want me to help you. He trusted me, and I hope you can trust me, too."

"I don't know if my father trusted you," she said, shaking her head.

Surprise and anger flared in his eyes. "Why would you say that?"

"Because he told me not to trust *anyone* from the Bureau, and since you're an agent, that includes you."

"When did he tell you that?"

She realized she'd said too much. "A while ago."

"Really? A while ago? Or was it today? What else did he say?"

"That's my business."

"Every word could be important, Sophie. You need to tell me."

"No, I don't need to tell you. If he wanted you to know anything, he would have left you a message."

"So, he left you a message?"

Damn, the man was sharp. "It doesn't matter how or when he said it, I'm still not going to trust you. I'm not going to go against him."

"I'm not just some agent from the Bureau, Sophie."

"Oh, please. Just because we've seen each other naked doesn't mean anything."

He frowned at her comment. "Look, we're wasting time. Here's what's going to happen. You're either going to tell me what your dad was worried about so I can help you figure out who killed him and keep you safe at the same time, or you're going to have to shoot me. Those are your options. Because I'm not leaving here without you."

"You think I can't pull the trigger?" she challenged. "Because I can."

"And where will that get you? Will you be any closer to finding your father's killer?"

She really hated his calm, pointed questions. She was running on emotion, and he was using logic. "Fine, I can tell you this much. My dad said that he was in trouble and that he wanted me to be safe. He told me not to trust anyone, to run away and hide. Do whatever I needed to do to stay alive." She deliberately left out the part about the key and the next step she was supposed to take.

"Was that it?" Damon challenged.

"There was some stuff about him being sorry and how much he loved me, but the last message ended abruptly." She drew in a shaky breath. "I think he was calling me from the car right before he went off the road. I heard a crash and then nothing."

"Did he say who was after him? Did he name names? Did he call out a case he was working on? Anyone who had a grudge against him?"

"No, he was quite vague. And I'm not lying about that. I wish he'd said who or what or anything specific, because then I wouldn't be running away without knowing who might be chasing me." She licked her lips. "I believe he really just wanted to say good-bye." Her eyes watered, and her hands on the gun began to shake as her shoulders grew weary.

"So, what are you going to do now? What's your plan?"

"I'm still trying to figure that out. I know I can't stay

here."

"No, you can't. I don't even understand why you came here at all. Surely, someone at the FBI knows about this place. Peter told me your dad brought him into the FBI. He must have made the trip up here at some point."

"No, he didn't come here. Only the Rowlands were here with us. They own the cabin next door. Vincent and my dad bought the cabins as safe houses a long time ago. When we were here, we used fake names. I thought it was a game back then. My dad never let his work touch our lives."

"Well, someone from the Bureau will talk to Vincent Rowland. Vincent may be retired, but he and your father were good friends; he'll be interviewed."

"I know all that, but I had to go somewhere," she said. "I needed to be alone to cry, to think. I wasn't planning to stay longer than a night."

The doubt in his eyes grew as his gaze moved past her to the fireplace, to the empty space and the brick she'd placed on the floor.

"You didn't come here to mourn—you came here to get something," he said.

"This gun," she lied.

"You drove all the way up here to get a gun? No way. I don't buy it. You're not telling me the whole truth, Sophie. And I can't help you if you don't."

"Damon, please, just go. Just leave me alone," she pleaded, desperate to get him out of the cabin before she did something even more stupid—like start to trust him. "I'll disappear. I'll go somewhere no one else knows about. You don't have to worry about me. You've done your duty. You came after me. You did that for my dad. Now do something for me—leave me alone. You've managed it for four years. You can keep going."

His mouth tightened. "I'm not leaving you alone. You won't be safe. You can't get help from a friend, because you'll put them in danger, and even if you are very careful, you'll make a mistake. You don't know how to stay off the radar, but I do. You're going to have to trust someone at some point. You're going to have to put your anger aside and let it be me."

Before she could answer, she was suddenly hit with a shower of glass from the nearby window.

What the hell had just happened?

Another pane blew out, and something whizzed by her ear.

Damon grabbed her arm and pulled down as a third window exploded.

Someone was shooting at her!

"Are you hit?" Damon asked, his gaze raking her face.

She shook her head, unable to find words. There was glass in her hair and her bare arms were bleeding, but she'd managed to escape the bullets. "Who is shooting at me?"

"Doesn't matter. We need to get out of here. There's a back door, right?" Damon asked in clipped tones.

"Yes, but what if they're out there, too?"

Another shot took out the last of the front windows, and she ducked closer to Damon. The shooter must have some sort of silencer on his weapon because she couldn't hear the blasts, only the glass breaking.

"Stay down," Damon said, as he crept closer to the window and took a look outside.

"Do you see anyone?"

"Yes. In the trees. Just one, I think. Looks like he shot out my tires. He probably thinks it's your car. Here's what you're going to do. You're going to run out the back, while I draw out our shooter." He pulled a gun out from under his T-shirt. He'd obviously had it tucked into the waistband of his jeans.

Her recent stand with her own gun seemed fairly ridiculous right now. Damon could have taken her out any time he wanted.

"Where's your car?" he asked.

"I hid it by a boathouse a mile away from here."

"Good. Go there. I'll meet you as soon as I can. Where's the boathouse?"

She hesitated for a split second.

"Seriously?" he demanded, anger in his dark-blue eyes. "Someone is trying to kill you, Sophie, and I'm the only one standing in the way."

"It's off Caldwell Road, past Kingston Lodge. What if you can't get away? What if there's someone at my car?"

"There won't be. I'll get away, and you'll wait for me. You need me, Sophie, whether you want to admit it or not."

The vase on the table shattered with another shot.

She picked up her gun, crawled over to the kitchen table, grabbed her bag, and ran through the kitchen toward the back door.

She took a peek outside. The back yard was enclosed, and she didn't see anyone inside the fencing.

She heard gunfire from the front of the house—*Damon was shooting back.*

As she went outside, she stayed close to the back of the structure until she could get through the gate and dash into a cluster of trees. She held her breath every step of the way, expecting to be taken down at any moment, but Damon was doing what he'd promised, keeping the shooter engaged.

When she reached the woods, she heard the distant sound of sirens. Someone had heard Damon's gunshots and called the police.

The shots abruptly ended. All was quiet except for the sirens. A car engine roared from somewhere nearby.

Had the gunman left at the sound of the cops? She really hoped so. She also hoped Damon was all right.

Five minutes later, she made her way past the old lodge to the boathouse. Her car was where she'd left it. She pulled out her keys, watching the vehicle for a long minute before making her way over to it. She slid behind the wheel, her heart pounding. She wanted to speed away. But would she be safer on the road? Her father certainly hadn't been.

Damon had asked her to wait. He'd told her she needed him, and she had the terrible feeling she did. She had no idea who had come after her—why anyone would try to kill her.

Her father's warning voicemails had just been jumbled words before this. Now they felt very, very real.

Her heart stopped as a man came around the side of the boathouse. To her relief, it was Damon. He slid into the passenger seat and said, "Drive."

"Where?"

"Wherever you're supposed to go next." He gave her a knowing look. "Your dad told you to come here, didn't he? I'm guessing his instructions didn't end there."

She hated that he was right and even more that he knew it. But his cocky arrogance and his powerful male presence made her feel a little safer. "What happened to the gunman?"

"He took off at the sound of the sirens."

"Did you get a look at him?"

"Not much of one. He had on jeans and a sweatshirt, a baseball cap on his head. Didn't see his face. He jumped into a truck and took off. I wasn't close enough to get a license plate. I could guess at the make and model, but right now it's more important that we keep moving. If your father's concerns about law enforcement are valid, then we need to leave before the police find us."

She hadn't even thought of that. "But you don't need to go with me. You're FBI. You can tell the police you went to the cabin, but I wasn't there. You can tell them about the shooter." She was actually proud of her suggestion, until Damon gave a quick shake of his head.

"Not a chance. The shooter saw me. I have to be able to defend myself, and I can't do that if I get tied up with the local cops, not to mention the fact that you need me, Sophie." His hard gaze met hers. "You may not want to admit it, but you do. You can't underestimate who's after you."

She shivered, and it wasn't just because of the recent gunshots. She still couldn't believe Damon had come after her.

"Like it or not, we're in this together now," Damon said. "Where are we going?"

"I'll tell you when we get there."

"Why don't you let me drive?"

Her hands were shaking and her heart was hammering against her chest, but there was no way she was giving up the wheel. It was all the control she had right now, and she was hanging on to it.

Six

Damon scoured the road as Sophie drove away from the cabin. Fortunately, she knew where she was going and was able to avoid the police activity at the house and the surrounding woods, but his pulse didn't slow down until they were at least ten miles away.

He was actually impressed with Sophie's steady hand on the wheel. She was terrified and probably still dealing with a huge adrenaline rush, but she was keeping it together.

He still wondered why she'd run from NYC to the lake house and what she'd gotten from the hiding spot in the fireplace; he was damned sure it wasn't just the gun. But that raised another question. If Alan didn't trust his fellow FBI agents, then why had he sent his daughter to a cabin he owned—a cabin next door to the one owned by the Rowlands?

Sophie had said it was a secret cabin, but Vincent Rowland knew about it, and he could have told any number of people at any time.

Vincent might not have believed there was any need for continued secrecy after he retired. And if Peter or Karen had contacted him last night and asked him if he knew where Sophie might run, he could have told them about the cabin.

Not that Damon wanted to believe Peter or Karen had sent someone to the lake with a gun to take care of Sophie. But he couldn't rule it out.

"When is the last time you spoke to Vincent Rowland?" he asked, glancing over at her.

Sophie shot him a surprised look. They'd both been silent for the past twenty minutes, each lost in their own thoughts, but now he wanted to talk. He needed more information, and he needed it fast.

"Vincent?" she echoed. "I don't think I've spoken to him since Jamie died. Why?"

"Still wondering how anyone found you at the cabin."

"Vincent wouldn't have told anyone. He and my dad had a pact. The cabins were their safe houses. And besides that, I've known Vincent since I was a child. The Rowlands were there for me and my father during the darkest days of our lives when my mom died. There's nothing you could say that would make me believe Vincent or Cassie would send a shooter to the lake to take me out."

"I'm not saying that's what happened, but if Peter or Karen or anyone else at the FBI called Vincent or Cassie after you disappeared last night and said they were worried about you and asked if either of them know where you might go, it's possible someone might have mentioned the cabin in an attempt to help you. They wouldn't know about your father's warning not to trust anyone at the Bureau."

"I suppose I could believe that," she conceded. "But Cassie is in London right now."

"She still has a phone. What about Vincent?"

"I don't know if he's in New York; he travels a lot."

His phone vibrated in his pocket, and as he pulled it out, he realized he should have disabled the phone before leaving the cabin. "It's Peter," he said.

"You can't answer that. You can't tell him where we are," she said, panic in her voice. "You shouldn't have even brought the phone with you. What if they're tracking us right now?"

"I'll get rid of the phone as soon as I see if he leaves me a voicemail." He waited a moment, then saw the message. "Looks like he did."

"Put it on speaker. If we're in this together, there can't be secrets between us."

He did as she asked.

"Damon, it's Peter Hunt. If you've located Sophie Parker, you need to bring her in. She's in serious danger. I'm extremely worried about both of you. Call me back."

"That was fast," he muttered. "Obviously, Peter knows about the shootout at your cabin."

Sophie glanced at her watch. "That was half an hour ago. How did they find out so quickly?"

"They obviously traced the car to me and notified the FBI. Peter put two and two together, figuring I'd come after you." He paused. "What's the deal with you and Peter Hunt? Why didn't you ask him for help? He has obviously been a long-time family friend."

"I told you—my dad said not to trust anyone. I didn't know if he was including Peter in that, but he certainly didn't tell me to go to Peter, so I didn't."

"You said your father's last message was cut off. Maybe he would have said more if he had time."

"He left me four voicemails before he got cut off, and he never mentioned Peter in any of them."

He was surprised that Alan had left her that many messages. Her words also led him to believe that she still hadn't told him the whole story, but he'd questioned enough witnesses in his time to know when to push and when to retreat.

Right now, Sophie was running high on emotions ranging from fear, to grief, to anger. He needed to let her burn some of that off before he tried to gain her confidence.

He also needed to get rid of his phone. He didn't have a removable battery, so he turned off the power, then rolled down the window and tossed it into the bushes on the side of the road. Hopefully by the time anyone got to his last known location, he and Sophie would be miles away.

As he disconnected from his phone, it felt both freeing and alarming. He'd gone undercover before and been without a phone, but he'd always had a contact at the Bureau, someone who knew where he was and what mission he was on. He could have called for backup at any point, and it would have come, but this was different. When he'd gotten into the car with Sophie, he'd chosen a side—her side.

It was a little shocking how quickly and easily he'd done that.

He told himself it was for Alan; that wasn't the complete truth. But motivation didn't matter. He and Sophie were on their own, and he needed to think about what to do next.

"Where did you get this car?" he asked.

"I rented it in New York. I paid in cash. I'm supposed to bring it back today, but I don't see how I can do that."

"No, you can't do that. We're going to need to switch cars at some point. The FBI will already be checking with rental car agencies in Manhattan. Your photo will be sent around, and if they don't have this license plate number yet, they soon will."

"How are we going to switch cars? We're in the mountains."

"We'll figure it out. Hopefully, we have a little time."

Several more minutes passed, then she said, "Will someone be worried about you, Damon? Someone you care about?"

He wished he had a better answer to that question. "I'm sure my abandoned car and shot-up tires will cause some concern, but I just moved to New York a week ago, so I haven't gotten close to anyone. I barely know my coworkers' last names."

"Why did you move? I thought you were a superstar in DC. My dad mentioned you a few months back, saying you were cracking some huge terrorism case. He was quite proud; he liked to brag about the successes of his students. You were one of his favorites." She cleared her throat. "I was happy to hear you were doing so well."

"Were you?" he asked dryly.

She shot him an indecipherable look. "Well, maybe *happy* is a little strong. But you didn't answer my question. Why did you leave DC?"

"Your father made me an offer. He wanted me to work on his taskforce in New York. It was time for a change, so I said yes." He paused. "You never told your father you knew me, did you?"

"I said I met you at the wake; that was it. I don't tell my father about one-night stands."

"So, I wasn't your only one-night stand?"

Something twitched in her gaze, then she turned her attention back on the road. "Does it matter?"

It didn't matter, but he knew the truth. That night had been out of character for her. He'd known it at the time, but he just hadn't cared; he'd wanted her too much. He'd taken her *yes* at face value, because asking if she was sure might have changed her answer, and that had been unthinkable.

"What was the task force my dad wanted you to work on?" she asked.

"I don't know. I assumed it had to do with the focus of his division—organized crime. But he never got a chance to tell me. I was wrapping up some details on my last case, and he told me we'd get into my new assignment next week. I wasn't worried about what it was. I wanted to work with your father. I respected him a great deal. He pushed me to do my best and I liked that. Whatever he wanted me to work on was fine with me."

"A lot of his students felt that way about him, and it was a two-way street. My dad really cared about the people he worked with. He used to tell me that his biggest flaw was getting personally attached. I didn't understand how that could be a flaw, but maybe it made him vulnerable to betrayal."

"You think he was betrayed?"

"Yes," she said without hesitation. "By someone he

trusted, and then he didn't know who to believe."

"What else did he say in his message to you, Sophie?"

Her hands tightened on the wheel, and she didn't look at him when she said, "I already told you. He was proud of me. He wanted me to have a happy and long life even if he couldn't be there. But he hoped he would be. He said he might be able to figure things out, but obviously he didn't have the time to do that."

"I wish I could hear the messages," he muttered.

"So do I," she said, a deep, wrenching pain in her voice. "You don't know how difficult it was for me to crush the phone, to destroy my last connection with him. I almost couldn't do it."

"But you did." He was starting to realize that the soft Sophie of his dreams had a steel core.

"I knew I had to. I couldn't be sentimental about it."

He couldn't imagine the difficulty of the choice she'd made to destroy her father's last message to her. That must have been agonizing; he knew how close they were. It would have been much easier for him, because he didn't feel close to either of his parents. Their actions had always been disappointing.

He'd been told that he'd disappointed them, too. That was probably true. Clearing his throat, he repeated his earlier question. "Where are we going, Sophie?"

"I'll tell you later."

"Why not now?"

"I don't know. It's just the way I feel."

He disliked the edge in her voice, the distrust. The Sophie he'd met at Jamie's wake had been sad, but she'd also been open, warm, and caring. It was what had drawn him to her. He'd wanted to wrap himself up in her softness, her kindness, her passion, and he'd done just that.

He wondered if he hadn't taken more from her than he'd given back. He hoped not. He hoped the night had been as good for her as it had been for him. He couldn't really imagine how it couldn't have been. It was the most memorable night of his life—maybe because it had just happened once. But that night was a long time ago now, and he needed to stay in the present.

He straightened and looked out the side view mirror, then glanced behind them. Since he'd last checked the road, a silver SUV had come into view.

"They've been there for a couple of minutes," Sophie said, looking into the rearview mirror.

He mentally cursed himself for getting lost in the past for even that long.

There appeared to be a couple in the front seat of the SUV: a man behind the wheel, a woman in the passenger seat.

"Do you think it's the person who shot at us?" Sophie asked with alarm. "What should I do? There's nowhere to pull off."

He could hear the panic in her voice and wished he was at the wheel. He would have forced that issue earlier, but Sophie had barely been willing to let him in the car; he hadn't wanted to push his luck.

"I don't think that's the shooter," he said. "But pick up your speed a little. Let's take the next turnoff, see if they follow."

"What if the turnoff is a dead end? Shouldn't we just try to outrun them?"

The curvy two-lane road didn't seem like a good option for a road race. "My gut tells me that they won't follow. Let's try turning off first."

The minutes ticked by as they both looked for an exit.

"There's a road," Sophie said with relief.

He put his hand on the side of the door as she took the turnoff a little fast. As they shot down the side road, he saw the SUV pass by on the main highway. Sophie drove another mile and then slowed down and pulled over to the side. She glanced in the rearview mirror. "I don't see them."

"Let's give it a minute."

As the road remained empty behind them, Sophie blew

out a breath and gave him an apologetic look. "Sorry. I guess I'm jittery."

"Better to be acutely aware of your surroundings than not. How about letting me drive?"

She hesitated. "I can't."

"Because you think I'm going to drive you somewhere you don't want to go?"

"Maybe. Yes. I feel like I have one tiny thread of control right now, and it's only because my hands are on the steering wheel."

He could have taken control of her and the car at any moment, but he wasn't going to tell her that. He needed her to stay strong and if that meant she was at the wheel, he could live with it. "Then you can drive."

She pulled the car back onto the road, made a U-turn and returned to the highway.

They didn't speak for a while, and he was fine with that. He needed to keep his head in the game and talking to Sophie was distracting.

As she drove through the mountains, he could see that they were taking a circuitous route south, probably back to New York City or at least somewhere in that vicinity. But the trip was taking a torturously long time. They often found themselves behind slow-moving motorhomes or they'd spend long minutes sitting in lines of cars waiting to get past road construction.

After almost three hours, Sophie took an exit and pulled into a gas station. "I need to use the restroom, and we're almost out of gas."

"I'll take care of the gas."

"I have cash."

"I do, too. Hang on to yours for now."

She nodded wearily as they walked into the convenience store. They both used the facilities, then he prepaid the gas while Sophie grabbed drinks and snacks and met him back outside as he finished filling up the car.

"I know you want control," he said. "But you're

exhausted, and I have a feeling we still have a long way to go. How about letting me take a turn driving?"

"I am tired," she admitted. "But I got energy drinks and candy bars, so I should be okay."

He smiled at her valiant effort to stay strong and to stay awake. "I'm sure we'll make good use of all of those, but let me drive. I promise I won't take you anywhere you don't want to go. Just give me some general directions, and I'm good."

He could see the conflict in her brown eyes, but eventually, she said, "All right."

He was relieved to win one battle, especially since he was very tired of being a passenger. Sophie might like control, but so did he.

As he got back onto the highway, a sign ahead offered several options. "Which way?"

"Stay to the right."

"We're not going back to New York City, are we?"

"No, we're going to Connecticut."

"What's in Connecticut?"

"You'll see when we get there."

"Do you know how annoying that answer is?"

She smiled for the first time, which was fairly incredible considering his words. "I know it's annoying, but somehow that makes this situation feel less terrifying. It's like we're normal; we're just two people annoying each other."

"Nothing about this is normal."

"I know. You're right. But in all honesty, my life has never really been normal. It has its moments, sometimes years, where things seem like they're going along smoothly, and then *bam*—everything changes. The floor drops out from under me. You'd think I'd be used to it by now, but it always takes me by surprise. I wonder when it won't."

He looked over at her, feeling a wave of compassion at her sad, bewildering tone. "I don't know, Sophie, but I don't think it's going to be this week."

"Me, either," she said with a sigh. "I might have to close my eyes for a minute, Damon. I feel so tired. I hardly slept last night."

"Take a rest. But before you do, can you give me a city? Otherwise, who knows where we'll be in Connecticut when you wake up?"

She hesitated, then said, "New Haven. Will you do what I was doing, Damon? Will you get off the highway occasionally, switch things up? It will take longer, but I think it will be worth it."

"I can do that. Don't worry. I'm very good at evasion tactics. I can spot a tail from miles away."

"What are we going to do about the car? A police officer might see the license and call it in."

"That's why I will take the back roads. We'll switch cars when I see the right opportunity."

"Okay," she said, settling back in her seat as her eyes drifted closed.

She was asleep within a second, and his gaze lingered on her face so long he almost went off the side of the road on the next turn.

Dragging his attention back to the highway, he told himself to concentrate on the mission—which, apparently, was taking Sophie to New Haven.

He'd never been there, but he knew Yale was there. Alan had gone to the university; so had Peter. That bothered him. If Alan was sending Sophie to another location that was tied to his life, then they might end up dodging more bullets.

He wished Sophie had been more forthcoming. While being an agent often required patience, he wasn't that good at waiting. He liked action. He liked results. But right now, all he could do was drive—and try not to look at Sophie.

She was getting under his skin again. Over the past few hours, the undercurrent of tension between them had been impossible to miss. Even with everything else going on, their past was lurking in the shadows.

It was easier not to think about that night when Sophie was awake, when someone was shooting at them, but now with her sitting so close, and with the endlessly long, empty road in front of him, he couldn't get her off his mind.

All the images he'd tried to forget were coming back in full, vivid glory. He could feel her body under his, and the memory of her taste made his lips tingle. It had been a night to remember but one he needed desperately to forget.

He thought he'd made some progress in that regard. He'd dated other women since Sophie. He'd kept busy building his career. He'd constantly reminded himself that love was for losers, and he wasn't going to be a loser ever again.

On the other hand, sex with a beautiful woman was just fine…it just couldn't be Sophie.

He blew out a breath, tapping his fingers restlessly on the steering wheel, trying really hard not to turn his head, not to admit that he wanted her again.

But even if he did want her, he wasn't going to have her. He wasn't going to cross that line.

He had to think of Sophie as a job. His only goal should be in getting her to safety.

So why couldn't he stop thinking about getting her back into bed?

Seven

They'd set up a bonfire on the beach, Jamie's friends sitting in beach chairs and on blankets, waiting for a special fireworks show that Cassie had arranged for Jamie's wake. Someone had handed out champagne glasses, which they really didn't need since they'd been drinking since sunset, and it was now past eleven.

"Mind if I share your blanket?" the tall, dark-haired man with the compelling blue eyes asked.

She'd been avoiding him since she'd first seen him in the house. He unnerved her with the way he looked at her, the way she felt herself looking back at him.

There was a part of her that screamed danger—send him away—but instead of saying no, she said yes. She moved over so he could sit down on the blanket next to her, her body tightening at his nearness. She felt all tingly inside, on edge, a little reckless—none of the emotions she should be feeling at a memorial wake.

This wasn't a date. She was supposed to be mourning her friend, not ogling a man, who seemed to be as alone as she was. But as the breeze blew off the lake, she could smell the musky scent of his cologne. She could almost feel his breath on her cheek. And his amazing blue gaze seemed to see right into her soul.

All of her senses were on fire. She twisted her fingers together, resisting the impulsive desire she had to touch him.

It had to be the champagne or the wine. She'd drunk too much.

But she didn't feel drunk. She just felt—needy, hungry, empty.

She turned her head and found him watching her, shimmering beams of desire in his eyes. She didn't know much about him except that his name was Damon, and he and Jamie had served in the Army together. He hadn't said much all evening. He'd just watched, listened, took everything in.

She supposed she'd done much the same. Except for Cassie, she didn't really know any of Jamie's other friends. He'd traveled a far different road from her in the past ten years, and while they'd kept in touch, they hadn't seen each other very often.

Realizing that Damon was staring back at her, she focused on the fire and took a long sip of the bubbly champagne. It tingled against her throat, and she wanted more of that feeling—anything that would take away the sadness of this night. Jamie had been like a brother to her, the one person who could make her laugh, tease her out of a bad mood, make her feel like she could make it, be whoever she wanted to be. She was going to miss him so much.

She drank her way quickly to the bottom of her glass.

"Maybe you should slow down," Damon said.

She gave him a defiant look. "Why? What are any of us waiting for? We put off doing things until later. We say maybe next year, there will be time, but there isn't always time."

"That's true enough," he said somberly, finishing off his own glass.

She leaned over and grabbed a half-opened bottle from another blanket and refilled their glasses. After her first sip, she said, "Jamie was good at living in the moment. I need to get better at that." She glanced over at him. "What about you?"

"I could improve."

She smiled, feeling rebellious and reckless, a bad but heady combination, especially considering the irresistible pull she was feeling to the man sitting next to her. "Want to work on it right now?"

"What did you have in mind?"

"A dance," she said, getting to her feet. She extended her hand, and after a moment's hesitation, he took it.

"No one else is dancing," he said, as he stood up.

"Then we'll be the first." She needed to move, and the music and the night were calling to her.

Everyone else faded away. She could hear chatter. She was vaguely aware of a few more people getting up to dance, but she couldn't seem to look away from Damon's mesmerizing gaze.

He pulled her against his hard, masculine chest, and she was happy to go into his embrace, her emotions changing from sadness into yearning, from anger to desire.

At some point, the music ended...but they couldn't let go of each other...

A horn blared in her ear. She didn't understand why there was a car in the cabin. But she wasn't in the cabin anymore, was she?

Blinking her eyes open, she sat up abruptly, realizing that while she'd been dreaming about Damon, the car had stopped, and Damon was not in the driver's seat. She was stunned by that revelation. *Where the hell was he?*

She'd told him to drive to New Haven, but this strip mall with a deli, yoga studio, real-estate office, Chinese restaurant, and a phone store wasn't at all familiar to her. Her heart began to beat faster as she searched for some sign of Damon.

Had Damon taken advantage of her unconsciousness to talk to the FBI—or someone else?

He'd told her to trust him, but what did she really know about him? He could have told someone she might be at the lake. He could have pretended to get rid of the shooter so that he could get closer to her. And she'd gone along with it. She'd even let him drive.

Anger ran through her at her own stupidity. She wanted to run away, but she couldn't drive anywhere, because he obviously had the keys.

She opened the car door and stepped out on the pavement. She could try to get a cab, but without a phone, that wouldn't be easy. While she was debating what to do, the door to the Chinese restaurant opened and Damon came out, holding a large, white paper bag in his hands.

A mix of relief and anger ran through her. "Why did you stop here?" she demanded. "And why didn't you wake me up and tell me where you were going?"

"Well, you woke up on the wrong side of the car," he drawled.

"Not funny, Damon."

"I stopped to get food, because I was hungry, and I thought you might be, too. I also wanted to get a phone that couldn't be traced to us." He tipped his head to the phone store. "And I didn't wake you up, because I didn't need you to take care of any of that. I thought you could use the rest. You were restless the last hour, mumbling random words in your sleep."

She felt heat sweep across her cheeks, as she remembered her last dream had been of their night together. "What did I say?"

"Nothing incriminating."

She supposed she should be grateful for that. "Where are we, Damon?"

"About twenty-five miles outside of New Haven. Want to tell me where we're going now?"

She glanced at her watch and couldn't believe it was a little past six. Where had the day gone? They'd left the lake sometime after ten, and, apparently, they'd spent eight hours driving through the mountains and across two states. Taking back roads might have prevented a tail, but it had also delayed them from getting to the next location before closing time. Staying off the highway and keeping to side streets would put New Haven at least an hour away.

"We can't go there until tomorrow," she said. "It won't be open by the time we get there."

"So, it's not a safe house?"

"No, it's not. We're going to need a place to stay the night."

"Agreed. First, we need to ditch this car, and I think this is a good spot."

"Here?" She looked around the parking lot in confusion. "Why is this good?"

"There are plenty of other cars around. There's an all-night liquor store over there, so the lot probably won't ever be completely empty, and the car won't stand out."

Damon was very good at situation analysis. "All right, but how are we going to get to New Haven?"

"We're going to worry about that tomorrow."

"What?" She didn't like that idea at all.

"We'll take a cab to a motel somewhere between here and there. We'll hunker down and stay out of sight until the morning. Then we'll look into getting another vehicle."

"You don't think the FBI has alerted every cab driver to our fugitive status?"

"Probably not in Connecticut," he said, placing the call.

She leaned against the car as he ordered the cab, feeling more clear-headed now that she was getting some fresh air. It also felt good to stand up after so many hours of sitting.

"Five minutes," Damon told her. Then he scrolled through his phone. "There's a group of motels about eight miles of here. There's a motel about two miles from here, but I think that's too close to this lot. Wait, I see four motels/hotels within a three-block radius about eight miles from here. That's a better spot for us. If anyone finds the car and tries to track us to a nearby motel, they'll have to figure out which one we're in."

"Your mind is a magical thing," she said. "Very clever."

"Not so much magical but well-trained," he said. "I'm

trying to stay one step ahead."

"That would be an amazing feat, because I think we're about ten steps behind."

"We might not be if you'd share a little more information."

"It won't change anything."

"I'd like to be the judge of that."

"Well, you can't, so…"

"All right, let's not talk about it now. Get your bag. I want to move away from this car before the cab gets here."

She took her purse out of the car and made sure she hadn't left anything behind. Then she followed Damon across the length of the parking lot. They were close to the entrance when a taxi turned in to the lot, and Damon flagged him down.

Other than giving an address to the driver, they didn't speak on their way to the motel.

When they reached their destination, she paid for the trip in cash, and they waited for the taxi to pull away before walking two blocks away to a different motel.

It was a cheap, run-down-looking building with outside hallways facing the parking lot, and it didn't stir a lot of positive feelings within her.

"You want to stay here?" she asked, unable to stop herself from wrinkling her nose in disgust.

"Yes. It's the kind of place where people don't ask questions."

"It looks like the kind of place where they rent rooms by the hour."

"Maybe, but that's not going to bother us." He handed her the bag of Chinese food. "Wait here while I check us in. I'm going to be less memorable than you."

She wasn't sure if that was a compliment, but she waited outside the lobby while he got them a room.

He'd been in the office only a few minutes when a truck pulled into the parking lot with two guys in it. She remembered Damon saying that the shooter at the lake had left in a truck, and she felt suddenly very nervous. She walked quickly into a breezeway and through a door labeled Ice Machine. Her heart rate sped up when she realized the small room had only one way out. Had she made a tactical error?

She should have gone into the office where there were people—where there was Damon—but it was too late now.

She heard footsteps outside, and she looked around for some kind of weapon, but there was nothing in the small room but a vending machine, an ice machine, and a plastic ice bucket.

She stepped to the side as the door opened, and blew out a breath of relief when she saw it was Damon.

"Looking for some drinks?" he asked with a raise of his brow.

"No. Two men drove into the parking lot. I didn't want them to see me. They were in a truck. I didn't know if it was the same truck the shooter was in."

"It wasn't. I saw the guys—an older man about fifty with a teenaged son and a mangy-looking dog."

She was relieved to hear that.

"I don't think they're going to bother us," he added.

"Okay, good. Where's our room?"

"Top floor. I got you a room with a view, princess."

She made a face at him. "I am not a princess. I'm fine with dirt—just not motel room kind of dirt."

"It's going to be fine. Let's get some drinks while we're here."

After grabbing sodas and water out of the vending machine, they made their way to the second floor.

The room smelled like beer and cigarettes and was as bad as she'd expected, with peeling paint, an old TV, and lumpy-looking mattresses, but if there was a silver lining, it could be found in the fact that there were two beds. Besides the danger tracking her steps, spending the night with Damon presented other challenges.

Damon set the bag of food down on a small table and

turned on the ancient air conditioning unit, which rattled and smoked a little as it struggled into action.

"Damn, it's hot in here," he muttered. "The AC feels like heat."

"Now who's being a princess?" she asked, as she sat down at the table.

He frowned and took the chair across from her. "I hate the heat."

"It's not that bad. Maybe it will get cooler the longer it's on." She opened the bag and began pulling out cartons, her stomach rumbling at the spicy smells. She hadn't eaten anything besides the convenience store snacks hours ago.

"I wasn't sure what you liked, so I got a little of everything," Damon said. "Too bad we don't have a microwave; it might be a little cold by now."

"I don't care, and I like pretty much everything. I'm also starving. Yesterday, I didn't think I'd ever be hungry again, but now I feel like I could eat every bit of this."

"Well, don't hold back."

She didn't, grabbing a plastic fork and digging into a carton of Kung Pao chicken. Damon went after the sweet and sour pork. Five minutes later, they switched, and when they were finished with those cartons, they moved on to chow mein, fried rice, and a beef stir fry.

Twenty minutes later, she sat back with a satisfied sigh. "That was excellent. I ate way too much."

"It's good to eat. You need to keep your strength up for whatever is coming next."

She frowned at his words. "Thanks for the reminder. I was having a nice little moment of denial, and you ruined it."

"Sorry. Maybe these will help." He pushed a bag of fortune cookies across the table.

She took one out and turned it over in her hand. "I can't imagine what could possibly be in this fortune cookie that I would want to hear."

"Something uplifting and positive," he suggested.

"Or trivial and pointless." She suddenly smiled.

"What?" he asked curiously.

"Jamie used to make up fortune cookie sayings. We'd get Chinese food during our summers at the lake at the Pink Pagoda—which by the way, was painted yellow, but apparently no one felt that was a problem. Anyway, Jamie never liked his fortune; he always got weird ones, so he started making up his own."

A light of recognition came on in Damon's blue eyes. "Damn! He did that with me, too, only we were in Shanghai together."

"So, it was a real Chinese fortune cookie?"

"I suppose. It was a touristy restaurant. We only had a few hours of leave left, and Jamie was hungry."

"He was always hungry," she murmured, wondering if anyone she loved would ever outlive her, which was a very depressing thought. "Do you remember the fortune that Jamie made up?"

Damon thought for a minute. "It was something like: *'Help! I'm a wise man trapped in a cookie.'"*

She grinned. "That sounds like Jamie. My favorite of his was: *'You want to change your life? Stop eating cookies.'"*

A smile slowly spread across Damon's lips, warming up his usually stoic, somewhat hard, expression, and she liked it—far too much.

"You don't do that very often," she commented. "Only every once in a while, and you fight it until you just can't stop it."

Damon raised an eyebrow at her words. "What are you talking about?"

"Your smile. It's rarely used."

He shrugged. "I smile when it's warranted."

"Do you? You don't seem like a man who likes to show his emotions, whether they're good or bad."

"Emotion is weakness in my line of work."

"I guess I can see that. I often wondered how my dad did the job, because when he was with me, he was so open and loving. I could never really see him going undercover, pretending to be someone else. He didn't seem like he could do it." She paused, as her father's last words ran through her head. "Obviously, he could. Maybe he was putting up a front with me. Maybe I didn't know him at all."

"You knew him. Don't second-guess your relationship."

"I can't stop myself. I'm not supposed to trust anyone but him, but what if I didn't really know him? What if I just saw the man he wanted me to see?" She reflected on everything that had happened. "Two days ago, I was living one kind of life and now I'm living another, and it's all because of my dad. I feel like there might be a lot of things I don't know."

"I'm sure there are a lot of things you don't know," Damon agreed.

She didn't like his reply. "I was kind of hoping you'd respond with something more reassuring."

"I don't think we should lie to each other, Sophie, not with everything that's going on."

He was right, but the truth seemed very elusive at the moment. She broke open her cookie and read her fortune. "Well, this isn't helpful at all."

"What does it say?"

"*Two days from now, tomorrow will be yesterday.*"

"Intriguing." Another one of his rare smiles appeared. "Maybe it means tomorrow will be better."

"Now, there's that optimism I was looking for earlier. It only took a cookie to get you there. I just hope it doesn't mean tomorrow is going to be worse."

"Speaking of tomorrow," Damon began.

"I told you I'd tell you when we got there, and that's still true."

"Why the delay? You think I'm going to tip someone off?"

"It has crossed my mind. When I woke up and you were not in the car, I felt a moment of panic. I don't know why. I should be used to waking up alone when it comes to you."

"Ouch," he said with a grimace. "That was a low blow. But I didn't leave this time; I bought you food and a phone."

"I know." She took a breath. "And I'm sorry for the crack. It was a low blow."

"I deserved it. One of these days, I'm going to tell you why I left before the sun came up."

"I already know why—the night was over. And that's all you wanted."

His gaze darkened. "Like I said, one of these days, we'll talk more about it."

"One of these days…why not now?"

"Because you're holding back on me. I can't put everything on the table unless you do, too."

"I'm not holding back on personal stuff."

"Holding back is holding back…"

She couldn't imagine there was any great mystery that he was about to reveal. "Fine. You keep your secret, and I'll keep mine. I'm not really that interested anyway."

A gleam came into his eyes. "I think you are—even though you don't want to be."

"And you're delusional. My father was just killed. I'm on the run. I'm not even thinking about the night we spent together. It's so far down the list of things I need to be concerned about, it's not even on the list. It was another lifetime. I don't even know why we're discussing it."

"Because you brought it up with your low blow," he reminded her. "I don't think it's that far down the list."

She really hated how often he was right. "Let's just drop it." She was overwhelmed with emotion right now, and discussing that night with the one man she'd spent four years trying to forget was only going to make things worse.

"Dropping it," he said, as he shoved his chair back and stood up. "I'm going to get another water. Do you want anything else from the vending machine?"

"No, thanks."

"Lock the door behind me, and make sure it's me before you let me back in."

While she didn't appreciate his ordering tone, she flipped the dead bolt after he left and let out a breath.

It was good to put some space between them—if only for a few minutes.

But as she looked around the seedy motel room, the silence suddenly seemed overwhelming. She'd spent most of the day wishing Damon would go away, and now she really wanted him to come back—and fast.

Eight

Damon didn't really want anything from the vending machine; he just wanted to get away from Sophie. He never should have gotten into a discussion with her about their night together, but there was a part of him that wanted to make her understand that his leaving had never really been about her. It was him—all him.

He only liked commitment when it came to his job, to the soldiers he served with, his fellow agents, the people he was trying to put away or those under his protection. In his career, he was willing to put everything on the line. But women were another story.

He had never been good at relationships. He didn't do long-term. He didn't make promises. He didn't believe in soul mates or even love, really. He certainly didn't believe in happily ever after. And usually he stayed away from women who thought differently than him.

Sophie should have been one of those women he stayed away from, but four years ago, he hadn't been able to do that. He'd been in a dark place, and she'd helped him get out of it. He thought he'd helped her, too. But staying with her after that night wasn't an option. He was just sorry he'd hurt her, and clearly he had.

She might say all the right things, pretend it was no big deal, but her eyes were too expressive. When she felt pain, she showed it, and knowing he'd put a little of the pain in her eyes gnawed at him. It was the last thing he'd ever wanted to do.

He wanted to tell her that. He wanted her to know that it wasn't anything she'd said or done, but he also knew that dissecting that night probably wouldn't get them anywhere and they definitely had more pressing problems.

He took a lap around the building to burn off the unsettled feelings, the reckless energy, wanting to tire himself out before he had to return to Sophie and the very small hotel room. Instead of thinking about her, he should be planning for tomorrow. He might not know exactly where they were going, but he could still come up with some contingency plans. He could get on his phone and research New Haven, figure out how they might get transportation, look into the best places to stay in case they were in town longer than a few hours.

Feeling better now that he had a specific plan that didn't include having sex with Sophie, he stopped at the vending machine and picked up more drinks and a few chocolate bars. Then he headed back to the room. He rapped once, saw her peek through the blinds at him, and then she opened the door.

He thought he saw relief in her brown eyes, but he didn't know if that had to do with his reappearance or the chocolate in his hand.

"I love Almond Joy," she said, grabbing the bar. "Coconut and chocolate are my favorite combination." She stopped in the middle of unwrapping the chocolate. "You didn't get this for yourself, did you?"

"You can have it. I'm not that into chocolate."

"I do not understand how anyone could not be into chocolate."

He was happy to see they were back on a more even keel.

He sat down at the table and took out the phone he'd recently purchased. On the long drive through the mountains, his only worry about being disconnected from the world was Wyatt. He was supposed to meet him tonight, and he wasn't going to be there. He needed to make sure Wyatt knew that, and he hoped he could get Bree to go in his place.

"What are you doing?" Sophie asked, peering over his shoulder as she munched on her chocolate bar.

"Checking something."

"Like what? Your mail?"

"No."

"Sports scores? Stock market? Latest news?" she asked cheekily.

"Chocolate definitely wakes you up."

She made a face at him. "Come on, Damon, talk to me. I need to know if you're going to compromise us in some way. You would be just as aggressive if I was the one on the phone right now."

"Relax, Sophie, I know what I'm doing."

"I'll relax when you tell me *what* you're doing."

"Several years ago, while I was at Quantico, a group of us set up a private chat forum, a place where we could exchange coded information if we couldn't get on a phone or meet in person. It was originally part of an assignment to set up a protocol for communication. But we kept it going after we graduated, a safety net so to speak."

"How many people know about it?"

"Six—well, five, now that Jamie is no longer with us."

"Why are you checking it tonight?"

"Because yesterday morning I received an SOS from one of the members of the group. We met up, and he told me that he'd escaped a recent attack on his life. He wanted my help, but before we could get any further in the conversation, he got spooked and ran. Last night he got back to me asking if we could try again tonight. Unfortunately, I'm not going to make it. I need to let him know and see if someone else can meet him."

"Is he in danger?"

"Yes."

"Maybe you should be meeting him instead of staying here with me."

He'd had the same thought, but there was no way he was leaving Sophie alone. Wyatt could take care of himself. "That's not an option."

He opened the forum, and while there was no further communication from Wyatt, there was a reply from Bree to Wyatt.

Bree had always used the moniker Knight after the Mets second baseman Ray Knight, saying it was about time a knight was a woman. Bree and Parisa, the other woman in their group, had never been particularly thrilled with the all-male baseball forum idea, but neither one of them wasted energy on things that didn't really matter, especially when they both knew they were as good, if not better, than any male agent.

Bree's message read: *I feel like taking a few swings tonight, too. Hope you show, Carter. You've been MIA too long. Team is looking to trade you.*

He was relieved that Bree was going to meet with Wyatt. That took the pressure off him. But he didn't care much for the second part of her message, which confirmed his belief that Peter and Karen knew he'd gone looking for Sophie. They might not know if he'd found her, but they'd be suspicious of his motives and his secrecy.

He typed in a reply: *Not going to make practice tonight. Working on a pitch with another player who needs the support.* He hesitated, wishing they could be more direct, but they couldn't. *Who's leading team trade talks? Coach's BFF or second in command? Might be hidden agenda.*

"What on earth does all that mean?" Sophie asked.

He glanced up at her and saw the confused look in her eyes. "I said I can't make the meeting."

"It sounds like you're talking about baseball."

"That's the way it's supposed to sound. It's set up to be a baseball chat about the 1986 World Series Mets team."

A gleam of understanding entered her eyes. "Because

Jamie was obsessed with the Mets."

"It was his idea," he conceded. "We all picked particular players to use as our monikers. I'm Gary Carter. He was a catcher."

"And Fernandez, who's that in real life?"

He hesitated. "It doesn't matter."

Her eyes widened. "You're really not going to tell me? You want me to trust you, but you clearly don't trust me. This is a two-way street, Damon."

"And my secrecy is not about you. I have a bond with these people that I can't break."

She didn't look happy with that answer, but she seemed to accept it.

"I can tell you this," he said. "The person who's in trouble has been working undercover for your father. He was supposed to meet Alan on Monday, but Alan didn't show, and my friend was attacked. He barely escaped with his life."

She paled. "Your friend's assault is connected to my father?"

"He seemed to think so, but he didn't know about your father's accident when we spoke. I'm not sure what he believes now."

"If his attack is connected to my dad, then that should give the FBI a clue as to who's behind everything."

"My friend hasn't told the FBI what happened to him. He was waiting for your father—his handler—to get back to him. I told him about your dad's death last night, and he wanted to meet. That's where we are right now."

"I don't understand. Why don't you tell the FBI what your friend said?"

"Because he's worried there's a mole. He thought he was set up." He paused, remembering how bad Wyatt had looked. "He was in terrible shape, Sophie. I've never seen him like that. He used to have swagger, charm, a never-say-die personality, but he was like a hyped-up junkie in need of a fix—paranoid, edgy, scared… It was like he was hanging onto a cliff by his fingertips."

"I know that feeling." She sat down across from him. "If your friend worked for my dad, then my father must have had a lot of faith in him, because he only brought people on to his team who he respected. Maybe we should both go meet him. Maybe holing up here isn't the best idea. We can come back in the morning—or I can."

"It would take us a few hours to get back to New York, and the place we were going to meet at would be closed by then. Plus, we need to be in New Haven in the morning. Another friend is going to meet him. Hopefully, she can get him to a safe place, and then we can figure out what's going on."

"What does that other line mean—about the team looking to trade Carter?"

"She's warning me that I'm under suspicion, probably because my car was found shot up at the cabin. They don't know whose side I'm on."

"Your decision to come looking for me has certainly complicated your life."

"Somehow, I always knew it would."

Their gazes clung for a long moment. Sophie swiped her dry lips with her tongue, which turned his body instantly hard.

He cleared his throat and looked back at the phone. "Anyway, there's nothing more to be done tonight."

"Getting back to your group," Sophie said. "It sounds like one of the members is a woman. I might be able to figure out who's in the group if I think about Jamie and his time at Quantico and who he talked about…"

"It's not worth expending your effort on that."

"Well, it's better than thinking about the fact that my dad called a meeting with an undercover agent, and he didn't show up, and then that agent was almost killed."

"We don't know why he didn't show up."

"What does your friend think?"

He didn't want to relate what Wyatt had said, not when he didn't know what was fact and what was theory, and especially not when Sophie's pain was so raw, the depth of her loss so deep. "I'm not sure."

"You said we weren't going to lie to each other, Damon. Does your friend think my dad was the mole?"

"He considered it to be a possibility," he said carefully.

She sucked in a breath. "I knew you were going to say that, but it's still not easy to hear."

"And we don't know if it's true."

"Someone killed my dad, so it doesn't sound like he was in charge of anything. Maybe he was a victim, too."

"That's a good possibility. We can speculate all we want, but we don't have enough facts to come to a conclusion."

She let out a frustrated sigh. "You're very logical, Damon."

"That usually works in my favor."

"I'm sure it does, but it's irritating at times."

"Because it makes me right more often than wrong?"

"And because it makes you cocky," she retorted. "But mostly because it makes me feel like I'm way out of my depth. I run on emotion; I always have. But all that emotion has landed me in the deep end of the pool. I'm treading water as fast as I can, but it wouldn't take much for me to drown. And sometimes I feel like it would be easier to let go."

He did not like that comment at all. "I'm not going to let you drown, Sophie. And you are not going to let go, because whether or not you run on emotion, you are a fighter. I've seen nothing but fight in you since we were at the cabin."

"I try to fight, but sometimes it feels futile. I watched my mother fight cancer. She battled for a long time, but she didn't win. I lost her when I was sixteen. And now I've lost my dad. I'm alone. And if that's not bad enough, there's a chance I'm going to find out that my father is not the man I thought he was. How can I lose faith in the most important person in my life in less than twenty-four hours?"

"No one is asking you to lose faith. Let's deal with the facts as they come."

She swallowed hard, her gaze still troubled. "What do

you think, Damon? I know you liked him, respected him. Do you think my father did something wrong? Is there any way he could be a—traitor?"

Her question hit him hard. She was forcing him to look at something he didn't want to look at. "It would be very difficult for me to believe that," he said slowly. "I don't see how Alan could sell out his country or a fellow agent. His life was the FBI."

"It was. He lived for his job," she agreed. "He was a patriot. He always talked about the importance of doing the right thing. Were those just empty words?"

He was a little surprised that she had as many doubts as she did about her father's innocence. "What aren't you telling me, Sophie?"

"Nothing."

"You just asked how you could lose faith in a person you'd loved your entire life in less than twenty-four hours, and I want to know the same thing. I don't think your doubts are based solely on what my undercover friend thinks about your dad, so what else is in play?"

He could see the conflict in her eyes, but finally she said, "On his voicemails, he kept apologizing, and he said something about not realizing he was down in the mud until it was too late. That makes it sound like he made a mistake; I just don't know how big a mistake it was. Obviously, it was big enough to get him killed." She got up from her chair and paced around the small room. "I wish I could listen to the voicemails again. Maybe I'm not remembering them clearly."

She paused in front of him, giving him a sad, helpless, frustrated look that made his heart flip over. He wanted to pull her into his arms. He wanted to tell her everything was going to be fine, that her father was not a bad guy, that they would find a way to prove that. But he didn't know if any of that was true. He'd already promised her he wouldn't lie to her. And he'd also promised himself that he wouldn't touch her.

"Maybe we should turn on the TV," he suggested.

"Really? That's all you have to say?"

"I don't know what else to say. I didn't hear the voicemails. You're feeding me piecemeal information. I have no idea if there's more you're holding back, since I still don't know where we're going tomorrow. I'm operating with less information than you are, unless you want to start sharing..."

Her mouth tightened. "Maybe we should turn the TV on. This conversation is going nowhere."

"It would go somewhere if you'd talk."

She walked over to the dresser and picked up the remote. Then she sat down on the bed and flipped through the channels.

"See if you can find some news," he said. "There might be an update on the investigation."

"We get like ten channels, Damon. You could have picked a better motel," she said grumpily.

He could have done a lot of things differently.

He looked back at his phone, as Bree answered his question: *Coach's BFF and second are tight. Manager also angry about your actions. You might not keep your job if you stay away too long. Any idea who tried to strike you out?*

He typed in an answer. *"Didn't get a good look. More important things to worry about than job. Hope you can get Fernandez back on his game. Think there's a link between us. Let me know next practice time. Don't get yourself benched. Think we're going to need you."*

Bree sat in her office cubicle Thursday evening and read Damon's message on her personal phone with a growing sense of uneasiness. After Damon's car had been located at a cabin in the Adirondacks, at a property purportedly owned by Alan Parker, a lot of questions had been raised about him. There had been a flurry of meetings, hushed conversations, and even a few suspicious looks sent in her direction, since several people knew that she and Damon were friends from

Quantico.

If anyone asked, she could truthfully say that Damon had not told her of any plans to drive north when they'd spoken the night before. When he hadn't shown up for work or responded to a text about lunch, she'd assumed he'd gone off to find Wyatt. She'd certainly never anticipated he'd go looking for Sophie Parker.

She remembered seeing Sophie at Jamie's funeral. Jamie had mentioned Sophie a few times in conversation, referring to her as his nerdy but beautiful childhood friend, who was obsessed with digging for relics from the past. It was clear that there had been a deep affection between them, so deep she'd once felt a little jealous... *How silly was that?* She'd only been Jamie's girlfriend for about five minutes. In fact, she didn't know if Jamie had ever really thought of himself as her boyfriend.

She shook those disturbing thoughts out of her head, and brought her mind back to the present.

There was a connection between Alan's death, Wyatt's attack, and Sophie's disappearance, and Damon had put himself in the middle of all three events. But now, with Damon laying low and Wyatt out of touch, it was on her to find out what was going on. If there was a traitor in the building, she needed to figure out who it was.

"Agent Adams?"

She looked up in surprise to see ASAC Karen Leigh standing by her desk. She'd had very little contact with Agent Leigh since she'd come to the New York field office three months earlier, because their teams rarely crossed paths. But Karen had an excellent reputation and was regarded as a rising star at the Bureau.

She got to her feet. "Agent Leigh, what can I do for you?"

"I'm going downstairs to get a coffee. Since we're both working late, I thought you might like to join me."

She could see by the purpose in Karen's eyes that it was more of an order than an invitation, not that she had to follow orders from Karen, but she was interested in what Karen had to say. "Of course. That sounds good. I can always use a shot of caffeine."

"Excellent."

They didn't speak on their way out of the offices or in the elevator to the first floor. When they got to the coffeehouse located in the lobby, they picked up their drinks and then took a seat at an isolated table against the wall.

She was actually happy to have coffee. She was still working on too little sleep from her last case, and she had a long night ahead of her.

"Have you heard from Damon?" Karen asked, not bothering with any polite chitchat.

"No, I haven't." She kept her expression neutral, her shoulders relaxed, her breath even. She'd taken enough polygraphs to know how to lie with the best of them. "Have you? I'm worried about him. I hope he's all right."

"I'm worried, too. Did he tell you he was going to look for Sophie Parker?"

"Is that what he was doing?" she countered.

"I would imagine so, since Alan owned the cabin in the Adirondacks where Damon's car was located," Karen said sharply.

"If you knew that Alan owned a cabin there, why didn't you send someone to the lake to look for Sophie? When I was in the office last night, it didn't appear that anyone had any idea where Sophie was. But a cabin owned by her father would seem to be a big lead."

She might be making a mistake to confront Karen, but she'd always been better at offense than defense.

"I didn't know about the cabin until the police notified us that Damon's car was found on the property," Karen replied. "It took us some time to dig through the property information to find the link to Alan. Apparently, Damon didn't need to do that, and I wonder why."

"Maybe Alan told him about the cabin," she suggested.

"Then Damon should have told us."

"I don't know why he didn't," she said. "But if I had to take a guess, it would be because he's new to the team, and he doesn't know who to trust."

"Everyone on Alan's team can be trusted. Alan handpicked each one of us. We are all extremely loyal to him. Did Damon doubt that in some way?"

"I really don't know. I spoke to Damon for about five minutes last night. We haven't seen each other in months. All he said was that he'd been here a week and didn't really know what Alan was working on."

"Well, that was by Alan's choice. He had some special project in mind for Damon that he didn't share with me."

She found that interesting. Karen couldn't hide that Alan's secrecy on Damon's assignment bothered her. And why wouldn't Alan tell Karen what he wanted Damon to work on? Maybe it was whatever case had gotten him killed.

"Do you have any theories on who killed Alan?" she asked, taking a sip of her coffee. Since Karen had instigated the conversation, she was going to seize the opportunity to find out what she could.

"Nothing I can talk about. We're keeping the circle small right now." Karen tapped her blue-coated fingernails on the table and said, "What about Wyatt Tanner?"

"What about him?"

"You know him, too, don't you? Have you heard from him?"

"I know him, but I haven't spoken to him since he went undercover almost a year ago. Why do you ask?"

"He missed a meet, and with Alan's accident, I'm concerned about him. I want to make sure that everyone we have in the field is safe until we bring Alan's killer to justice. I know that you and Damon and Wyatt went through Quantico together, and Alan spoke highly of all three of you."

"We're friends, but our assignments have taken us in very different directions."

"Yes, I know. Alan actually wanted you for our team, but he said you had a passion for finding missing children."

"I do," she admitted.

"That's a tough job. A lot of heartbreak."

"I'm a tough agent. As are you. You have an excellent reputation."

Karen's tension eased at her compliment. "I do my best. Alan taught me a lot."

"How long have you worked for Alan?"

"Two years—ever since he left Quantico and came to New York. I'm really going to miss him. He wasn't just my boss; he was a mentor and a friend."

There appeared to be genuine emotion in Karen's eyes, and Bree couldn't help wondering just how deep Karen's friendship with Alan had gone, but she certainly couldn't ask her that.

"Alan was a good man," Karen added. "He didn't deserve to die."

"No," she murmured, feeling now as if Karen had gone somewhere else in her head, a distant look in her eyes.

Karen suddenly straightened, squaring her shoulders and tilting up her chin. "If you hear from Damon or Wyatt, please tell them to get in touch with me. Now that Alan is gone, it's my responsibility to make sure that all the agents in our department are safe."

"I don't expect to hear from them, but if I do, I will certainly pass the message on. I would assume that Wyatt would get in touch with his handler. Was that Alan?"

"It was. I've tried to contact Wyatt through our emergency protocol, but he hasn't replied."

"Maybe he still will."

"I hope so."

"So do I," she murmured. Glancing at her watch, she realized time was quickly passing, and she had her own meet to make. "I should get back upstairs. I have some work to finish. Are you coming?"

"Actually, I'm going to stay here for a few more minutes. I haven't been out of the office all day," Karen replied. "I could use a break."

She got to her feet. "Then I'll see you later."

After leaving the coffeehouse, she paused in the lobby of the building, and glanced back at Karen through the glass doors. She was on her phone, and Bree couldn't help wondering who she was calling and if it had anything to do with their conversation. Karen had definitely been pumping her for information, but she'd gotten nothing, so what did she have to report?

Turning away, she made her way to the bank of elevators. She stepped to the side as the doors opened to allow people to exit and was surprised to see Peter Hunt with a man she knew only by reputation and from the news, Senator Greg Raleigh from Connecticut.

Peter gave her a brief nod as the men walked out of the building together.

As she got in the elevator, she couldn't help thinking that senators rarely came to the FBI; usually the FBI went to them.

It could be nothing…but right now everything had the potential to be something…

Nine

After scouring the Internet for news stories about Alan's accident, Sophie's disappearance and the shootout at the cabin, Damon found little new information. Police were still asking for witnesses to Alan's accident. Sophie was still missing and possibly in danger, and gunshots were heard near a cabin, sometimes used by the Parkers. There was no mention of his presence at the cabin, and he was quite sure that someone at the FBI had put the lid on that.

Frustrated at being in the dark and cut off from the Bureau's resources, he set down the phone and glanced over at Sophie who was changing channels every few minutes. She hadn't had anything to say to him in the last hour, which was probably a good thing, but he had a feeling there were a lot of ideas running through her head.

He needed to make sure he knew what she was thinking of doing before she did it.

"Can't find anything you like?" he asked.

She shook her head. "Nope. Not that the choices are great: a game show, a rerun of *I Love Lucy*, an episode of the *Real Housewives of Somewhere* and some sitcoms with laugh tracks so loud they must have brought in a hundred people to feign amusement."

He smiled at the disgust in her tone. "Not much of a TV watcher, are you?"

"I like the History Channel, travel documentaries, and shows with substance. I mean, who cares how this woman gets her lips to look plump?" She waved the remote toward the screen, which showed a middle-aged brunette at a plastic surgeon's office.

"Certainly not me," he said, getting up from the hard, uncomfortable chair. He crossed the room and sat down on the other bed. Thank God, the motel had had a room with two beds. It was hot enough in here without having to deal with the heat between him and Sophie. At least they could keep a good several feet between them.

She muted the sound on the television and said, "I feel like I want to call someone, Damon."

"Who?" he asked warily.

"My aunt Valerie—my mother's sister. She lives in Sydney, Australia, so maybe the news about my father hasn't gotten down there yet, or it might not be important or big enough for her press to cover, but I don't know for sure, and it's bothering me."

"You can't call her."

"She's the only family I have left, Damon. It's one thing to leave my friends hanging, but Aunt Valerie was there for me when my mom was sick. How can I let her think something might have happened to me?"

"If you call her, something *might* happen to you," he said forcefully. "We can't risk it. The Bureau could have a tap on your aunt's phone."

"All the way in Australia?" she asked doubtfully.

"With technology, the world is not that big anymore. Look, it's only been a day. You can wait awhile longer."

She let out a sigh. "Has it really only been twenty-four hours? It feels like much longer than that."

It did to him, too. "Tell me about your aunt, your relationship," he said, thinking that if she talked about her family, maybe she could wait on actually talking to them.

"Valerie is my mother's younger sister by seven years. She came to live with us when I was eleven. That's when my mom was diagnosed with cancer. She was only thirty-five years old."

"That's rough."

"It was horrible. The other moms were jogging and taking yoga classes and helping their kids with homework and art projects, driving carpool and doing all the things that moms do, but mine was having chemo and trying not to throw up. Valerie came for a visit and realized that we needed help. My dad was there for my mother, of course, but he was working, too. So, Valerie moved in. She gave up her single, twenty-eight-year-old life to take care of us, and she stayed with us for five years. I don't know what I would have done without her. She made it okay to laugh when everything seemed really bad."

"I'm glad you had someone like that in your life."

"Me, too. Valerie fell in love with an Aussie a year before my mom died, and she did long-distance with him until after the funeral. Then it was finally her turn to have a life. She got married and had three little girls. I haven't seen them since they were babies, but I keep in touch through text and email." She gave him a pleading look. "I really want to talk to my aunt."

"Tell me about your mom," he suggested, offering another distraction. "Your dad always spoke of *his Maggie* in almost reverent tones. She sounded like an amazing woman."

"She was amazing, and after she died, she became a saint in my dad's eyes, probably mine, too. Not that she wasn't wonderful, but I think we did embellish just how wonderful she was after she was gone."

"How did your parents meet?"

"They met at Yale their junior year. Mom was a history major and Dad was pre-law. He was going to be a lawyer back then. They both said it was love at first sight. They got married a year after college. Neither set of grandparents was happy about that. My mother's parents were wealthy, and they didn't think my father, who came from very blue-collar roots, was good enough for their blue-blooded daughter. They had a huge fight and basically told my mom she could choose him or them, and she chose him."

"They sound terrible."

"They weren't nice. They were full of stubborn, arrogant pride, and worried incessantly about what the world thought of them. They did make amends with my mom after she got sick, but it was too little, too late. After my mom's funeral, I never saw them again. My grandfather died a few years ago, and my grandmother moved to Australia to be near Aunt Valerie. She's probably driving my aunt nuts, although Valerie married a man my grandmother approved of, so maybe it's not so bad."

"I don't understand how anyone could disapprove of your father. He didn't have a lot of money, but he did graduate from Yale."

"He was a scholarship kid at Yale. They acted like he was gifted his diploma, which was ridiculous."

"What about your father's parents? Why didn't they approve of the marriage?"

"I think they were put off by my mom's family and their snobbishness. They were around somewhat when I was little, but they died young. My grandfather had a heart attack when I was about five and my grandmother was killed in a car accident a few years later." She paused. "What if I just text or email my aunt?"

"No."

She sighed. "Fine, then let's talk about your family. Are your parents alive?"

He really didn't want to talk about his family, but if it kept Sophie from doing something stupid, then he had to do it. "Yes," he said shortly.

"And well?"

"Last I heard. Why don't you throw the remote control over here? I'll see if I can find a better show."

"Hang on, we're talking, Damon."

"I don't like to talk about my family."

She gave him a speculative look. "Why not? What's the deal with them?"

"There's no *deal*. We're just not close."

"Now or always?"

It was clear that Sophie wasn't going to let the subject go without getting more information. She really did like to dig, even if she didn't have her hands in actual dirt. Unfortunately, his family history was not his favorite subject.

"Always," he said. "Can we talk about something else?"

"After we finish talking about this," she said stubbornly. "Come on, Damon. We have hours to kill. What are your parents' names?"

"My father is Cameron Wolfe. He's an entertainment lawyer in Beverly Hills."

"That sounds fancy."

"It can be. He works with a lot of celebrities."

"And your mother? What's her story?"

"Her name is Suzanne Cummings. She never took my father's name as she was a soap opera actress in her twenties when they met."

"No kidding?" she asked in surprise. "What soap opera was she on?"

"I think it was called *Now and Forever*. It ran for about five years. At any rate, my parents' relationship was as fake as the daytime drama she starred in, filled with secrets, lies, and betrayals—all the things that make for a good show. Only it wasn't a show, it was my life." He cleared his throat, realizing how much his bitterness was showing. "They got divorced when I was nine. I'm quite certain my father made sure that the divorce happened before their ten-year anniversary, when my mother would have gotten a bonus settlement, as noted in their pre-nup."

"That's sad and cynical."

"It's also the truth. Their divorce played out in the tabloids. My mother was a drama queen and my father was a Hollywood deal-maker. He was also an SOB. There were rumors of other men with my mother, other women with my father, alcoholism, drugs, whatever would make for a better story. At different points, one of them would petition for full custody of me, claiming that the other was a bad parent. I'd get dragged into court or sent to my grandparents' while everyone had a cool-down. I thought for a long time they were fighting about me, that they loved me so much they couldn't bear to give me up."

"Maybe that was the reason," Sophie said quietly.

"No, I was just a pawn in their divorce game."

"I'm sure they both loved you."

"They loved themselves more."

"Who did you end up living with?"

"I went back and forth, and back and forth, and back and forth. Summer was the worst. I could never just be in one place, hanging with my friends. I was always in a car, on a plane, headed to somewhere else, some place usually hot and sweaty. Speaking of which, the air conditioning in this room sucks."

"It's not great," she agreed. "We could have afforded a better place."

"And drawn more attention."

"Did your parents remarry?"

"We're not done with them yet?" he asked with a groan.

"Almost there."

"Yes, my mother remarried when I was twelve. My stepfather was a studio vice president of something. He moved us into a Beverly Hills mansion with a great pool."

"And good air conditioning, I'll bet."

"It did have that. But the house was so big, sometimes I wasn't even sure they were in it with me. Then they had three girls, one right after the other, and it was baby-land around there."

"And your dad? Did he also remarry?"

"The first time when I was about thirteen. Second time I was twenty. He got divorced for the third time last year. In case you haven't guessed, he's not much of a prize as a husband...or a father. But he is charming. Everyone likes him." He stopped talking, surprised at himself for having said so much to her. "Now that you're sufficiently bored, can I have the remote?"

"I'm not bored at all." She licked her lips. "We kind of skipped the getting to know each other part when we first met."

"We did do that," he agreed, meeting her gaze. His body hardened as he saw the memories in her eyes, the same memories running through his head. "Now, the remote?"

She ignored him—again.

"How did you get into the Army? Did you enlist at eighteen, or what?" she asked.

"No, I went to college. I didn't know what I wanted to do, but it was going to be far from Hollywood and the film industry. Then 9/11 happened, and it changed me. After that horrific event, I was drawn to the military. I joined the ROTC, which horrified both parents for the five minutes that they chose to care about it."

"Maybe they were worried about your safety?"

"I doubt that, but I didn't pay attention to them. I got my degree and went into the Army as an officer and finally found something real—sometimes too real at times," he muttered, thinking that going from Hollywood to boot camp had been like going from Earth to Mars. He hadn't been at all prepared for real hardship, for physical and mental tests, but he'd come out a much better and stronger person.

"You met Jamie in the Army, right?"

"Third year in. We were on the same team—as close as brothers. When our tours were up, it was Jamie who suggested we look at the FBI."

"I never thought he'd follow his father into the FBI," Sophie said. "As a kid, he was adamant about not doing that."

"He told me that, too. Jamie wanted to make his own way in the world, but when his dad retired, he felt like he could join the Bureau without having to worry about nepotism or people thinking he was getting favors he didn't deserve." He paused. "Did you ever want to follow your dad and work at the Bureau?"

"Not even for one second."

"Okay, that's a no."

She gave him a sheepish look. "It's not that I didn't admire what my father did. He was a true patriot. He believed in country, duty, faithfulness, the good of all people. He devoted his life to that, and I was super proud of him. And sometimes I felt selfish for not wanting to do the same, but I've always been more interested in ancient history than current events. For me, piecing together someone's story from what little might be left behind from their home, their city or their grave is fascinating."

He liked the way her brown eyes shimmered with gold when she felt passionate about something. He liked it even more when the passion was focused on him.

"One time I found a small, engraved gold ring," she continued. "It took me almost two years to figure out that it belonged to a very young prince in a very old country. He'd died on his wedding day, shot by a rival for his wife's attentions. He was seventeen years old."

"What happened to his killer?"

"Of course, you would ask that," she said with a laugh. "That's your special agent training. I was more interested in what happened to his wife."

"Well, did you find out?"

"His wife was forced to marry her husband's killer. But interestingly enough, that man died by poison a few years later. No one ever knew who did it. I think it was her."

"Sounds like one of my mother's soap operas. How did you learn all that from a ring anyway?"

"I traced the ring through the engraving back to the prince's family and then I researched my way through old manuscripts and tales of that time period and put it all together. I'm making it sound easy, but it wasn't."

"That's impressive. You must be great at puzzles."

"I do like the challenge. When I find something like a

ring or a bone, I develop a rather obsessive compulsion to know everything about it. Every person has a story and so many are never told, but every now and then, I get to tell one. It's how we inform history. It's how we learn from our pasts." She let out a breath. "And I'm getting super carried away."

"You love what you do. That's great. Not everyone can say that."

"I do love it. I wanted to be an archaeologist from about age six on. You don't know how many times I dug up our backyard."

"Did you ever find anything?"

"The bones of somebody's family pet. After that, my parents put a moratorium on digs in the backyard. But they did sign me up for summer adventures, so that helped."

"Your dad told me that you teach, too, is that right?"

"Yes. I teach in the fall and go on digs in the summer. I'm supposed to be in Egypt next month."

A look of concern flashed through her eyes.

"What's wrong?" he asked.

"I just remembered that it's finals next week. I was going to spend this weekend writing the tests for my classes. I'm supposed to have office hours on Monday and the final is next Wednesday. But I'm sitting here in a seedy motel room without any way to communicate with anyone. What are my students going to do? Are they going to get incompletes? Some of them are graduating. And some of them have worked two jobs to afford to go on the dig with me in July. I'm letting down so many people, Damon. I feel terrible about it. Am I being selfish?"

"No, you're being smart. You could have been killed this morning. Hell, you could have been killed last night if you'd gone into your apartment instead of running away. This isn't a game you're in. Your father is dead, and we're trying to keep you alive. Don’t forget that. I'm sure the university is aware that you're missing. Someone will step in for you. They'll take care of your students."

"You're probably right," she said slowly. "I just don't

want any of them to get hurt by this."

He was touched by the generosity of her spirit, the softness of her heart. She cared about people, and that was somewhat rare in his world. He had his core group of friends, people he trusted with his life, and the danger they were perpetually in intensified their loyalty to each other. But Sophie felt loyal to her students, her employers, her friends, even an aunt she hadn't seen since she was sixteen.

He wondered what it would feel like if she felt that way about him...

But he didn't want that kind of caring relationship. He didn't want someone he had to check in with, someone to worry about and to have worry about him. That's why he'd left her all those years ago. He'd known if he stayed past dawn, she'd spin a web around him that he wouldn't be able to get out of—or want to. And he'd made a promise to himself a long time ago that he wouldn't let anyone else control what he did, who he saw, where he went.

It had been a promise he'd kept.

Sometimes it felt like a lonely promise.

But he'd always told himself it was better to be the one who left and not the one left behind.

"You're suddenly quiet," Sophie said. "What are you thinking about, Damon?"

"Your students," he lied. "The only way to protect them is to stay away from them."

"That's true. Look what happened to you when you got close to me—you almost got shot."

"Wasn't even close. Which bothers me," he added, thinking about the firefight at the cabin.

"It bothers you that you weren't hit?" she asked in amazement.

"Just wondered why our attacker didn't wait for a better shot…or why there weren't two people to box us in."

Her brows knit together. "You're unhappy with the skill of our attacker?"

"You were standing in front of the window, but you

weren't hit. Was that on purpose? Was it a warning shot?"

"I never thought of that," she said slowly. "But why would he be warning me?"

"No idea. I'm just speculating."

"One of my favorite pastimes," she said. "I am good at putting puzzles together, Damon, but I don't think we have enough pieces."

"We'll start getting them tomorrow."

"I hate waiting."

"So do I, especially for the details on where we're going in the morning," he added pointedly.

"It will be tomorrow soon enough."

It didn't feel that way to him. A long, hot night loomed ahead of them, and talking to Sophie had only made him like her more. He was also bothered by some of what she'd shared with him.

"Sophie," he said abruptly, swinging his legs off the bed as he faced her.

"What?" she asked warily, obviously picking up on his change of tone.

"You said we weren't going anywhere that could be tied to your father or your past, but that's not true. We're going to New Haven, where your parents went to school, where Peter Hunt went to school. I'm guessing your father might have had an apartment there at one time. Or a house. Or a life."

She drew in a breath. "We're not going into New Haven. There's a storage place on the outskirts of town." She reached into her pocket and pulled out a key.

"I knew you went to the cabin to get something besides a gun. Why didn't we go straight to the storage unit? They don't usually close that early."

"This one closes at seven. I checked before I got rid of my phone. I was trying to figure out if I could get to the cabin and then get to New Haven all in one day. I could have done it if I'd found the key faster or if you hadn't arrived or if someone hadn't tried to kill us, making us take a tortuous route to get here."

"You should have told me. We could have switched up our route, gotten to the site before it closed."

"We had to stay off the main highways," she argued. "That was more important."

She might be right, but he was still pissed off that she had kept the information from him. "What's in the storage unit?"

"I have no idea. He just told me to get the key and go there."

"In his voicemail, he specifically told you where to go? Because if he did, there's a chance the Bureau has been able to retrieve those voicemails from the phone carrier. Maybe that's how they tracked you to the cabin."

"He didn't mention the cabin. He spoke in code, like the way you do on your baseball forum. He used references to places only I would understand."

"Like what? Tell me exactly."

"You know, I don't like you ordering me around," she said with irritation.

"I don't like getting shot at. Let's see if we can work together."

"He told me to go to my favorite place in the world—that was the cabin—and get a key. He asked me if I remembered the story about his beer bottle collection and that he'd left me something there—the storage unit."

"Beer bottle collection?" he queried.

"In college, he started a collection of beer bottles, and he kept it up in his twenties. But once he married my mom and they had me, apparently my mother decided the beer bottle collection had to go. My mom loved to do spring cleaning. Twice a year, she'd make me go through my closets. One day I was really mad because she wanted me to give away something I wanted to keep, and my dad told me he had a secret place where he would stash things he didn't want to get rid of. So, I put my stuff in a box like my mom wanted me to, and my dad and I were supposed to drop it off at a charity collection box. Only, we didn't go there, we went to New

Haven and put it in his storage locker where he still had his beer bottle collection."

"Did you live in New Haven at the time?"

"No, we were in Woodbridge then, which isn't far. Anyway, that was the one and only time I went to the storage center. After my mom died, one day my dad showed up with all my boxes. He said he wanted to give me some of my memories back and make me feel better." She paused. "I didn't know he still had the storage unit. It wasn't something I thought about, that's for sure. But I guess he kept it all these years. Maybe he needed it after he sold the house I grew up in."

He was beginning to think that Alan had a lot more secrets than anyone could imagine. "So that's it, that's the whole story? Was there anything else on the voicemails?"

"No, just vague apologies and telling me to be careful and to run as fast and as far away as I could once I did the two things he asked me to do—get the key and go to the storage unit."

"I still don't like that the unit is in New Haven where he went to school. Maybe Peter Hunt knew about his beer bottle collection and where he stashed it."

"I don't think my father would send me into trouble."

"Well, the cabin didn't work out so well." He got to his feet and walked around the room, thinking about all the different scenarios that could play out. His gut was churning, his instincts telling him they could easily be walking into some sort of a trap.

"What are you thinking?" Sophie asked worriedly.

"That we should abandon the storage unit and just lay low until we figure out what's going on."

"But I have to go there. My dad told me it was important. I have to follow what he said. It was the last thing he asked me to do."

"When he asked you, he didn't know someone was going to find you at the cabin. He wouldn't want you to go into danger."

She stared back at him with determination in her eyes. "We can argue about it all night, but I'm going there in the morning. My father left me something, and I have to know what it is."

"I can stop you."

She got to her feet and walked over to face him. "You could probably do that, but you're not going to."

His heart thudded against his chest. "Why wouldn't I?"

She didn't answer right away, and the tension between them tightened so much he felt as if something was about to snap—maybe him. He shoved his hands into his pockets to stop himself from grabbing her, because with her standing so close, he could barely remember what they were arguing about.

"Because you want to know what's in there as much as I do," she said finally.

He blinked, forcing himself to refocus on the conversation.

"And you know that if we don't find the storage unit first, whatever is there could be gone forever," she added.

"It could already be gone," he said. "We don't know if we're ahead or behind."

"We'll find out tomorrow. You should take a shower, Damon; you look hot."

He was hot all right, fired up by the situation, by her, by the damned summer heat. "Finally, one of your ideas I actually like."

He went into the bathroom, shut the door and took a deep breath. He never had trouble concentrating on a mission, but Sophie was making it almost impossible to think and act logically. He could not run on emotion the way she did, or they were both going to end up dead.

Stripping off his clothes, he got into a cold shower and felt a rush of relief.

Unfortunately, he had a feeling the heat would be back as soon as he left the shower, because he and Sophie still had to get through the night together.

Ten

Sophie sat down on the edge of the bed as she heard the shower go on. She took a couple of deep breaths, trying to slow down her racing pulse. Damon had definitely gotten her worked up. She felt like she'd just finished a ten-mile run. Not that she ran enough to know what that would feel like, but it was probably like this.

She got back up, adrenaline and something else making her want to move.

The *something else* was, of course, Damon.

For a moment there, she'd thought he was going to kiss her. And for a moment there, she'd wanted him to. She'd wanted to go back to the night they'd spent together when everything bad had faded away, when only good feelings had washed over her, when she'd felt desired and adored and connected…

But look how that ended...

She'd woken up alone. Even though she didn't regret the night, she did wish he'd given them a chance to see if they could have had more than a night.

But she didn't need to be thinking about that now.

She had bigger problems—much bigger problems.

She wasn't stupid. She knew that someone else might

know about the storage unit, but she had to trust in someone, and right now the only person she could absolutely trust was her father.

Still, as Damon had reminded her, the cabin had been attacked and surely her father had not anticipated that happening. *Was she going to walk into another dangerous situation?* But if she didn't go, she'd never know what was there, what her father wanted her to have, and that was unthinkable.

So, she'd go and hope that Damon wouldn't try to stop her.

That thought made her wonder if she shouldn't leave while he was in the shower. She could get a cab, leave Damon to find his own way back to New York. Although, he'd probably track her down at the storage unit. There weren't that many in New Haven. She really should have kept that piece of information to herself, but it was too late now.

Run or stay...the decision seemed suddenly huge.

And then the bathroom door opened and Damon walked out in jeans and no shirt, beads of water clinging to his broad shoulders, the perfect amount of dark hair drifting across his chest and down his hard abs. Right now, he looked a lot less like a federal agent and very much more like the incredibly hot guy she'd had sex with four years ago.

She swallowed hard as he crossed the room and stood in front of the air-conditioning unit, shaking out his damp hair with his fingers.

Yeah, leaving really wasn't an option.

She sat down on her bed, starting to think of the lumpy, uncomfortable mattress as her island of sanity in the midst of her turbulent life.

She grabbed the remote and turned up the sound on the television. The local news was on, the first story about a protest at Yale over a new increase in tuition fees. Nothing particularly earth-shattering there, and that was fine with her. She was trying to calm down, not get amped up over more bad news in the world. Maybe they'd do the weather next or sports, things that wouldn't change the course of her life.

"We have breaking news," the female anchor said, interrupting her co-host, who was about to talk about an upcoming art festival. "Out of New York," she added, then paused, as she listened to whoever was talking in her ear.

Damon turned away from the air conditioning to look at the television.

A photo came up on the screen, and for a split second she was terrified it might be a picture of her father or of her, but it was a man she didn't recognize. She blew out a breath. "Thank God, it's not my dad or us," she murmured.

"Don't thank God yet," he said tersely.

"What do you mean?"

He didn't answer as the news anchor continued with the story. "The body pulled from the Hudson River earlier tonight was that of thirty-six-year-old Lorenzo Venturi, the youngest son of the infamous Mafia leader, Giancarlo Venturi, who died in prison last year after serving half of a life sentence for murder, racketeering, money laundering and a long list of other criminal activities. He is survived by his older brother Stefan and his mother Venetia."

"Damn," Damon said, his profile turning hard. "That's not good."

"What does this guy's death have to do with us?"

"Your father ran the organized crime division, Sophie."

"I know that. Was this guy part of one of his cases?"

"Yes. And I'm fairly certain that my friend who's in trouble has been undercover with the Venturi family for the last year."

"What does this mean then? Is it such a bad thing when one of the bad guys ends up dead?"

"Depends on who killed him and why. And whether or not they were also responsible for your father's death."

"I can't imagine it's the same person. This man was a criminal. My dad was a federal agent."

"Venturi could have been turned into an informant by your dad. He could have been passing him critical information."

"And that's why they're both dead?" she asked.

"Possibly. Or it could have been a power grab between the Venturi brothers, who resurrected the business after their father died."

"That makes more sense. If you look back through history, brothers killing brothers to attain power is quite a common theme."

"It's a plausible theory," he said. "But all we really know for sure is that the body count is going up fast, and we don't want to add to it."

"No, we don't," she said heavily, his words reminding her just how precarious her life was right now.

"You wanted another puzzle piece, Sophie. We just got one. Now we have to figure out where it fits."

"Maybe there will be an answer in the storage unit."

He met her gaze. "I still think it's a bad idea. Maybe I should go alone."

"No way. That's not happening."

"I could take the key from you. I could figure out where it goes."

"You could, but you're not going to, because we're in this together. You asked me to trust you, and I have. You're not going to let me down, are you?"

His expression hardened. "No, I'm not going to let you down."

"Good." She flipped the channel to a sitcom rerun, desperately needing some canned laughter and happy music.

"I'm going to see what else I can find out about Lorenzo Venturi's death online," Damon said, reaching for his phone.

"Are you sure your search won't trigger some FBI flag? You're using the motel Internet. Can't it be traced?"

"It can, but with news organizations reporting on Venturi's death, I think there will be thousands of searches on the subject tonight. We won't stand out."

"You always have an answer."

He looked up from his phone, his blue eyes unusually

dark. "Not always, Sophie."

"What question can't you answer?" she asked daringly, knowing she probably shouldn't, but she couldn't stop herself.

"How we're going to keep our hands off each other tonight."

Her breath stuck in her chest. "Well, it would be easier if you put your shirt back on."

A slow smile spread across his face. "But it's so hot in here."

"Yeah, and you're not helping." She turned up the sound on the television again until it was almost blaring.

Damon retrieved his shirt from the bathroom, covering up just the way she'd asked. *She just wished she hadn't asked...*

"You don't have to worry, Sophie," Damon said a moment later, a gleam in his eyes. "Nothing is going to happen that you don't want to happen."

Which only made her worry more...

When had his life gone so wrong? Wyatt walked through the 8th Street arcade which was housed in an old warehouse. The arcade was crowded with kids, and it reminded him of when his biggest goal had been to break the record on whatever video game he was playing. But that life felt like a lifetime ago and yearning for it was pointless, so he quickly made his way to the back of the building where the batting cages were located under an array of bright lights. There were five cages, the first two being used by high school boys. Bree was in the last one.

He paused, watching her adjust her helmet over her ponytail, then her batting stance, as she waited for the ball machine to start. The first pitch came in hard and fast. She swung and connected in the sweet spot of the bat, sending the ball soaring into the netting behind the machine. If they'd been on a baseball field, it might have gone over the fence.

That was Bree—always swinging for the fences.

He felt another odd wave of nostalgia. Watching Bree reminded him of when they'd all first met at Quantico, how filled with hope and optimism and energy they'd been. They were going to run the world, but now the world was running them—or at least him. Perhaps Damon, too. He'd read the messages in the forum, and he knew Damon was in trouble. He couldn't count on him for help.

Could he count on Bree?

He'd never really known her that well. She'd had a fling with Jamie and been partnered with Damon on a lot of team assignments, so she'd been closer to them, but as for him and her—they'd always been on the periphery of each other. He did know that she was smart, fearless, and fiercely loyal. He needed all three traits about now.

Taking another look around, he saw no one who rang any alarm bells, so he walked over to the fence, standing behind her.

"Took you long enough," she said, without looking at him. "I'm almost out of quarters."

He didn't know why, but the normalcy of her words lightened the load he'd been carrying the past few days. "Looks like you'll be ready for summer softball."

"No time for games." She hit one last shot into the nets before setting down her bat and walking over to him. As she got closer, her frown grew. "You look awful."

"Good thing I don't have a mirror."

"Damon said you were messed up."

"You talked to him?"

"Yesterday—before he went looking for Sophie Parker, and ran into a barrage of bullets. But he's okay—for now. Did you see his messages?"

"A few minutes ago. He doesn't say—is he with Parker's daughter?"

"Not sure, but I think so. She's still officially missing." Bree paused, her blue eyes getting more serious. "Damon didn't tell anyone at the Bureau he was looking for Sophie.

He's put himself in a bad position by not bringing anyone else in on the information he had. Peter Hunt was furious when Damon's car was found shot up at a cabin apparently owned by Alan, although the ownership was buried beneath layers of LLCs. Peter told everyone in the office today that the next person who goes off on their own is going to be fired, no questions asked. I've never seen him so worked up, but then he did just lose one of his best friends."

"Which begs the question—if Peter and Alan were close, why didn't Hunt know about Parker's cabin?"

"A good question. Maybe it was Parker's safe house."

"How did Damon know about it?"

"Probably from Jamie. He used to go to the Adirondacks in the summers. That's why his sister had Jamie's wake there. I'm guessing Damon met Sophie at the lake that weekend."

"Right. You didn't go to Jamie's wake, did you?"

"No. Just the funeral," she said, a shadow flitting through her gaze. "At any rate, Damon and Sophie are not at the cabin anymore. Where they are now, I have no idea, but Peter has a lot of people looking for them."

"What do you think of Hunt?"

"He has a good reputation and a lot of powerful friends. I saw him leaving the office today with Senator Greg Raleigh."

"That's interesting," he muttered. "Senators don't usually come to the office."

"That's what I thought. I looked him up. Raleigh went to Yale the same time as Alan and Peter. I'm sure he was there to find out what's going on in the investigation."

"To make sure justice will be served…or not."

"You've gotten very jaded, Wyatt."

"Can't deny that. Been undercover too long."

"Speaking of which, I just heard that they pulled Lorenzo Venturi's body out of the river. Does that mean anything to you?"

She knew he was working with the Venturis? Sudden doubt stiffened his spine. *Had he made a tactical error?* "Should it?" he challenged.

"Well, Alan works on organized crime. You work for Alan. He's dead, and now, so is a known mobster. Seems like there could be a connection," she said with cool confidence. "I doubt I'll be the only one to make it. Any idea who killed Venturi?"

"No. But it was probably the same person who killed Alan and tried to take me out."

"That sounds like another Venturi. Why are you so afraid of coming into the office, Wyatt? If you're made, you need protection."

"I don't know who to trust at the Bureau."

"Why? What happened?"

"Alan set up a meet with me on Monday. Someone was waiting for me, and it wasn't Alan. There's no way anyone would have known about our meet if they didn't get the information from Alan or didn't know how to hack the system. It was an inside job. I'm sure of it."

She frowned, not looking completely convinced.

"You want more?" he asked. "Then add this into the equation. The attack on me was on Monday, two days before Alan died. Where the hell was he when I was fighting for my life? Why didn't he respond to the emergency protocol I initiated after that?"

"Is it possible he didn't get the message?"

"If he didn't, then someone close to him was keeping him from getting the information."

"Like Karen Leigh?"

"She's his right hand."

"Okay. What else can you tell me? I can try to help you from the inside, but I need more information, Wyatt. You're going to have to trust someone, and I'm all you've got."

She was right, but he didn't like it. "There's a new player in the Venturi operation. I overheard an argument between Lorenzo and Stefan two weeks ago. Lorenzo told Stefan he was selling out the family, that his father was probably dying a second death in heaven watching him work for his enemies. Stefan told him it was a new world and to get used to it or get out." Wyatt paused. "It's possible that the new player decided to eliminate Lorenzo."

"But what part does Alan play in any of this? Aside from missing the meet, why don't you trust him?"

"I've been feeding him evidence for months, but he kept saying he didn't have enough. I also gave him information to use in busting a smaller side group, who could probably produce more evidence on the Venturis. He agreed to run a sting, but someone tipped off the group, and the bust went south."

"That might not have been Alan's fault."

He drew in a breath. "Look, I don't know if Alan was playing both sides, but I have to find out. Unfortunately, I have no resources and it looks like Damon is in as much shit as I am."

"Well, lucky for both of you, there's a woman around to bail you out," she said with a cocky smile. "First things first—where are you staying?"

"On the street."

"That must be why you smell like garbage. You'll stay at my apartment."

"No. Someone could be watching you."

"Why would they be watching me? I'm not in Karen's division. I don't work with you or Damon."

"But you were at Quantico with us. Alan was your instructor, too. He brought you into the New York office, just like he did with me and Damon."

Her gaze narrowed. "You think that means something? He brought in a lot of people, and we all went through Quantico."

"There's a link. I don't know what it is, but my gut tells me that the three of us being in New York is not random."

"You can't sleep on the street, Wyatt. There's an underground garage in my building. I can sneak you in through there. No one will see you come in. We need to work on this together."

He was tempted. A bed and a shower were starting to

feel like desperate needs, but he didn't want to put Bree in danger.

"I can take care of myself," she said, obviously reading his mind. "I also have food there. You look like you haven't eaten in weeks."

"I could eat," he admitted.

"Then it's done. 53rd and Hayes, walk between the first two buildings. There's a side door into the garage. I'll meet you there in twenty minutes." She paused. "You can trust me, Wyatt."

He walked back through the arcade and onto the street. He hoped he wasn't about to make a huge mistake.

Eleven

Damon woke up before Sophie on Friday morning. It was his second restless night in a row, and his mood was not the best, especially since the air conditioning seemed to have kicked off. The sun was just coming up, so he took another shower, before quietly re-entering the room.

Sophie was asleep, her golden hair laying in beautiful tangles across the white pillow, one hand tucked under her chin. She'd thrown off the covers and her top had crept up her torso, revealing a beautiful patch of creamy skin.

His cold shower quickly became a distant memory.

Grabbing the phone, he searched for a car rental place. There was one only four blocks away. That was good news. And it opened at seven—five minutes from now. He'd rent the car, find them some breakfast and by the time he got back, Sophie would be awake, dressed, alert, maybe even a little annoying, so he could get rid of the very inconvenient desire he felt for her.

He didn't really know how he'd made it through the night, but endless episodes of sitcom television had finally sent them both into a stupor. Since he'd told her nothing was going to happen that she didn't want to happen, he'd waited for her to make a move, but she hadn't.

That was probably the smartest thing she'd done in the past two days.

Now it was time to start thinking about what was ahead.

He checked the parking lot, which didn't take long, since there were only a few cars, all of which were empty. There was an older man in the office, sitting behind the desk. Through the blinds on the window, he could see the television was on.

He walked quickly down the street. Hopefully, nothing would go wrong before he got back.

Damon was gone—again.

Sophie walked over to the window and looked out. There was no sign of him.

He wanted her to trust him, but he continued to keep her out of the loop, and she was getting a little tired of him calling all the shots.

Where on earth had he gone? They didn't have a car. Had he called a cab? Walked somewhere? Had he looked up the storage unit address online and gone without her?

She quickly put her hand into her pocket, relieved when her fingers curled around the key. If he'd gone to the storage area without her, he'd have taken the key. Although he didn't know which unit it was; she had that information in her head.

She didn't really believe he'd abandoned her. He seemed to be determined to stay as close to her as possible.

Unless their personal chat the night before had made him nervous?

She smiled at that thought. Damon was a tough, fearless guy—a soldier, a special agent, a man no doubt fully prepared to die while carrying out his duty. But when it came to talking about anything personal, he spooked pretty easily.

Having learned more about his family, his selfish parents, his back-and-forth childhood, she had a better understanding of why he might stay away from relationships.

He hadn't had good role models growing up. Love in his life probably looked like a battlefield. And Damon didn't want to die on that field, so he stayed out of love.

At least, she thought he did.

He hadn't mentioned any women in his life. And he'd said there was no one to worry about him, but perhaps she was making assumptions.

Turning away from the window, she told herself to stop thinking about his love life and concentrate on what was ahead. The storage center opened in an hour. In a very short time, she'd learn exactly what her father had left her. Hopefully, it would give her some sort of peace, closure…something to help start the healing process. It would be even better if it also provided information and clues as to who had killed her dad.

Taking advantage of Damon's absence, she got into the shower and let the water and shampoo clean away some of the grime of the last two days. She hadn't taken a shower since before she'd left for work on Wednesday morning, and it felt good to feel clean again.

It also felt like she was taking the first step back into her life, although that was probably an optimistic thought. There would be no return to normal for her, because even when they figured out who had killed her father and tried to kill her, her dad would still be gone. At the end of the day, she'd be alone. There would be no dad to call after an exciting discovery on a dig, or a bad day at work, or something funny a student had told her. No dad with a shoulder to lean on when life got tough or she felt sad. No dad to walk her down the aisle, hold her first child, tell her future husband he better be good to her or else…

Her mouth trembled as all the sadness she'd been holding at bay came back with the power of a rushing waterfall. She bit back a sob, telling herself it still wasn't time to cry. But the dam was breaking and here in the steamy shower with the water pounding down, it was easier to let the tears fall.

She cried for her loss. She cried out her fear. She cried

for the injustice of it all. And when she finally ran out of emotion, she let the water stream down her face and wash it all away.

By the time she was done, the hot water was gone and it was almost a relief to feel nothing but cold. The chill brought back the protective numbness that would keep her going, allow her to do what she needed to do.

She grabbed a towel, dried off, then blew-dry her hair, used some blush and lipstick that she happened to have in her bag, and put her sad, sweaty clothes back on. Picking up another outfit might have to get on the schedule at some point.

When she stepped out of the bathroom, Damon was sitting at the table with more bags of food, and the smell of bacon made forgiveness a little easier. "So, you're back."

"You can't be too angry," he said with a pleading smile. "I brought you bacon, pancakes, waffles, and eggs."

"And what did you bring for yourself?" she asked, as she sat down across from him.

He smiled. "Not in a sharing mood?"

"You should have woken me up and told me where you were going, Damon. You left me here without a note or a phone."

"Sorry. I didn't see any paper, and I thought you could use the sleep. I was only gone twenty minutes. Eat, you'll feel better."

She frowned but decided eating would get her further than arguing. She opened the carton holding three buttermilk pancakes, lathered each with a slab of butter, and poured on some maple syrup. Then she took a buttery bite and almost sighed with delight. "This is good."

"Excellent," he agreed, as he munched on a piece of bacon.

She noticed his concerned gaze, and wiped her mouth with her fingers. "What? Do I have something in my teeth?"

"Are you all right, Sophie?"

"Don't I look all right?" she countered.

"I thought I might have heard you crying."

"That was just the shower running," she lied, hoping her red eyes didn't completely give her away. "I'm fine. I'm ready to get on with the day. Do you think we should take a cab to the unit?"

"I rented us a car."

"What? Already?"

"There was a place not far away. I had enough cash to cover it."

"But it's in your name. How can we use it?"

"We won't use it long, but I wasn't sure how far away the place was, and I like having a car with us, in case we need to make a quick exit. Or in case your father wants you to go somewhere else."

"Okay." She did wonder if there would be another stop after this one, if her dad had left her more instructions to follow, but she'd find that out soon enough. "Did you check your forum this morning? Did you hear from your friends?"

He nodded. "Yes. Bree said they met up last night. Everyone is safe for the moment." He paused. "Do you know Senator Raleigh?"

"He went to school with my dad. Why?"

"He met with Peter at the office yesterday."

"I'm sure he's trying to find out what happened." She saw something in Damon's eyes. "Why does it bother you?"

"It doesn't bother me; I'm just trying to figure out if it's an important detail or not. What do you know about him?"

"Not much. My dad probably saw him once a year at a golf tournament for Yale alums. I don't think they had much contact beyond that." She racked her brain to think of any other details. "He's married. He lives somewhere in Connecticut. That's all I know."

"Who else goes to this golf tournament?"

"Peter Hunt; he's a very good golfer. Harrison Delano and Michael Brennan usually go."

"Delano—he owns the hotel chain, right?"

"Delano Hotels, yes. I think Harrison owns a lot of other

things as well—boats, planes, small islands. Karen told me that my father had a dinner on his calendar with Harrison for this week, but, of course, he didn't keep it. She wanted to know what that was about. I had no idea, and I told her that. I was a little surprised, because I know my dad had a bit of a falling-out with Harrison a while ago, something to do with a botched anniversary weekend at one of his hotels. I think my dad wanted to surprise my mom with something special before she died, and Harrison charged him over the moon for it. There was definitely some kind of misunderstanding, and I know Harrison didn't come to my mom's funeral. But somewhere along the way, they must have patched things up."

"Interesting. Who's Michael Brennan?"

"Michael runs a hedge fund. He's a finance guy, somewhat on the serious side. He has a daughter around my age and a son a few years older. We used to see them for holiday parties back in the day. My mom and Michael's wife were friends for a time." She paused, thinking how long ago that life seemed now. "All those friendships kind of disintegrated after my mom died, which is kind of weird, because they were my dad's friends, but I think she was the one who liked to socialize. My dad was always working. She had to make sure he'd take time off once in a while. Otherwise, he never did."

"Your father ran with a rich crowd," Damon commented.

"He graduated from an Ivy League school—what do you expect? But they're not all rich. Peter certainly isn't. And Diane is definitely not."

"Diane?"

"Diane Lewis. She's a long-time friend and a professor at Yale now. She gave me a lot of advice when I was deciding what degrees to get and whether or not I should take my teaching position at NYU. She was a big help." She paused, thinking about how sad all of her father's friends must be, especially Diane, who had such a big heart. "I wish I could talk to Diane, too. She's a lovely person, and I know she must be worrying about me."

"You'll be able to talk to her when this is over."

"Will I?" she challenged. "My dad's messages made it sound like I was going to have to disappear for a long time."

Damon frowned again. "I don't know how he thought you were going to manage that on your own with the entire FBI looking for you, and God knows who else."

"I don't, either. Maybe the answer is in the storage unit." She wiped her mouth and stood up. "Let's go."

Sophie grew more nervous the closer they got to the storage center, and she was actually glad she wasn't driving this morning, since she couldn't seem to stop the waves of unsettling unease rocketing through her body. Was this a good idea? Was she crazy to make another stop at a place her father had owned? Was Damon right?

Damon suddenly put a hand on her thigh, and she almost jumped out of her skin.

"Take a breath," he said, glancing over at her.

"I just have this terrifying feeling that my life is about to change again. Not that I can even imagine how it can get any worse."

"Don't try to imagine that."

She nodded, but she couldn't help noticing that he hadn't told her everything was going to be all right.

"Is this the place?" he asked a moment later.

"Yes," she said, as he slowed down.

The storage center sat on a half-acre of land. A large two-story building housed the office and a one-story structure of about fifty eight-by-ten foot units formed a U-shape next to the building. The property was on the outskirts of town by the interstate and was surrounded by a chain link fence. It was a few minutes past eight, and the front gate was open, but Damon didn't drive through the entrance, continuing on for another few blocks.

"What are you doing? That was the place."

"Just taking a look."

"What are you looking for?"

"Anything I don't want to see," he said vaguely.

"There was a white Jetta by the office. It could belong to the manager. I didn't see any other cars."

"Nor did I. Where's the unit?"

"It's around the back. It faces the interstate."

"Okay." He made a U-turn and then returned to the storage center, driving through the entrance gates, then turning right to get to her unit.

"It's there," she said, pointing to the third one in.

He parked in front of the unit. "Let's do it."

She got out of the car and met him by the padlocked door. Her fingers were shaking again, so bad she could barely put in the key. To her dismay, it didn't work.

"Try again," Damon said.

She drew in a breath and inserted the key again. It worked. She removed the lock and put it aside.

Damon pulled up the roll-back door, and they walked into the space. There were a couple of large boxes in the unit, a bicycle she remembered from her dad's limited fascination with bike racing that had probably been part of his way of escaping from the grief of her mom's death. The beer bottle collection that had once been a source of contention between him and her mom was in an open crate on the floor. There was a filing cabinet that had once sat in her father's study and a small table that had been in their family room. A signed bat from Barry Bonds, one of her dad's favorite ballplayers, was propped up against the wall. But it was the silver aluminum suitcase next to the table that drew her attention. It was the one thing in the unit that she didn't recognize.

She moved toward it, Damon right behind her. She was going to lift it, but it was heavier than she expected. Damon grabbed it and put it on the table.

"You want to open it, or do you want me to?" he asked.

She felt suddenly paralyzed. "I don't know if I should

look inside."

His deep-blue gaze was filled with understanding but also determination. "I can do it if you want."

"No," she said quickly, realizing she couldn't make that choice. "My dad left it for me. I have to be the one to look at it first."

Damon took a step back and motioned her forward.

She licked her lips, then unzipped the case and lifted the lid, not sure what to expect.

"Oh, my God," she murmured.

Inside the case were stacks of hundred dollar bills.

"Shit!" Damon swore. "What the hell were you thinking, Alan?"

She was silently asking her father the very same thing. Then she noticed the mesh pocket on the inside lid of the suitcase. She unzipped it and pulled out passports and driver's licenses, her shock mounting as she saw her face, but different names, on each item. "I don't understand. What is all this?"

"Your exit package," Damon said tersely. "Your dad knew you were going to need this to start over."

She met his gaze. "Where—where did he get all this money?"

"Do you really want me to answer that?"

She could hear the anger in his voice, the betrayal…

"No. No." She threw the passports and IDs back into the pocket and zipped the suitcase shut. "Let's just leave it here."

"We can't do that," he said, grabbing the case.

"I don't want it."

"Your father left it for you, and we're not coming back for it when you change your mind. Now, let's get out of here."

Before they could leave the unit, two men rushed inside. They wore black T-shirts and black jeans, ski masks covering their faces, a gun in each of their hands.

Her heart thudded against her chest.

They were trapped. There was no way out.

Twelve

He should have closed the door while they were inside.

He should have left Sophie in the car.

He should have done a lot of things.

Instead, he'd let them get caught like mice in a trap.

"Hand the case over," one of the men said in a deep, gravelly voice.

He couldn't see their faces, but by their athletically powerful body types, he imagined both to be in their thirties.

"Do it, or she dies," the second man said, aiming his weapon at Sophie.

He could feel Sophie inching closer to him. *Good.* He wanted her behind him when he made his move. And he would make a move, because there was no doubt in his mind that these men were not going to leave them alive whether he gave them the case or not.

It would be risky. He was fast, but he might not be fast enough to fire off two shots before a bullet took down Sophie.

As he adjusted the suitcase in his hand, the weight and the metal exterior made him realize it could be a weapon, too. Or at least a distraction.

That's all he needed…a split-second could make the difference.

"Do it now," the first man ordered.

"Okay," he said, putting up his free hand. "You can have it. Just don't shoot."

He took a step forward.

"Stop right there and drop it. Then shove it over here," the man closest to him ordered.

"No problem."

He leaned forward as if to set the case down, then quickly changed directions, hurling the case at the man in front of him. It hit him in the legs, knocking him down.

Then Damon whipped out his gun, shooting the second guy in the chest.

The man's gun went off as he fell to the ground.

He heard Sophie scream. He prayed she hadn't been hit, but he couldn't take time to look.

The man he'd temporarily disabled with the suitcase was getting up.

He fired his next shot at that man's heart. He staggered and fell backward, his gun falling out of his hand.

The sound of the gunshots felt incredibly loud, echoing off the walls of the unit. He was sure they would bring someone running in their direction at any second.

He turned to Sophie, who was gripping her dad's baseball bat in her hands, her face white with fear and shock. He didn't see any blood on her, thank God. "Are you all right?"

She nodded.

"Let's go." He grabbed the case and sprinted toward the car. He would have liked to check the men for IDs, but there was no time. He put the case in the backseat, then jumped in as Sophie did the same.

He gunned the engine, speeding out of the parking lot as Sophie fastened her seat belt.

He heard sirens as they left the lot, and he took the next corner on two wheels. They needed to get away, because getting caught by the cops with a suitcase of unexplained money and two dead bodies behind them would put them both in an interrogation room, with no chance of finding who killed Alan or who was after them. The FBI would take over their case, but that might put them in even more danger if there was a mole inside the Bureau.

Sophie braced her hand against the center console as he took another turn and sped through an intersection. Thankfully, they were in an industrial area with large warehouses and semi-trucks to get lost behind.

The sirens seemed to be getting more distant, but they weren't out of the woods yet.

"Do you think they're dead?" Sophie asked.

He looked over at her shocked, white, bloodless face. Her brown eyes were huge and terrified. "Probably."

"Oh God, oh God," she murmured. "I think I'm going to be sick." She rolled down her window, fanning her face with her hand.

He wanted to tell her to duck down, not hang her very pretty face out the window, but he had to give her a minute.

"What are we going to do? You just killed two people," she said, rolling the window back up.

"It was them or us. They weren't going to leave us there alive, Sophie."

"What are we going to do now? The person in the office might have seen our car. Someone heard the gunshots. They're going to find the bodies. They're going to trace the unit to my dad, to me. How are we going to get out of this?"

She was quickly spinning out of control. He had no idea how they were going to get away, but he would take it one step at a time—problem solve.

"First, we need to ditch this car," he said.

"Where? And what will we do then? Are we going to take a train or a bus or a cab? Won't the police put our pictures out on the wire or whatever they do? How are we going to use any public transportation?"

She was right; public transportation was not a good option. Nor was continuing to drive around in the vehicle they were in. The license plate had most likely been captured on the security cameras at the storage unit. The only thing he felt remotely good about was that the bodies of the men he'd shot might later provide a clue as to who was after them, and hopefully Bree could get access to that information. But that was something to deal with later.

Spying a long block of office buildings, he drove into a parking lot packed with cars and pulled into a spot between a sedan and an older model SUV, which wouldn't have any alarm protection.

"What are we doing?" Sophie asked in alarm, turning her head to see if anyone was behind them. "Are we hiding here? It's too close. We need to get farther away."

"We're not staying here. We're going to borrow a car."

She looked at him in confusion. "Borrow—as in *steal*—a car? Do you know how to do that?"

"I do."

"But someone will call the cops when they realize their car isn't here."

"It's early in the morning. I'm guessing whoever parked here won't be checking on their car until at least lunchtime or maybe after work. That gives us a few hours to get somewhere else, then we'll drop the car off, and eventually they'll get it back. Don't worry."

"Don't worry?" she echoed, a high-pitched, squeaky tone to her voice. "Why would I worry? We've killed two people. Now we're going to steal a car. Oh, and we have a suitcase filled with a freaking ton of money and fake passports. There's certainly nothing to be concerned about. It's just a normal, average day for me."

He grabbed her arm. "Stop. I promise that you will have a chance to lose it, Sophie. You'll be able to rant and rave and scream and cry—whatever you want to do, but not now. Now, we have to get to a safe place. Can you stay with me?"

She stared back at him. "Yes," she said tightly. "But how are you going to break into that car? Throw a rock through the window?"

"Way too noisy." He pulled his keys out of his pocket and wrapped his fingers around a small black gadget. "This will get us into the vehicle and start the car."

"Really? They make things that do that?"

"The FBI does. I needed it on my last job, and I never gave it back. Come on."

He got out of the car and grabbed the suitcase from the backseat. He took a sweeping glance around the lot and then opened the SUV next to them. As he'd predicted, the device he had was able to start the car. Within minutes, they were on their way.

Despite his outward confidence, he held his breath until they got on the interstate and blended in with the traffic. For another five miles, he watched his rearview mirror like a hawk, but there were no police cars on their tail.

Sophie wasn't talking, her gaze fixed on her side view mirror.

Another five miles passed; the traffic got heavier, and his pulse started to pound again. Getting stuck in a traffic jam was not part of the plan.

"There's a police car," Sophie said suddenly. "It's coming up behind us."

"I see it." He noted the flashing lights and the increasingly loud siren.

"It's for us. They've found us. What are we going to do?"

He heard the panic in her voice, and he did not have a good answer. They couldn't make a run for it, not with traffic coming to a standstill. "Get down as far as you can," he told her. "They'll be looking for two people."

She unbuckled her belt and dropped as low as she could in her seat. "What's happening?" she asked him. "Can you change lanes, get off?"

"I don't want to do anything to draw suspicion." He paused. "The police car is coming down the left side. Cars are moving over for him."

The siren screamed in his ear as the police car drew level. He snuck a side glance at the vehicle, enormously relieved when it went by, the officers inside obviously responding to another call.

"It's not us," he told Sophie. "They're gone. I think there might be an accident; that's why the traffic is so slow."

"They're really gone?"

"Yes. You can get up."

She eased back into her seat and refastened her belt. "I thought that was it."

"I think I'm going to get off, take the frontage road for a while."

He drove the streets adjacent to the interstate for a few miles, noting firetrucks and police cars on a bridge at the scene of an accident.

He turned on the radio, searching for a news station. He wanted to know if anyone was talking about the shooting at the storage unit, but a weather update and a traffic report were followed by political news from Washington. He turned it off, feeling somewhat relieved now that they were thirty plus miles from the scene and hopefully in a vehicle that no one was looking for yet. "I think we're good—for now."

He looked over at Sophie. The color was starting to come back into her face, but she still appeared shell-shocked, and he couldn't blame her. She'd seen two men killed right in front of her. They were running for their lives, and they hadn't even had a second to talk about or deal with the suitcase her father had left for her, which raised another big set of questions. But he didn't want to get into any of that now.

"I can't quite believe we got away," she said. "Everything has been happening so fast. You shot two people in less than a minute, and you did it before they could shoot us. How did you manage that?"

"Training and a little luck."

She shook her head in bemusement. "I thought we were trapped. I didn't see any way out. But you did. You saved my life."

"I saved both our lives."

She gazed back at him. "There were security cameras—do you think they caught what happened?"

"I'm sure they caught us leaving."

"So, now the police could arrest us for murder." She glanced toward the backseat. "And for having what looks like hundreds of thousands of dollars in cash."

"We need to talk about that, but let's put it on the back burner until we get to a safe place."

"Is there a safe place?" she asked with despair.

"Somewhere. We just have to find it."

"And then what? We hide out for a day, a week, a month?"

"You're thinking too far ahead, Sophie. Just stay in the moment. Right now, we're okay. We're alive. That's all that matters." He looked at her and saw the valiant effort she was making to hold it together. "I'm going to keep you safe. I promise."

Her brown eyes shimmered with unshed tears. "I know you're going to try," she whispered.

"Not just try. I will make it happen, and together we're going to dig our way to the truth. I'm going to need you and your brilliant, deductive mind for that."

"I don't feel smart right now; I feel—numb."

"That will wear off. Just keep breathing. Some days that's all you can do."

Sophie's pulse slowed down with each passing mile, and after an hour and a half, she was starting to feel like an imminent heart attack was no longer a possibility. But she was still worried and while she was trying to stay in the moment as Damon had suggested, she knew they were going to have to make some moves to stay ahead of the authorities and whatever bad guys were coming after them next.

"Where are we going?" she asked. Damon had been driving side streets, keeping somewhat parallel to the interstate, but his turns appeared to be completely random.

"I'm not sure, but we're going to be out of gas in about fifteen miles, so we'll have to make a stop soon, and that would probably be a good time to get rid of this car."

"And steal another one? It feels so risky, even with your handy-dandy little gadget."

"It's not my first choice. But public transportation is out."

"I know." She thought for a moment. They were headed south toward New York, and while she was excited to leave Connecticut, New York didn't feel any safer, not while things were so hot. "I feel like we need to lay low for a few hours. Maybe we should drop off the car and find a library or a bookstore, a place where we could sit for a bit without anyone noticing," she suggested.

"Those places sound too crowded."

"But having people around might prevent someone from taking another shot at us. A deserted location doesn't feel safe." She blew out a breath of frustration. Being cut off from her entire life was starting to wear on her. "We need a friend." She didn't realize she'd spoken the words aloud until Damon gave her a quick look.

"We can't bring friends into this," he said. "At least not your friends. If we get back to New York, I can get my friends to help us."

"That will take hours at the rate of speed we're traveling and getting back on the interstate could be dangerous, not to mention we'll have to steal another car, and then that theft could get reported."

"What do you suggest? I'm open to ideas."

She thought for a few minutes, happy that her brain was starting to work again. A road sign gave her an idea. "Greenwich, Connecticut is about twenty-five miles from here."

"So?"

"So, the Rowlands have a house in Greenwich. It's where Jamie and Cassie grew up. You remember—it's where they had the catered lunch after Jamie's funeral, before we went up to the lake for the wake."

"I remember the house, but why would we go there? Vincent is former FBI, and someone also tied to your dad."

"Yes, but he's probably not there. He has an apartment in Manhattan where he stays when he's not traveling. He kept the house because it's where Jamie's things are, but he told my dad it's difficult for him to be there." Her idea began to pick up steam as she considered all the angles. "Cassie's mom has been in California since before Jamie died; she's not around. Cassie moved to London last year, so she's not using the house now, either. It could be empty, Damon." She looked over at him, feeling a surge of optimism. "There could be a car there, too. I know Vincent didn't want to get rid of Jamie's car. It might still be there." The more she thought about it, the more it seemed like the Rowland house was the perfect solution to their problems. "What do you think?"

"It's sounding better than I first thought," he conceded. "We'd have to determine whether or not Vincent is at the house, though. I'm also betting that there's a security system. Most FBI agents, even former ones, have them."

Her heart sank at that thought. "True. I don't suppose you have a handy-dandy gadget to get past that, do you?"

"No gadgets, but I might be able to disarm it, depending on how sophisticated it is. I can't remember—is the garage attached or separate?"

"It's separate. Even if we can't get into the house, maybe we can get into the garage."

"We still need to know if Vincent is there."

"Good point." She thought for another moment, then said, "You won't like my next idea, but think about it before you say no."

"You want to call Cassie," he said, meeting her gaze.

"Yes. You don't think they'd tap her phone, do you? I haven't seen her in a few years. She's living in London. They can't possibly tap into all my friends' phones, can they?"

He shrugged off that question. "It bothers me more that Cassie is attached to Vincent. Even though he's retired, he still has friends at the Bureau. Peter Hunt might be one of them. I'm sure Peter called Vincent to ask him if he knew where you were, if not before we showed up at the cabin, then definitely afterwards."

"And I'm sure he said he didn't know, because he doesn't."

While Damon was considering the pros and cons of calling Cassie, she asked the question that had been rolling around in her head the last thirty minutes. "Do you think those men at the storage unit were hired by someone at the FBI to kill us, or were they attached to some crime family my dad was investigating?"

"I don't know, Sophie," he said somberly. "I wish I'd had time to pull off their face masks or take a photo or look for ID. We might have been able to get my friend to identify them."

"I'm sure the police will do that."

"But we may not get the information quickly. It depends on how much access my friend can get."

The men's images flashed into her head. "The one closest to me had a tattoo on his neck. It had snakes and vines and a weird symbol in the middle." She paused. "It's weird, but I think I've seen it before; I don't know where. I could try to draw it if I had some paper. Would that be helpful?"

"Absolutely," he said with an approving nod. "Good job on noticing that."

"I wasn't trying to notice. It just drew my attention. It was creeping out from under his face mask, and I couldn't look away." She felt the tension return as she thought about those frightening moments. "I should have taken my gun out of my bag when we went into the unit. I don't know why I didn't think about that."

"Probably because you're not used to carrying a weapon. I should have made sure you had it ready to go. You would have had a better chance of surviving."

"I doubt that. You were more effective than any weapon I might have had in my shaky hand." Seeing Damon in action—so quick, so purposeful, so deadly—had definitely changed her impression of him. And while the fact that he could kill two men so fast and so easily probably should have scared her, right now it just made her feel safer.

"You did good back there, too, Sophie. You didn't panic."

"I didn't have time. I don't even think I was breathing."

"And yet you noticed a tattoo that might prove to be a valuable clue."

"I did do that," she said. "So, what about Cassie? Shall I call her? I know her number. I can feel her out about her dad's whereabouts without revealing anything."

He hesitated, then slowly nodded. "All right, but keep it short. You're calling to let her know the tragic news about your dad. That's it."

"She might have questions if she's heard I've disappeared."

"Say you needed time away, and the FBI was asking you a lot of questions that you didn't want to answer, so you went off on your own." He pulled the phone out of his pocket and handed it to her.

Even though it was her friend she was calling and her idea to make the call, she felt suddenly nervous. She wasn't used to lying to people, especially people she cared about. But she had to do it. She was in survival mode.

She tapped in the number and put the phone on speaker. The phone rang once, twice, three times…and then Cassie picked up.

"Hello?" Cassie said shortly, as if she didn't recognize the number and was anticipating the call to be from a telemarketer.

"It's Sophie."

"Oh my God, Sophie." Cassie's tone immediately changed. "I've been so worried about you. My dad told me your father was killed in a car crash, and you're missing, and everyone is looking for you. Where are you? Are you all right?"

"I'm okay. Well, I'm not okay, but I'm hanging in there. I didn’t know if you'd heard the news about my father. I wanted to call you and tell you personally, but a lot has been happening really fast."

"My dad said everyone thinks you've been kidnapped by whoever killed your father. I've been really afraid for you, Sophie." Cassie's voice choked on the end of her sentence.

Cassie's emotion almost made Sophie lose it, but she couldn't do that.

"What happened?" Cassie continued.

Damon squeezed her leg, giving her a silent reminder not to reveal too much.

"I saw some men going into my apartment building," she said, deciding to stick close to the truth. "I got scared, so I ran away. I probably shouldn't be calling you, but I just had to hear a friendly voice. And I thought maybe your dad could help me. I don't have his number, and I wasn't sure if he was in Manhattan or Greenwich or somewhere else."

"Oh, no, I'm sorry. He's not in New York or in Greenwich. Dad just got on a plane to Paris. I'm meeting him there tomorrow for my birthday. It will be the first time I've celebrated my birthday with him in a few years, but he's not seeing anyone right now, and neither am I, so we decided we should do Paris together."

Cassie's plans with her dad for a birthday celebration almost broke her heart again. "That sounds lovely."

"But if you need us, Sophie, we will help you. Maybe you should come to Paris, too. I can wire you money, buy you a ticket, whatever you need."

She would love to run away to France, but that wasn't an option. "It's all right. I have someone who is helping me here. But maybe I'll call you tomorrow and I can talk to you and your dad together."

"Absolutely. We can call you as soon as we get together. Is this a good number?"

"I'll call you. I'm not sure if I'll have this phone tomorrow."

"What does that mean?"

"It's too long of a story to get into."

"Sophie, I'm really worried about you. Why don't you go

to the FBI? They'll protect you."

"I can't trust anyone right now."

"You can't trust the people who've worked with your dad for twenty-something years?" Cassie asked doubtfully. "That doesn't make sense."

"Nothing makes sense, but that's where I'm at."

Damon tapped her leg again. He wanted her to wrap it up.

"I'll speak to you tomorrow," she said. "Don't worry about me. And, please, don't tell anyone about this call."

"I won't. I promise. Stay safe."

"I'm going to try." She clicked the phone off and looked at Damon. "I didn't think it would be hard to hear her voice but it was. At any rate, the house in Greenwich should be empty. Should we go for it?"

"It sounds like our best bet. We need to get another phone. See if you can find a place on the map where we can buy one, before we drop this car off."

"Why do we have to get another phone now?"

"You just made a call to the daughter of a former FBI agent."

"Cassie wouldn't know how to trace a call."

"Not saying *she* would. Just see if you can find anything."

She used the phone map to search. "There's a shopping center a mile and a half from here."

He followed her directions, and several minutes later, he pulled into a busy retail center that boasted a supermarket, a drugstore, and a bunch of small shops, including one that sold phones.

"I'm going to need some cash," he said.

"We have plenty of that," she said cynically.

"Not that cash."

She dug into her bag and pulled out some bills.

"I'll be right back," he told her. "Keep the doors locked."

She did as he asked, but she felt like a sitting duck as soon as he left the car. She shifted down in her seat, hoping no one would notice her or the stolen vehicle she was sitting in. It seemed to take forever for Damon to complete the transaction, but finally he came out of the store. He took the wrapping off the new phone and dumped the box into the trash along with the old phone they'd been using.

When he got to the car, he motioned for her to get out. He grabbed the suitcase from the back and suggested they walk to the other end of the lot to call for a cab.

"So, we're not stealing another car?" she asked.

"I like the idea of using Jamie's car, if it's at the Rowlands' house. We'll get a cab to drop us a few blocks away."

"Okay. Good idea." She felt very conspicuous as they walked across the crowded lot. She felt terrified to be in the open, but she kept telling herself that no one was paying any attention to them. Still, it felt like there were eyes everywhere. They'd tried to hide their tracks, but how successful had they been?

They stopped by the entrance to a clothing boutique, and Damon called for a cab. "Five minutes," he said, as he got off the phone.

"That feels like an eternity right now."

"We'll be fine," he assured her.

She wondered if he really thought that, or if he was just saying it for her benefit, but she decided to let it be, because she really wanted to believe they would be fine. "That suitcase feels like it's drawing attention."

"Only because you know what's inside," he replied. But even so, he pushed the suitcase toward a garbage can so it wasn't as noticeable.

"I don't want to think about what's inside."

He nodded, his expression grim. "Neither do I."

Despite what she'd just said, she couldn't help thinking about the money, the fake IDs, the men with the guns who had almost taken their lives. Which brought up another question.

"How do you think they found us?" she asked. "How did

they know we were at the storage unit?"

"The manager of the storage center could have called someone when we accessed the unit."

"Wouldn't that have taken longer for someone to get there if they were waiting for a call?"

"They could have been nearby."

"But if the manager was in on it, he could have opened the unit at any time. If they just wanted the cash…" She stopped, seeing the truth in his eyes. "It wasn't just the cash. It's me."

"Or both of us, at this point. If they just wanted the case, they would have just shot us without asking for us to hand it over."

That didn't make her feel good at all, but she couldn't deny that it made sense. "If the manager didn't make the call, is there some way we're being tracked? We've been so careful. But first the cabin, then the storage unit…"

"We weren't that careful," he said with a shake of his head. "We were in New Haven, Sophie, close to where your dad went to school, going to a storage unit he'd had for years. Even if it wasn't in his name, it's tied to him. I told you I was concerned about that last night. At any rate, we need to get some place where we can think without looking over our shoulders every second."

She couldn't agree more. "There's a cab," she said, hoping her idea to use the Rowlands' house was as good as she thought, because certainly there was a link between her dad and the Rowlands, too.

Thirteen

They had the cab drop them off a few blocks from the Rowlands' house, and then they walked the rest of the way. Damon hadn't paid much attention to the house the one and only time he'd been there for Jamie's funeral, but it was an impressive two-story stone and clapboard colonial on a half-acre of land with a winding driveway and a three-car garage set back from the house. It matched the other large and stately homes in the upscale neighborhood, most of which were set apart from their neighbors by tall trees and thick brush.

"I like the privacy level," he muttered to Sophie, as they walked up the drive. He was a little surprised there were no electronic gates on the property, but since the Rowlands didn't appear to spend much time in the house anymore, maybe they'd gone lax on security.

They walked up the front steps and paused by the front door.

"Should we ring the bell?" Sophie asked nervously.

"Yes. Let's see if anyone answers. We know it won't be Cassie or Vincent."

Sophie pressed the bell and they waited. She hit it again when no one answered. As he looked around, he was relieved to see that the front door could not be seen from the street.

There was a coded lock on the door, which he might be able to break, but he wasn't ready for that yet.

"Let's go around the back," he said. "We'll check the garage."

Unlike the front door, the door leading into the garage had just a simple lock on it, and he was able to lift the mechanism with another small tool that he carried with him.

"You're like Inspector Gadget," Sophie murmured.

"I'm not sure that's a compliment, but okay," he said dryly, pushing open the door.

They walked into the large garage. There were two cars parked inside. One was a silver BMW SUV and the other was a dark-red Chevy Camaro with a convertible top. His gut clenched at the sight of that car, memories of driving down to Quantico with Jamie behind the wheel, the top down, the music blaring, and the open road filled with possibilities in front of them. That day seemed like a lifetime ago.

"Jamie's car," Sophie said, walking over to the vehicle.

She put her hand on the hood, a yearning sadness in her expression, and he completely understood the feeling. Jamie had been a bright spot in both of their lives, and he doubted Jamie had even known how much of an impact he'd made on them.

"Jamie always liked driving a convertible," she continued, giving him a quiet smile. "When he got out of the Army, right before he went to Virginia for FBI training, he came by my apartment, and we took a ride down the Jersey Shore. We hadn't seen each other in years, and I thought he'd changed in some ways—there were more shadows in his eyes, more lines on his face, even a little gray in his hair—but in other ways he was just the same Jamie—optimistic, carefree, happy. I thought being a soldier would make him more serious. I'm sure he saw some horrible things, but he never talked about them."

"He was good at compartmentalizing and letting bad memories go."

"You're good at that, too."

"It comes with the job we both did. It's hard to survive if you don't lock some things away."

"I'm starting to understand that. My emotions are all over the place," she said. "I can't let grief over my dad's death take hold. I can't let fear of whoever is trying to kill us paralyze me. I can't worry about where my dad got all that money, because I'll get lost in all the questions, and I won't be ready for whatever is coming next. My life is a spinning top right now, and if I stop spinning, I might crash and end up in an even worse place." She paused. "And then…there's you."

His pulse quickened as she turned to face him. "What about me?"

"You know," she said helplessly. "I really did think I was over you."

His mouth went dry at her words. He'd thought he was over her, too. Before he could utter a reply, the sound of voices in the yard sent him rushing across the garage. He grabbed her hand and pulled her around to the other side of Jamie's car. They squatted down, hidden in the space between the car and the wall.

"The suitcase," she whispered.

He suddenly realized he'd left the suitcase where he'd been standing. He crept out of hiding to get it and then slid it behind the car next to her.

The voices were louder now. They sounded female.

"Who do you think is out there?" Sophie asked in a hushed voice.

He listened closely. The women were speaking Spanish—or maybe Portuguese. "Stay here. I'm going to take a look."

"Maybe you shouldn't. What if they see you? What if they come in?"

"I'll be right back. Just stay hidden."

He walked over to the side door of the garage. The top half was a window covered by a decorative fabric curtain. He lifted it and saw two women on the back deck. One was sweeping, and the other was shaking out a small rug. A moment later, they both went into the house, but the back door was still open.

If they were going to get in the house, this was their best chance. He walked quickly back to Sophie.

"Housecleaners," he said, squatting down next to her. "Two women. There could be more inside, or that could be it."

"Why didn't they answer the door?"

"Maybe they just arrived."

"Do you think they'll come into the garage?"

He looked around, doubting that cleaning the garage was part of their routine. "I don't think so. They left the door to the house open. I'm going to see if I can get inside."

"What?" she asked sharply. "You're going to sneak into the house while there are people there? Are you crazy?"

It was a risk, but one he felt he needed to take. They needed a place to stay, and this garage was not going to be comfortable for longer than a few hours. "It's a big house, and I doubt the crew has more than two or three people. I'll find somewhere to hide, and when they're gone, I'll let you in."

"What if they see you and call the police?"

"I can do it, Sophie."

She stared back at him with unhappy eyes. "Don't get caught. I—I need you, Damon. I know I acted like I didn't before, but I do."

Her heartfelt admission stirred him. She wasn't talking about needing him in a sexual way, but he couldn't stop himself from going there.

Impulsively, he leaned in and kissed her lips. Her sweet, hot taste brought back all the memories between them. He framed her face with his hands. He wanted to linger, explore the warm depths of her mouth, slide his tongue down her neck, feel her curves with his fingers, and lose himself in her, the way he'd done before.

The temperature in the garage went up by twenty degrees. It had always been like that between them—hot, passionate, reckless.

It took all his willpower to drag his mouth away from hers.

Her eyes glittered with desire, her cheeks awash with pink, a nice change from the paleness he'd seen earlier. Her blood was definitely pumping again, and so was his.

"I'll be back," he promised.

"Hurry," she murmured.

He wanted to believe it was because she wanted him to come back and keep the kiss going, but more likely it was because she was worried about being left alone. That wasn't going to happen. He was not leaving Sophie until she was safe.

But as he slipped out the side door, he couldn't help thinking it would be difficult to leave her even then.

Sophie sat down on the floor, leaning against the wall of the garage, her position protected from view by the side of Jamie's car. Her breath was coming fast and ragged, and while she told herself it was fear, it was also something else—it was Damon.

The last thing she'd *expected* him to do was kiss her. The last thing she'd *wanted* him to do was kiss her.

Actually, that wasn't true.

She'd been wanting him to kiss her since he'd first shown up at the cabin.

Closing her eyes, she leaned her head back against the wall, letting the feelings he'd stirred up run through her.

It had been just like before. One kiss—and then searing, unexpected, overwhelming need.

But this wasn't like before. They couldn't have a night and walk away from each other. They were tied together for God knew how long. They were fighting to stay alive. The last thing she should be thinking about was sleeping with Damon. *But wouldn't it be nice to forget about everything for just a little while?*

She'd told him she'd begun to understand the importance of compartmentalizing, and that was definitely true.

Why not lock everything else behind their own separate doors and just keep the one open with him? She was tired of being confused, sad, scared, angry…she just wanted to feel happy, positive emotions, release the tension, float away on a sensual cloud of goodness.

She knew she'd feel that way with Damon. It had been great between them before. They'd been in sync from the first kiss, the first touch. It was as if their bodies had been waiting for each other—made for each other. If ever a night had been close to perfect, it had been that one.

Until he'd left.

Opening her eyes, she reminded herself that they were better in the dark, in the shadows, and not in reality, not in the cold light of day, which was probably why Damon had abruptly ended the kiss he'd impulsively started.

She shouldn't be worrying about having sex with Damon; she should be concerned about whether he could hide out in the house until the cleaners left. The last thing they needed was for the police to arrive and arrest them for trespassing. If that happened, they'd get split up, and who knew what other charges they would face?

As her gaze moved to the suitcase her father had left her, she knew she should also be worried about the money. She'd been trying hard not to think about it.

She had no idea how much cash was inside, but she knew it was a lot. *Where had he gotten all that money?* She hoped he'd cleaned out his bank accounts and stashed the money in the case and hid it in the storage unit before getting in his car and ending up in northern New Jersey. But that seemed doubtful.

They'd always lived a comfortable life, but not a rich life, and money had gotten tighter after her mother had become sick.

She'd also drained some dollars out of her father's bank account with all her educational expenses. He'd always told her that he wanted to pay for college and grad school, that he didn't want her to graduate with debt, and he'd made that happen, but now she couldn't help wondering how he'd managed it. She had no idea what he got paid, but she didn't think it was an exorbitant amount. *So where had the money come from? Had he liquidated some investments that she knew nothing about?*

Her father's rambling voicemails ran through her head again…The first words he'd spoken to her had been, *"I'm sorry."* He'd said he'd made mistakes, that he'd ended up in a bad place, that he wanted to still fix things and maybe he could, but if he couldn't, he wanted her to run. He wanted her to live a happy life, to be safe. But he'd also told her to get the key, go to the storage unit. He'd wanted her to find the money. She was a hundred percent sure of that. He'd wanted her to use it and the passports and start a new life—as if that would be easy to do.

She couldn't teach without using her real identity, her real degrees. She couldn't go on digs without credentials.

But she could live. And maybe that's all he'd been able to arrange for her.

She laid the suitcase down flat and opened the lid again, secretly praying she'd imagined the amount of money inside, but she hadn't.

Pulling out a stack of hundred dollar bills, she counted one hundred bills. And there were at least fifty stacks of bills, maybe more. Her father had probably stashed away half a million dollars in cash.

She examined the first passport again. He'd used her fake name from the lake—Rebecca Framingham. Her photo looked like it might have been taken recently. Her gaze narrowed as she tried to remember when he'd last taken her picture.

He'd brought out his camera at Christmas, and, yes, she was wearing the dark red sweater she'd bought for Christmas Eve. Had he been planning this six months ago? The driver's license also matched the passport, and there was a credit card with Rebecca's name on it, too.

The other trio of passport, driver's license and credit card belonged to a Charlotte Bennett with a different photo of her. In this picture, she'd had her hair pulled back in a ponytail and she'd been wearing a dark-green top. *Had he wanted to give her two options of how to look?*

As she studied the IDs, it occurred to her that the address was the same on both—an apartment in Brooklyn. *Did the address exist? What was there? Her dad wouldn't put just any address on the ID, would he?*

Her mind grappled with the information. It was possible it was a random address or an empty lot. *But was it? And did it matter?*

The garage door opened.

She dropped the IDs and slammed the lid of the case down. Then she jumped to her feet, relieved to see Damon. She didn't know what she would have done if it had been someone else. She'd been so lost in thought, she'd lost track of where she was.

"The cleaners are gone," he said. "Looks like they just did a quick dust and a vacuum."

"And no one saw you?"

"No. I noticed that they'd damp-mopped the downstairs bathroom, so I figured they were done in there. I hid behind the shower curtain until I heard the door close. Then I turned the alarm off and came to find you."

"You're good at the secret agent stuff."

"It's my job. Let's go inside."

She leaned over and zipped the case back up as Damon came around to take it. "I started counting the money. It might be half a million or more."

He nodded, his mouth tight. "I figured."

She noticed he didn't comment on where or how her dad had gotten the money, but she suspected that conversation was coming. She grabbed her purse and followed him out of the garage.

The house was just as she remembered it: well-decorated

with expensive furniture, nice art, and a very formal feeling in the living room and dining room. At one time, she thought there had been more personal items, but those seemed to be gone.

She insisted on checking every room of the house, even though Damon told her he'd already done that. She had to be sure that they were alone before she could let herself breathe freely again, although after what had happened earlier in the day, that might be optimistic thinking.

The upstairs bedrooms that had once belonged to Cassie and Jamie tugged at her heart. Even though they were both fairly empty, there were remnants of the past: board games in Cassie's closet, baseball posters of the Mets on Jamie's walls. Damon seemed a little bothered by those posters, too.

She noticed that when he spoke about Jamie, his jaw turned to rock, his eyes darkened from blue to black, and his voice came out clipped and sharp. She doubted he thought he had any tells, but he did, and over the past several days, she'd watched him closely enough to notice. It was ironic that they'd both loved the same person, and it was that person who had brought them together, but only in death, not in life.

She felt better when they returned to the first floor where there were less memories, but that good feeling ended when they walked into Vincent's study. While most of the other rooms had been stripped of photographs, this room had not. Along one wall was an enormous built-in bookcase/entertainment center. In addition to a small television, there were a dozen or so framed photographs on the shelves.

They were mostly family pictures of Vincent and his wife as well as Cassie and Jamie. But there was one that caught her eye and made her heart squeeze tighter once more.

It was a photograph of her parents with the Rowlands. It had been taken at the lake, and judging by her parents' ages, they'd probably been in their early thirties. Vincent and her father stood near the wheel of a boat while the women were sitting on a bench in the background.

The men looked handsome and young. Her father wore a short-sleeved shirt hanging open over a pair of swim trunks, his light-brown hair blowing in the wind, his smile lighting up his face. Vincent didn't have a trace of gray in his black hair and no extra weight around the middle, which seemed to have crept on in later years.

She couldn't see her mom that well, but her blonde hair and blurry smile resembled the hazy image she carried in her head. Jamie's mom had on a big beach hat to cover her red hair and pale complexion.

"They had no idea," she murmured. "Of what was coming."

Damon came up next to her to look at the photo. "Good looking group."

"In this moment, they were happy," she said. "The Rowlands were still together. My mom wasn't sick. My dad was alive." She shook her head, giving Damon a helpless look. "I don't know when it will stop hurting."

"It hasn't been that long, and it probably won't ever completely go away, Sophie. But you already know that. You've been carrying around your mom's loss for a long time."

"True."

"You will find a way to go on, to smile again, to be happy."

"I want to believe that. It's certainly not easy right now."

"I know." He put his arm around her shoulders. "Maybe that picture should remind you of what I said earlier."

"About staying in the moment?"

"Yes."

"Easier to say than to do, but I will try. I just need to stop thinking that the good things will last, because they usually don't. Maybe if I were less optimistic, I wouldn't get hit so hard by disappointment."

"You're an optimist. That's not a bad thing."

"It is when you're constantly getting hit in the face with reality. I'm like a cartoon character, who keeps taking a pie in the face because she can't seem to figure out when to duck."

He smiled. "You have been pretty good at ducking. And there's no way you could have predicted all this was going to happen."

"Is that true?" she challenged. "I'm starting to feel like I missed some big signs, especially where my father is concerned." She stepped away from Damon and returned the photo to the shelf. "However, I don't want to talk about him right now. I know we have to do that eventually, but I'm not ready."

"Then why don't we go into the kitchen and see what's in the pantry?"

"I doubt there's much food here. I don't know when anyone was here last. It could have been months."

"Maybe there are some non-perishable items we can turn into a meal."

"We should have gotten food when we left the car in that lot."

"That would have been a good idea. I was more concerned with putting some distance between us and the stolen car."

"Me, too." She put a hand on his arm as he started to turn away. "Are we staying here, Damon? I thought we were going to take one of the cars and go."

"That was my original thought, but I think we should stay here tonight. Cassie and Vincent are in Europe. Cassie's mom lives in another state. The housecleaners have already been here. I think we're good for a while."

"Someone else could come by or see us—a neighbor, a delivery person."

"Well, I don't plan on answering the door, and I think if we stay in the back of the house and don't turn on the lights when it gets dark, no one will know we're here. Luckily, the Rowlands enjoy having privacy from their neighbors."

He made a good argument, and she wasn't really in the mood to be out on the open road again where anyone could follow them or stop them. "It would be nice to stay here. It's comfortable."

"And cool," he said with a smile. "Even without the air conditioning on."

She couldn't help but grin at that remark. "You and heat—it's a love-hate relationship, isn't it?"

"More like a hate-hate relationship. Everything bad in my life has happened during a heat wave, and this weekend has been no exception."

"What kind of bad things?" she asked curiously.

"It's a long story."

"Give me the short version. You owe me. I have to listen to you complain about the heat every single day."

He tipped his head. "I will try to do better."

"Just give me an example."

He let out a sigh. "Let's see. My dad left my mom on one of the hottest nights of the year. We were living by the beach, but there was no sea breeze and no air conditioning to battle the surprising ninety-degree-plus heat. It was sweltering. My parents started yelling. It was becoming a nightly fight, so I went on the deck and tried not to hear them, but all the windows were open, and I heard every word—every hateful, horrible word. I was happy when he left, because it was quiet again."

She was surprised by his words, by the image he'd evoked of himself as a young, scared boy. Damon rarely let her see any side of himself that wasn't strong and powerful. "That's awful," she said quietly.

"It wasn't great."

"I'm guessing there were more bad, hot nights after that."

"Between them—yes."

"And with other people?" she prodded.

"A few more—some while I was in Afghanistan—which often felt like hell on earth—and the last when Jamie died." He cleared his throat. "And that's all I'm going to say about that for now. Let's go find some food."

"Okay." With Damon and personal revelations, she felt like it was one step forward, two steps back, and she was learning when to retreat.

While Damon went into the walk-in pantry, she opened the refrigerator. There was a six-pack of soda there, probably left over from Cassie's last visit. She had had a diet cola habit since she was a teenager. There were condiments: mayo, ketchup, mustard, pickle relish, and salad dressing, but nothing else of note.

She grabbed two sodas and pulled them out as Damon came out of the pantry with an assortment of items, including soup, rice, canned vegetables, and some potato chips.

"Score," she said, taking the chip bag out of his hand. "Want a soda?"

"Sure. I'll get it in a second. We're a little short on fruits and vegetables, but we won't starve," he said.

"It all looks good to me." She opened the bag of chips and grabbed a couple, happy with the salty flavor. Then she popped open her soda while Damon went back into the pantry to forage for more ingredients. "The soup is probably fine," she said.

He came out with olive oil and crackers.

"What are you going to do with those?" she asked.

"I haven't decided yet, but it's going to be good."

"And here I thought I was the optimistic one. It looks like olive oil and crackers to me."

He smiled. "You have a better imagination than that."

His easy demeanor was starting to take the edge off, but she wondered how he'd gotten to that state so fast. It was taking her a lot longer to decompress.

"I feel like this day is surreal," she said. "It's weird that it almost feels normal now, when hours ago—"

He raised his hand, cutting her off. "No thinking about that. Lock it back in its compartment. Hours ago was hours ago."

"You killed two people and stole a car. I feel like we're Bonnie and Clyde."

"Only, we're the good guys."

"Are we?"

"Yes." He put down the ingredients and grabbed her by the arms. "Those men were going to kill us, Sophie, and if we hadn't stolen that car, the police would have arrested us. We'd be sitting ducks in a jail cell, with no opportunity to figure out who killed your father and who's trying to kill us."

"Maybe we'd be safer in a jail cell."

"Not for a second. We're dealing with organized crime, and probably more than one person working on the inside at the FBI, NYPD, DEA, and who knows where else? We'd never be safe in jail. I'm sorry I had to kill anyone. But I'm not sorry that we're the ones who are still alive."

"Well, I'm not sorry about that, either. I just never saw someone die before. It was so fast. It didn't seem real, but I know it was." She paused, licking her lips, as she gazed into his eyes. "Damon…"

"What?"

"Are we going to make it out of this? Are we going to be okay?" It was silly to ask him for a reassurance that he couldn't give her, but she needed him to say it.

"I'm sure we will," he said confidently. "But...it might get worse before it gets better, Sophie."

"Can it get any worse?"

"That's not a question you want to ask."

A shiver ran down her spine. He was right. She shouldn't have asked it, because the possibilities sent another wave of fear through her.

"I promise I will do everything I can to protect you," he added.

She looked into his deep-blue eyes and saw nothing but truth and purpose. "I know you will." She drew in a deep breath, her body starting to shiver for another reason. Damon must have sensed a mood change, because his gaze darkened, and his fingers tightened on her arms. Then he let go, and stepped back. "I'm going to see what I can make us to eat. If you want to take a shower or lie down…"

"You want to get rid of me?"

"I want to focus, and it's difficult to do that when you're

close."

"You're the one who started things up again in the garage." She licked her lips, feeling the reckless feeling come roaring back. "Maybe we should eat later…"

"No, and that was a mistake," he said with a definitive shake of his head.

"It didn't feel like a mistake."

"Well, it was. I shouldn't have done that. I'm sorry."

"I'm not. I've been wondering if it would feel the same now as it did before."

She could see him fighting the desire to ask her if she'd gotten the answer to that question.

"We should not go down this road. Go take a shower, Sophie. It will be safer."

She found herself smiling at the irony of his words. "Safer? I can't imagine anything we do could make our lives any less safe than they are right now."

"Let's not find out."

Fourteen

Something had happened, Bree thought, as she responded to an all-hands-on-deck call to the large twenty-third floor conference room at the FBI field office just before two. It was standing room only, at least thirty people crowding into the room. She squeezed past another agent to see Peter Hunt and Karen Leigh at the front of the room. Both wore serious expressions and looked like they were about to deliver some very bad news.

She drew in a nervous breath. She hadn't heard from Damon all day, despite checking the forum several times. She hoped he was still all right.

"We have new information," Peter said heavily. "This morning in New Haven, Connecticut, a storage unit was robbed, and two men were killed. If you direct your attention to the screen..." He motioned to the large monitor behind him.

She saw two cars outside of an open storage unit door. There was a sudden burst of fire from inside the unit and out of their range of vision. But at the edge of the frame, she could see someone on the ground. Then a man and a woman came running out of the unit.

Her heart thudded against her chest.

Damon!

He threw a silver suitcase into the back of a vehicle. A blonde woman jumped into the passenger seat, and they sped out of the lot.

Peter stopped the footage there. "As most of you know, that is Special Agent Damon Wolfe and Sophie Parker, Alan Parker's daughter. There were two deceased males found at the scene."

Peter hit a button on the computer to replace the storage unit security feed on the monitor with photographs of the deceased.

"The man on the left," Peter said, "has been identified as thirty-two-year-old Carl Rucker from Queens. Rucker has a long record of gang violence and armed robbery. He got out of prison eight months ago, and since then he's been working as an auto mechanic in a garage operated by the Venturi family. The second man's prints are not in the system. He had no identification and we were not able to get facial recognition. As you will note, he has a distinctive tattoo on his neck that our analysts are researching. Both men were wearing ski masks and weapons were found at the scene."

The fact that Damon had taken both men out and kept Sophie Parker safe was impressive. But she couldn't help wondering where Damon and Sophie were now and how much more trouble they were in.

"Agent Wolfe and Sophie Parker are in the wind," Peter continued. "Their vehicle was found abandoned in a parking lot several miles away. We have no other information on their current whereabouts." He paused. "This is a department-wide endeavor. As you can imagine, having an agent involved in a double homicide, regardless of the circumstances, is not a position we care to be in. We appreciate those of you in other divisions offering to help with this investigation, and we're going to take you up on it. Karen will be speaking to each of you as to how you can help."

Peter stepped back, and Karen came forward, giving him a brief nod of thanks as she took his place at the front of the room.

Karen's position at the Bureau had definitely gone up a notch since Alan had died. Before then, Karen had been seen as Alan's protégée, his rising star, but now she was running his entire division.

Karen cleared her throat. "Before I get to your assignments, I want to update you on another aspect of our investigation into the Venturi crime family and their possible involvement in the events of the last several days." Karen put a new photo up on the screen—*Wyatt*!

Bree was surprised to see Wyatt's official FBI picture. *What was Karen thinking?* If he hadn't been made before, he was now. It didn't make sense for Karen to out Wyatt in a group that included not just Alan's division but two other divisions as well, but then Karen might now know there was a possible traitor among them. Still, it was a huge risk for her to take.

"This is Special Agent Wyatt Tanner," Karen said. "Agent Parker brought Agent Tanner into the Venturi investigation ten months ago. He's been working undercover in construction for the Venturis' real-estate development firm. A CI has informed us that Agent Tanner's cover is blown and that there's a hit out on his life. He missed his last meet, and he is not answering emergency protocols." Karen paused, her cool demeanor cracking just a little. "We need to find Agent Tanner, as well as Agent Wolfe and Sophie Parker, as soon as possible. If any of you have any knowledge of their whereabouts, please come and talk to me or Peter immediately. It could be the difference between life and death. We cannot have one more person going out on his or her own. The stakes are too high. We are a team, and we will be better if we work together."

Bree felt as if Karen was looking directly at her as she finished her statement.

She didn't flinch or waver under Karen's pointed gaze. There was no way she was giving Damon or Wyatt up, and she had no intention of releasing their secret communication protocol, either. Right now, it was the only lifeline Damon and Wyatt had. And she didn't understand why Karen had told the group that Wyatt wasn't responding to emergency protocols when Wyatt had had a different story.

Before he had fallen asleep on her couch the night before, he'd told her that he'd initiated the protocols as soon as he'd escaped from his attacker on Monday, which was two days before Alan died. Had Alan ignored Wyatt's urgent need for a meet? Or had Karen or someone else intercepted the message?

She'd wanted to press Wyatt for more information, but he'd been exhausted. So, she'd given him a meal as well as a blanket and a pillow for her couch and told him to get some rest. When she'd gotten up for work a little past seven, he'd been gone, and she hadn't heard from him since. She had left him a burner phone to use, and he'd taken it with him, but he hadn't answered her call or text. She really hoped he was all right.

"What about the storage unit?" Seth Hanford asked. Seth was another agent in Karen and Alan's division, and he seemed to be jockeying a bit with Karen for more power.

Bree made a mental note to look into his background a bit more.

"Who rented the unit?" Seth asked. "Do we know what Agent Wolfe and Ms. Parker were doing there? And does anyone know what was in the case Wolfe was carrying?"

Peter Hunt stepped forward to take the questions. "The unit was rented by Justin Lawrence fifteen years ago. It now appears that Lawrence was another alias for Alan Parker. We have no idea what was in the suitcase, but it was obviously important enough for Agent Wolfe and Sophie Parker to go after it."

It suddenly all made sense. Alan had left something in the unit for his daughter…or for Damon—something that was in that silver suitcase.

But what didn't make sense was why Alan had rented the unit under an alias fifteen years ago, and no one had known about it, including his good friend Peter Hunt.

Unless Hunt had known about it.

Had Peter staked out the storage center? Had he sent someone to wait for Damon and Sophie to show up? Had he done the same thing at the cabin? Was Peter the one relaying information to the Venturis?

"That's it for now," Peter said. "Let's get back to work."

Since she was closest to the door, she was one of the first ones out of the conference room, but she'd barely taken three steps down the hallway when Peter Hunt called her name.

"Agent Adams," he said.

"Yes?" she asked, turning back to face him.

"I understand you are friends with Agents Wolfe and Tanner."

"We were at Quantico together."

"And you were all recruited by Alan for this office."

"Yes. But, as you know, I didn't work for him."

"I am aware of that." His sharp gaze raked her face. "Are you in contact with Damon or Wyatt?"

"No," she said, keeping her expression neutral. "I wish I was. I'm extremely concerned for them, especially in light of this new information."

"If you hear from them, you need to let me know."

"Of course. But there is something I'm curious about."

"Walk with me to the elevator," he said. "I have a meeting outside the office."

"All right."

Once inside in the elevator, Peter pushed the button for the lobby level. But before they'd gone two floors, he hit the stop button and the elevator came to a lurching stop.

She stumbled and had to brace her hand against the wall. "Why did you do that?" she asked, suddenly alarmed by the isolation and the possibility that Peter Hunt could be the FBI mole.

"Because you want to ask me something that I don't think anyone else needs to hear," he said, steel in his hard, dark eyes.

She didn't know Agent Hunt. He was way above her pay grade, but he had a good reputation for being extremely perceptive and very dedicated to the job. Now, he seemed almost…menacing. But she wasn't going to let him intimidate her. Alan Parker had trained her to be tough, and she'd only gotten tougher since she'd left Quantico.

"So, ask," he ordered.

"You were friends with Alan Parker for more than twenty years, but you didn't know about his cabin in the Adirondacks or the storage unit in New Haven. That seems odd."

"Does it? Alan went to great lengths to hide his interest in those properties."

"But the lake—Sophie and her dad went there with the Rowlands. How did you not know that? Even I knew that."

"You knew about the lake house?" he asked quickly. "Why didn't you say anything?"

"I didn't know there was a house, but I knew the Rowlands held a wake at the lake for their son Jamie a few years back and that Sophie attended it."

A gleam came into his eyes. "That must have been how Agent Wolfe knew where to find her. Yet, he didn't say anything when I spoke to him."

She ignored the comment about Damon. "Did you speak to Vincent Rowland? I would assume he would have been one of the first people you would contact, since he and Alan were friends. Surely, he would have told you about the house."

"I have not been able to connect with Vincent. And while I knew Alan and Vincent sometimes vacationed together, I wasn't aware there was a particular place they went. I wasn't a part of that. I certainly didn't know Alan had bought a cabin there under an assumed name."

She might be able to believe that, but pleading ignorance about one location was one thing—two locations felt suspect. "The storage unit in New Haven is close to Yale, the school you and Alan attended. You didn't know about that, either?" she challenged.

She was taking a huge risk with her career right now, speaking so impulsively and boldly to a man who could get her fired, but if Hunt was the mole, then she needed to shake him up enough to take action, to possibly make a mistake. That might be their only chance to catch him.

"Why don't you say what you want to say, Agent Adams?" he suggested.

"I believe someone at the FBI might be leaking information to the Venturis. Wherever Damon and Sophie go, someone else seems to show up, and not too far behind."

"And you believe that someone is me?"

She stared back at him. "I hope not. I'm also disturbed that Agent Leigh put Agent Tanner's picture up on the monitor. If there's a leak at the Bureau, she just put Wyatt in more danger."

"Agent Tanner's cover has been blown. Given his work relationship to Alan, and the fact that he's been unreachable since before Alan's death, it's possible he's no longer alive."

She sucked in a breath at his chilling words. She knew Wyatt was alive, but she needed to pretend she didn't. "How can you say that so coldly? He's one of us."

"And we're doing our best to find him. If you have proof there's a leak, by all means bring it to me. But I've got three people missing—all of them extremely important—and my first priority is finding them." He paused, as he pushed the start button. "You've got more guts than brains, Agent Adams. I know now why Alan recruited you. He liked that combination. He liked agents who tested the boundaries, but I do not. I like agents who follow the rules, because those rules will keep all of us alive and build cases that will not get thrown out of court. You might not be wrong about a leak, but unless you have a name and some evidence to back it up, it's just a theory, and I don't deal in theories; I don't have time."

When they reached the ground floor, Peter exited the elevator and strode toward the exterior doors. She thought about going back upstairs to her desk, but she couldn't help wondering where Peter was headed. He'd said he had a meeting outside the office. *With who? About what?*

Using more of her guts than her brain, she impulsively headed out the door after him. It might be a stupid move, but two people she cared about were in trouble, and she wasn't going to stand by and do nothing. She just hoped she wouldn't make things worse.

"I'm surprised, Damon." Sophie set her fork next to her empty plate and rested her arms on the kitchen table. She felt so much better now. She'd showered, washed her hair and had found black leggings and a T-shirt in Cassie's old bedroom. She'd been extremely happy to shed the clothes she'd put on before going to work on Wednesday, before her entire life had gone to hell. It was difficult to believe that was only three days ago.

Damon finished off the last spoonful of rice. "Is there really anything left to be surprised about?" he asked dryly.

"Yes. You can cook. And you're not just average—you're good."

"After everything that has happened the past few days, that made the shock meter?"

"It did. You took a box of rice, olive oil, stewed tomatoes, canned peas and made a delicious meal. Not to mention the chicken noodle soup appetizer with the shredded crackers on top. I am impressed."

"I made do with what we had. It wasn't a big deal."

"Where did you learn to cook? Your parents?"

"Definitely not from my parents. I had a nanny who was from El Salvador. She also cooked for the family, and she could make magic out of anything. Not that she had to make magic in my parents' pantry, because they truly had every ingredient imaginable, but she used to tell me stories about growing her own food and feeding her kids on next to nothing. Sometimes, while she was making dinner, she'd give me three ingredients and tell me I had to come up with something."

"That sounds fun."

"It was fun, until my mother came in and looked at my tomato and avocado toast and yelled at the nanny for not making me a real meal."

"Tomato and avocado toast sounds amazing, especially with a little olive oil on it."

"And black pepper. I was always allowed to use salt and pepper for seasoning my three ingredients."

She smiled at the proud gleam in his eyes. "You do like to win, don't you?"

"Can't deny that."

"I'm sorry to say that your mom does not sound that great."

"She was hard on the help," he conceded. "Not really that hard on me. She didn't want to risk me telling some judge I'd rather live with my father, so I usually got whatever I wanted, unless she was in some mood and wanted to pretend she was a disciplinarian. It didn't really matter. Whatever punishment she threw out was forgotten five minutes later."

"Did you play that for all it was worth?"

"Sometimes, especially when I got older, when I realized the power I had."

"I have a hunch you could have been a lot worse if you'd wanted to be. But you have a strong sense of what is right and what is wrong. I wonder where you got that from."

"I can't imagine. Neither one of my parents has ever met a rule they thought applied to them. They were always the exception."

"But not you. You always followed the rules."

"I wouldn't say always, but growing up the way I did, I liked structure. It felt good to know what the boundaries were. That's why I liked the military. It was straightforward. No games. No manipulation of emotions. I knew what my job was, and I did it."

"The FBI has a lot of rules, too."

"Not as many as the military, but, yes, it does."

She tilted her head as she studied him. "I get why you would like structure because your childhood was so unpredictable, but I have to say, Damon, that you've done nothing but break the rules since you heard my father was dead. Why didn't you tell anyone that you thought I might be at the lake? Why did you come alone? Really?"

"I already told you; I was worried about you. I didn't know if you were there. It was a long drive to find out."

"But you still could have told Karen or Peter where you were going, even if you thought it was a wild-goose chase. It would have made sense to let them know."

"I had met with my undercover friend right before I found out about your father, about the search for you. He'd put some doubts into my head as to who I could trust. I don't know Peter beyond the one short conversation I had with him before I left."

"What was that about?"

"He asked me if I knew you or your friends. I said I didn't. He had some questions about what Alan had brought me in to do, but I couldn't give him much information on that, either."

"Why did you say you didn't know me?"

"You know why. You never told anyone about that night, and neither did I. It was between us—that's it."

She nodded, appreciating his words. "Yes, it was just between us."

"I've had very little contact with Karen since I arrived and barely know the team," he added. "They weren't exactly inviting me into the inner circle. I decided I'd check out the lake and if you were there, I'd figure out the rest later."

"Well, I'm glad you came to find me. I might not have made it out of the cabin alive. It's weird to think I wouldn't have known about the suitcase of cash or the fake passports or anything if I'd died there." She sighed. "Maybe in some ways that would have been better."

"Not for a second. You have a lot of life left to live,

Sophie. A lot of archaeological digging to be done, discoveries to be made."

"My job has really been my whole life the last few years," she admitted. "Now I don't know when I'll get back to it or if I ever will."

"You will."

"I hope so." She paused. "When I was upstairs changing, I looked around a bit more, and I did notice that Jamie had left some clothes in his closet, if you feel like wearing something new. It felt good to me to get out of the clothes I've been living in."

"That's great news. I would love to change."

"Go ahead. I'll clean up."

He nodded but then made no move to get to his feet. "Sophie, we need to talk about the money."

Her gaze strayed to the suitcase on the floor. "I know. My dad must have drained his bank accounts. Or maybe he borrowed some money. Or he sold something and was paid in cash."

Damon's gaze settled on her face. "Is that really what you think?" he asked quietly.

"My dad is dead; he can't defend himself. I have to defend him."

"So, that's not really what you think."

"No, it's not what I think," she said in annoyance. "It looks like someone paid him off or he stole the money. I don't want to believe that either of those things could have happened, but I keep remembering how he started out his voicemail to me with an apology, only he never said how he'd gotten into trouble or what exactly he'd done. Why didn't he just say? Obviously, he was sending me to get the money. Why didn't he just tell me what he'd done?"

"Perhaps he couldn't bring himself to say the words. I think the last thing Alan wanted to do was disappoint you."

"I never thought that could happen. We had our fights as daughters and fathers do, but they were petty, small arguments about nothing. In my heart, I believed my father was the best person in the world. I loved him so much, Damon. He was my rock. He held me when my mom died. He was in the front row at every graduation. He took me to get ice cream when I got my heart broken. He even let me dress him up as a pumpkin on the first Halloween after my mom died, because I was so sad. Does a bad person do that kind of stuff?"

Damon didn't answer, which was good, because she didn't want him to say anything yet. She had to get her thoughts out.

"I was proud of my dad," she continued. "He put terrible people in jail. He made the world safer. I don't want him to turn into someone else now that he's gone. I want to keep believing in the man who taught me how to ride a bike and encouraged me to go for everything I wanted." She took an emotional breath. "But I'm not stupid, Damon. I know my father was not making that kind of money as an agent. I just want there to be a good reason behind him having that money. Like maybe he stole it from a criminal. Or maybe he was going to use it for leverage or evidence or something…"

"It's possible," Damon said slowly.

She gave him a grateful smile. "Thanks for saying that, even though you don't believe it. Your logical brain has already come up with a different equation."

"I respected him, too, Sophie, and I would like to prove his innocence. I don't know if that will be possible, but we don't have the whole story yet. Until we do, I'm keeping an open mind." He pushed back his chair. "I'm going to take a shower."

"Okay. Don't take too long," she said impulsively. "I kind of like having you nearby."

"I'll be back before you know it, but in the meantime." He tipped his head to the gun he'd placed on the counter. "Keep that close. And don't open the door, no matter what."

Fifteen

Bree followed Peter Hunt to a bar in Midtown about a mile away from the office. Peter hadn't seemed to notice her on his tail, walking at a brisk pace and making several calls along the way. He only glanced once over his shoulder at an intersection, but she was able to duck out of sight.

He stopped in front of a bar called the Golden Goose to finish whatever conversation he was having. By his body language, he appeared to be angry. Apparently, she wasn't the only one pissing him off these days.

As he returned his phone back to the pocket of his gray slacks, a black Escalade double-parked in front of the restaurant.

She took out her own phone, pretending to be listening to something as she hid in the doorway of an office building. Peter moved toward the curb as the car door opened.

A skinny man with dark hair and glasses, dressed in an expensive suit and tie, got out of the Escalade. On impulse, she turned on her camera and snapped a photo. She didn't recognize him, but he certainly exited the vehicle like a man expecting attention.

After him, Senator Raleigh stepped out of the car. Another meeting with the senator? Was this about Alan or something unrelated? Raleigh and Hunt had gone to Yale together; maybe the other man had as well.

She snapped a shot of the three men shaking hands. Then they walked into the bar. Glancing at her watch, she noted the time—three forty-five. A little early for happy hour, but the bar would probably be quiet before the after-work crowd came in.

Through the front windows, she saw them sit down at a table where a fourth man was already seated. She slipped out of her hiding place and moved a little closer, discreetly snapping a few shots of the fourth man as she got closer. All she could really see was the back of his head and his stark-white hair.

Then she moved down the street and crossed at the corner, spending another few minutes pretending to peruse some magazines at a newsstand with a good view of the bar. She stayed there for about fifteen minutes, not sure how long she wanted to keep her stakeout going. What might serve her better was identifying who else Peter and the senator were having drinks with.

She turned in the opposite direction and walked to her apartment, which was a mile and a half in the opposite direction.

She hoped Wyatt would be there. She had information for him and also some questions. She hadn't pressed him too hard the night before, but that was going to change. It probably wouldn't be easy to get him to talk. Not only was he distrustful and skittish right now—for good reason—out of the guys in their Quantico group, Wyatt was the most aloof, the most elusive, the one no one really knew, not even after a long conversation. Maybe that's why he was a good undercover agent. He gave nothing away.

Unfortunately, he wouldn't be back undercover any time soon, at least not in this city.

She entered her apartment building, keeping a close eye on her surroundings. She had a gun in her bag and knew how to defend herself, but she was hoping trouble had not found its way to her door. She walked up the stairs to her second-story apartment and knocked three times before using her key.

She didn't want Wyatt to shoot her before she could identify herself. But when she entered the room, she knew he had not come back. The apartment was exactly as she'd left it. She checked the bedroom and bathroom just to make sure he wasn't there and that there weren't any signs of a break-in.

As she moved over to her kitchen window, she glanced down at the alley between her building and the one next to it. She saw someone moving through the shadows. *Was it Wyatt—or someone else?*

Grabbing her bag, she pulled out her gun. If someone had tracked Wyatt to her place, or if Peter Hunt had decided her questions needed to be silenced, she better be ready.

While Damon was showering, Sophie took their dishes to the sink. She washed and dried everything by hand, wanting to leave the kitchen as spotless as they'd found it.

When that was done, she got a notepad and a pencil out of the kitchen drawer and sat down at the table.

She'd told Damon she thought she could draw the tattoo she'd seen on the gunman, and she wanted to give it a shot. But thinking about the tattoo also made her remember how close she'd come to losing her life. She shivered, the terror she'd felt still very close to the surface. She was trying to compartmentalize, but the experiences she'd been through over the past few days were beyond anything she'd ever had to deal with before.

But this was the kind of thing that Damon dealt with all the time—the kind of situation her father had dealt with, too.

As she thought about that, an older memory came into her head—her mom and dad arguing over something late one night. It had been unusual, because unlike Damon's parents, her parents had rarely raised their voices over anything. But that evening, her mom had been upset, worried, wanting to know why her father had to have such a dangerous job, why he couldn't quit after the years of service he'd already put in, why he had to be the one to keep putting his life on the line.

She'd never really thought of her dad as having a dangerous job. He was FBI, but he wore a suit when he went to work. He didn't come home with bruises and gunshot wounds. He'd never been almost killed—at least, she didn't think he had. But at this point, she wasn't sure about much of anything.

She'd thought she could read people. She'd thought she was a good judge of character, but the person she'd been closest to was quickly becoming a stranger, making her question everything about her life, her relationships.

But those questions weren't going to be answered until they found out who had killed her father and who was after her.

She picked up her pencil, closed her eyes and tried to remember what she'd seen.

The image started to come to life…

Opening her eyes, she sketched one snake and then another, trying to intertwine them in the way she remembered, but it wasn't quite right.

She ripped off the page and went to the next one. After several more attempts, she felt she had the snakes right. Then she tried to duplicate the vine that had wound around them. There had been tiny leaves on that vine. She felt as if there was a pattern to the leaves.

Were they spiked at the ends? She thought so. And they were bunched in twos, growing into a cluster as they wound up and down and around the middle.

Excitement ran through her as the picture developed. Now that she had the snakes, the vines and the leaves, she took a stab at the pattern in the middle. It had had six points, a circle inside, then a triangle and in the center of the triangle was an eye—a red eye.

The eye that she'd felt was looking at her.

A chill coursed through her, and it wasn't just because of the eye she'd drawn. It was because the symbol, the snakes and the vine reminded her of something.

She felt sure she'd seen the design somewhere before, but where?

She'd studied art and history and anthropology where symbols played important roles in many cultures. She could have seen this particular image anywhere. She might not have seen it as a tattoo but rather in a picture or on a piece of art.

Maybe she could find it on the Internet now that she'd put it down on paper. She looked around for the phone, but Damon had taken it with him. She'd have to wait until he was done changing, unless she could find another computer in the house.

Setting the drawing aside, she walked down the hall and into Vincent's study. There was no computer on the desk. She looked through the drawers and found nothing beyond envelopes, paper clips, pens, and some more notepads. She was about to close the last drawer when a black-and-white photograph caught her eye. She pulled it out. It was actually a photocopy of a picture of six people. They stood in front of a sign that said Quantico. Jamie was in the middle. Damon was next to him. She didn't recognize the other two men or the two women, but she was guessing this was the group of friends who used the baseball forum.

Someone, probably Jamie, had written a note across the bottom: *The next superheroes*.

She smiled. Jamie had always wanted to be a superhero—first the Army, then the FBI. Was that what drove Damon, too, beyond his appreciation for structure?

Maybe it was more about control than structure. Damon had been used as a pawn between his parents. They'd forgotten that they had a child who needed both of them. It had been more about winning than parenting. And Damon had not had the power to change that.

He'd said it was patriotism and 9/11 that made him join the Army, and she didn't doubt that at all, but she suspected it was also about wanting to be his own man, to do something important with his life, to make a difference—perhaps even be a superhero.

He'd been a superhero today at the storage unit. He'd taken down two gunmen with two shots fired in rapid succession. He'd been so quick, only one man had been able to get off an errant shot that fortunately hadn't hit her. She still didn't quite know how he'd done it.

Jamie would have been proud of his friend, she thought, as she looked back at Jamie's smiling face in the photo. He'd had a military haircut at the time the picture had been taken, and there was purposeful determination in his expression. The two women were quite attractive, one with very dark hair and an exotic beauty, the other more girl-next-door with lighter brown hair and light eyes. The other men were handsome, both dark-haired, rugged in appearance. They definitely looked like they were ready to take on the world. Especially Damon—his dark-brown hair and blue eyes could shine, even in a black and white copy of a photo.

A step brought her head up, and she was relieved to see Damon come through the doorway.

"It's you," she said with relief. He'd changed into a pair of clean jeans and a light-blue button-down shirt that made his eyes look even bluer. His hair was still damp, and he must have found a razor somewhere as his cheeks were smooth again, so smooth she wanted to run her fingers along his jawline. "You took your sweet time."

"What are you doing in here?"

"I was looking for a computer."

"To do what? We can't use anything here in the house. Too risky."

"Really? Would Vincent or Cassie know someone was in here using the computer? Anyway, it doesn't matter, because I couldn't find one, but I did find this." She handed him the photo. "Superheroes, huh?"

"That's what Jamie called us. This photo was taken a few days before Jamie died." He sighed at the end of his statement. "Tragic."

"I never really understood what happened. No one would tell me."

"The mission we were on was classified."

"But I thought you were training. Aren't all those missions fake?"

"Not this one. All I can tell you is that it was a horrific accident. But what Jamie did that day made a difference. It changed something important, and I try to hang on to that. Otherwise, it eats away at me."

She could see the pain in his expression. "Do you hold yourself responsible in some way?"

"I think we were all responsible in some way—even Jamie. If he were alive, he'd probably be the first to say that. You should put this back where you got it."

"Before I do—want to tell me who you've been talking to in the forum? Can we use names yet?"

He hesitated, then nodded. "I think we're there. This is Bree Adams. She's my inside-the-FBI contact." He pointed to the woman in the middle with the light-brown hair and light eyes. "And this is Wyatt Tanner, the undercover agent who was working with your dad." He identified the man on the far right with the dark hair and unsmiling eyes.

"And the others?"

"Parisa and Diego. They're both currently working out of the country; that's why they haven't responded."

"Thanks. It helps to put faces to names. I remember seeing some of these people at the funeral, but no one from Quantico came to the wake but you."

"No. They felt the wake was for closer friends. Jamie and I had a longer history together, so, of course, I went. Bree was close to Jamie but only for a short time. They had a fling during training. She was torn-up after he died, but she wasn't sure she'd be welcome at the wake, so she stayed away."

"He never mentioned her to me." She paused. "Did you have a fling at the academy?" she asked curiously.

"No, I don't mix business and pleasure. The people in this

picture are my friends. That's it. Keeps life simple."

She smiled at his words, then took the paper from his hand and returned it to the desk. "While you were showering," she said, changing the subject. "I drew what I think is the tattoo. I feel like the design is familiar. I want to go on the Internet and see if I can find the image. That's why I was looking for a computer since you can't seem to leave your phone unattended."

"Sorry. I didn't deliberately keep it from you. It was just in my pocket." He handed it to her and then followed her back to the kitchen.

She gave him the drawing, and he perused it for a long moment.

"What do you think?" she asked.

"That I wish I'd noticed even a tenth of what you did. This is good, Sophie. You're an artist. You see not just the big picture but also the details."

"I wouldn't say I'm an artist, but I do like to sketch. I have a feeling this design means something, and if we find out what it means, we might be able to close in on who this person was." She paused. "Although, maybe the police already know. Can Bree find out what the police report says?"

"I just sent a message to the forum with that very question. Hopefully, we'll learn what the police know very soon."

The mention of the police put her nerves back on edge. "You shot those men in self-defense. Even if the police arrest us, they'll have to believe that, right? The guys were wearing ski masks. They were there to rob us and probably kill us."

"I would hope that would be taken into consideration—if that's the way the police report the scene."

She didn't like the suggestion behind his words. "How could they not report it that way?"

"If there's an FBI mole, there could also be someone in the Connecticut Police Department. But let's not worry about that. I'm not as concerned about the police as I am with who sent those shooters and who's coming next. I don't think anyone is giving up."

Bree positioned herself behind her kitchen island, gun in hand, as three sharp knocks came at her door. It was a signal from their Quantico days. She walked over to the door and looked through the peephole. It was Wyatt. It must have been him she'd seen in the alley.

She lowered the gun and let him in. As he entered, she said, "I wasn't sure you'd be back."

"I probably shouldn't be, but I wanted an update."

"Where did you go early this morning?"

"To find someone."

"Who?" she asked curiously.

"A friend of mine."

"I thought you were all out of friends."

"She doesn't know who I am. She's a waitress. We've hung out a few times. She works the early shift at a diner."

She gave him a considering look. Wyatt was attractive when his face didn't boast three shades of purple bruising, and she had no doubt that he could find a woman whenever he wanted one, but she hadn't seen him getting involved while undercover. "Wasn't that risky?"

"She was part of my cover. I had to bring someone to parties. I couldn't always show up alone. It would have raised suspicion."

"Why did you go see her today? You're obviously in a shitload of trouble. Why take that to her?"

"Because there's a part of me that wonders if she knew more than I thought she did."

"Did you talk in your sleep?"

"We didn't do a lot of sleeping," he retorted.

"Of course not. So, what happened when you went to the diner?"

"She wasn't there. The manager said she called in sick today. I went by her apartment. She wasn't home, either."

She saw the grim expression in his eyes and realized he wasn't so much suspicious of this woman as worried. "You don't think the Venturis would go after her, do you?"

"I don't know. I only took her to two parties, but it's definitely possible. I shouldn't have waited so long to look for her."

"Maybe she was just taking a personal day. When's the last time you saw her?"

"Two—three weeks ago." He sat down on the couch and propped up his feet on her coffee table. "Do you have any news?"

She took the chair across from him. "Well, Damon shot two people this morning at a storage unit in New Haven. Both are dead."

Wyatt sat up at that piece of information. "Was he arrested?"

"No. He and Sophie Parker are on the run. They were caught on security footage at the storage place. I don't quite know how they got away, but they did."

"Good. Although, I don't know how innocent Sophie Parker is."

"She seems like a pawn in all this. One of the deceased males was identified as Carl Rucker, who was employed by one of the Venturi companies."

His expression turned grim. "And the other?"

"No ID. No facial recognition. He has a tattoo. Analysts are working on it." She paused. "Karen Leigh also showed your photo to everyone. She said that a CI told her you were made, and if anyone has contact with you, they should tell you to come in. She looked right at me when she said it."

"I probably shouldn't stay here," Wyatt said. "I'll find somewhere else to sleep tonight."

She couldn't deny that moving around might be the best choice for him. "Also, Peter Hunt and I had a bit of a confrontation in the elevator. He came at me about having information on you and Damon, and I decided to turn the tables."

Wyatt raised an eyebrow. "What did you do?"

"I poked the bear."

He groaned. "That sounds like you, Bree."

"And you," she retorted.

"I can't argue with that."

"I asked him why he hadn't known about the lake house where Sophie went, since he was friends with Alan and also with Vincent Rowland. He said he hadn't spoken to Vincent and mumbled something about not spending vacation time with Alan. I'm not sure I buy it. Also, the storage unit from today's ambush was rented by Alan under an alias, and since it was in New Haven where both he and Peter went to school, I was surprised Peter didn't know about that, either."

"Peter is looking more suspicious by the day."

"So is Karen. I don't know why she put your photo up in front of the entire office, not just your division. It felt like she had an ulterior motive. I'm wondering if she is going to frame you for something. If the investigation gets too close to FBI involvement in Alan's death, who better to pin it on than someone who might have been turned by the crime family he was sent to investigate?"

Wyatt stared back at her through unblinking serious dark eyes. "I can't think of anyone better."

"Do you know Seth Hanford? He seems to be a little put out that Karen has more power now. He has been asking a lot of annoyed questions in our meetings, as if he's angry he's out of the loop."

"I met him once. He worked closely with Alan on some projects. But he and I never had direct contact after I went under." Wyatt paused. "Getting back to the storage unit, why do you think Damon went there."

"Well, he came out with a silver suitcase, so I'm thinking he went for that."

A gleam entered Wyatt's eyes. "Maybe inside is the evidence we need to break this wide open."

"I hope so. I just sent Damon my update and some photos I want to ask you about as well." She grabbed her phone and moved over to the couch. "After I spoke to Peter, I followed him. He met three men at a bar in Midtown." She showed him the first photo of the tall, skinny guy with the glasses. "Do you recognize this man?"

He slowly shook his head. "I don't."

"Okay, the next one is Senator Raleigh. This is Peter's second meeting with the senator in a couple of days." She flipped to the last photo. "When they got inside, they met another man. I didn't get a good picture, but he has very white hair."

"Nope. No one on my radar," Wyatt said with a shake of his head.

"They were all about Peter and Alan's age, so maybe they're just friends."

"Could be." He paused. "We need to ask Damon what's in the suitcase."

"Already did that. We'll see what he says."

Sixteen

Sophie had been sitting at the kitchen table for over an hour, searching the Internet for tattoos similar to the one she'd drawn, but she'd come up with nothing even close. The phone was also not getting the best reception so every site seemed to take forever to load.

She got up from her chair and moved into the adjoining family room, where Damon was seated on the couch, his bare feet up on the coffee table, as he flipped through channels on the television. It was the most relaxed she'd seen him. The simple fact that he didn't have his shoes on made her feel like there was a little less danger around them.

"Are you done research?" he asked.

"For the moment. I wish I had a computer and some faster Wi-Fi. The phone doesn't move very fast."

"I'm assuming you didn't find anything then."

"Nothing that was a really good match, but I haven't given up yet. The snake is one of the most widely used symbols and it crosses many different cultures. Because the snake sheds its skin, some view it as a sign of rebirth and fertility. Others use the snake as a guardian of valuable and precious artifacts or to ward off intruders from their religious temples. The venom of the snake symbolizes poison, danger, even the divine. Some believe the snake bite leads them into immortality. It's going to take me a while to figure out what the snakes entwined in vines with that strange symbol and the red eye mean. It could be a combination of designs made into one." His smile made her pause. "That was way more than you wanted to know, wasn't it?"

"Let's just say I know more about snakes now than I did five minutes ago."

"Well, it was a teachable moment, and I'm a teacher."

"Is that how you see yourself, Sophie? As a teacher? Or as an archaeologist?"

"Both, really. I love to impart knowledge, as evidenced by my recent monologue on snakes. But there's nothing like the thrill of discovery. At any rate, I am going to figure out the meaning of that tattoo. It may not help us in any way, but it gives me something productive to do and to think about. Plus, I don't like to quit until I have the answer I'm seeking."

"I have definitely learned that you are not a quitter. You don't give up easily on anything."

"I've had a few moments where I wondered if I should give up."

"But you don't give in to those short periods of doubt. Why don't you take a break on your research? I'd like to check the forum to see if there's news from Bree or Wyatt."

"Sure." She sat down next to him and handed him the phone. "I'm surprised you were so patient. Probably checking the forum is more important than my research."

"You never know. You had the tattoo design fresh in your mind; I didn't want to mess with that."

"I appreciate that." She tipped her head toward the television. "Have we made the news yet?"

"Not the world news. There was another missile test from North Korea, so reports have been all about that."

"Sometimes it feels like the world is becoming a very scary place."

"You don't want to know the half of it," he muttered, a dark cloud passing through his eyes.

She couldn't imagine all the bad things Damon had seen. "I don't think I could handle it as well as you do."

"You would do what you had to do—just like you did today."

"I suppose, but in reality, you did everything. I just followed along."

"You picked up the bat. I'm not sure what you were going to do with it, but I liked the idea."

She smiled. "I didn't know what I was going to do with it, either. Against a gun, it wouldn't have been much protection, but I just instinctively reached for it."

"You have a lot of courage, Sophie."

"I never thought I did, but I guess I've never been tested until now. I'd like the tests to be over." She tilted her head, giving him a thoughtful look. "Does it ever get to you—the constant danger? The darkness? The bad people?"

He didn't answer right away, taking his time with her question. "Sometimes, but in the short-term, I try to focus on the mission at hand, and in the long-term, I try to believe in the good that I'm doing. If I can make a difference, save even one life, it's worth it."

She met his gaze, thinking how lucky the world was to have someone like Damon willing to take the risks, fight the danger, run forward when everyone else was running away. She was lucky, too.

"Something else you want to ask me?" he questioned, a curious look in his eyes.

"No. Go ahead and look at the forum. I'm curious to know if there's any news."

While Damon was accessing the forum, she looked toward the windows.

The sun had gone down a while ago, and they'd drawn all the curtains and blinds in the part of the house they were using, so the only light in this room was coming from the phone and from the television. They'd also closed the doors leading into the hallway, and Damon had even gone out front to make sure no light could be seen from the street or from a neighbor's house.

She knew they were in the best possible location they could be in. None of the Rowlands were close enough to drop in, and on a Friday night, she doubted any service people would show up at the house unexpectedly. They should be fine until at least tomorrow, but it still felt a little spooky.

"Bree sent a message," Damon said.

She moved closer, so she could read the screen with him, but the sentences didn't make a lot of sense. "You're going to have to translate your baseball code into words I can understand."

"Security cams caught us at the storage unit."

"We figured that," she said, her heart still sinking at the confirmation.

"They traced the ownership of the unit to your father."

"What about the men who tried to kill us? Any ID?"

"One is a known associate of the Venturi crime family, so it's looking like they're definitely involved in this. The other, the one with the tattoo, has not been identified, and they're checking to see if they can match the tattoo to any other known criminal organization."

"I'm glad they're working on it, too. They have far more resources than I do."

"They also have more people to bury whatever information they come up with."

She frowned at that reminder. "Did Bree say anything else?"

"She confronted Peter Hunt about the possibility of a leak, and he didn't deny it."

"Confronted? Was that smart?" she asked worriedly.

"Bree is good at reading people. She probably wanted to push him and see if she could get a reaction. She also followed him and took some pictures. She wants to know if we recognize these people." He brought up the photos on the phone. "Here's the first guy."

"That's Michael Brennan," she said, recognizing her father's friend. "I told you about him before. He's the financial, hedge fund guy who went to Yale with my dad."

"Okay. I know this is Senator Raleigh," Damon said, flipping to the next photo, then moving on to a third picture. "This isn't a clear shot, but what do you think about this guy? Do you know him?"

"That looks like Harrison Delano. He has really white hair. I can't see the man's face, but I'd bet that's him." She paused. "This is the Yale group that Peter and my dad were a part of, minus a couple of people. Maybe they're just trying to find out what happened to my father, or Peter is giving them an update."

"That's probably it," Damon said, as he typed in what she'd told him and then posted it in the forum.

"Probably?" she echoed. "Why does it sound like you think there's another reason?"

"I don't have another reason. I just don't know if that's what they're talking about."

"You don't think there's a chance they conspired against my dad in some way, do you? Those men are some of his best friends in the world."

"And they're all powerful people."

"So? I don't see how my father could have been a threat to any of them. Why would they have had him killed? No." She shook her head. "I think it's more likely they're all upset that he's dead and want to make sure he gets justice. They might also be worried about me."

"I'm sure they *are* worried about you, Sophie."

She didn't know if he meant they were worried because they cared about her or because she was a loose end. "Did Bree have anything else to report?"

"No, but she has a question—she wants to know what's in the suitcase. Apparently, they saw that on the security footage as well."

"Don't tell her," she said impulsively.

Damon lifted his gaze to hers, a question in his eyes. "We can trust Bree."

"I don't know her."

"You know me. We can trust her."

"All right, but I still don't want you to tell her—not yet anyway."

"Okay, we'll wait."

She let out a breath, not sure why she didn't want the money to come out now when it would certainly come out later, but she was still trying to make sense of it. "Thanks."

"No problem. Bree understands *need to know*." He sent a reply, then set the phone on the coffee table. "I told her we'd be in touch tomorrow."

"Tomorrow," she echoed. "I can't imagine what tomorrow is going to bring." She licked her lips, her thoughts tumbling around in her head. "I want to put my dad's killers away, Damon. I want to get my life back. I want you to have your life back. But I'm afraid of where the truth is going to take me. I'm terrified of where all this is going to end. Am I going to work hard to prove my father's innocence only to find out he's guilty? And then what? Do I try to cover it up, protect his reputation, his legacy?" She paused. "I shouldn't have even said that to you. Covering up his illegal actions would be a crime, too. I feel like I'm floundering, and it would be really easy to drown. I know you just said I'm not a quitter, but this is a lot to handle."

"I know, Sophie. It is a lot for you to deal with. You haven't even had a chance to mourn your father. But I can tell you this—you're not going to drown, because I won't let you. And you don't have to decide what you're going to do until you have all the facts, until you have to make a decision. I wish I could tell you not to be afraid of the truth, but I can't. I don't want to believe Alan is guilty of anything, but it's not looking good for him."

She appreciated his honesty, and it made her feel less guilty knowing that he had the same doubts she did. "I feel the same way. I keep thinking that if my father was innocent, he would have named names or given me specifics and leads to help prove his innocence. But cash and fake IDs and his voicemails saying he was sorry and telling me to run…paint a different picture. On the other hand, I can't understand why he didn't have more money if he was taking bribes or stealing cash. He didn't buy a big house or a boat or a fancy car. He lived simply." She took a breath, realizing what her father had spent money on. "But he did pay for all my schooling, all my living expenses. That added up."

"This isn't on you," Damon said sharply. "Your father didn't have to steal to send you to school."

"What if he did? I never asked him if he had the money for grad school; I just assumed. What does that make me?"

"Normal. Like every other kid in the world."

"And selfish."

"Like every other kid in the world," he repeated.

"I bet you didn't take money from your parents."

"That was different. Their money came with strings. I didn't want the strings, so I didn't take the money." He sent her a pointed look. "I am happy to go around the circle of questions with you, Sophie. I will help you analyze every little detail. I will speculate and theorize, but I won't listen to you try to blame yourself for what your father might have done. You are not responsible for any of this. Got it?"

Judging by his stern expression, there was only one answer. "Got it," she said, happy to have his reassurance. "I feel like I need to say thank you again."

"Please, don't."

"Then I'll just think it."

"Works for me," he said with a flash of relief.

"Speaking of your parents—"

He groaned. "We don't need to speak of them."

"I was just wondering if you keep in touch. Do you see them on holidays? Has time changed your relationship from when you were a kid?"

"Not really. I saw my mother two Christmases ago and my father probably the year before that. We exchange the occasional text or email. They send me pics from their vacations."

His parents really sounded like narcissists. "What about

your half-siblings? Do you communicate with them?"

"We also text once in a while. I try to remember their birthdays. That's about it. I was thirteen when my first half-sister was born. There's a big age gap between us, and frankly we don't have a lot in common. My life with my parents was a different world. They only know the world of their mom and dad, and it's a happy one. They don't need me dragging it down."

"You wouldn't do that."

"Well, it doesn't matter. Everyone is very happy with the way things are."

"I bet your parents miss you more than you think."

"That's because you like to believe the best in people, Sophie."

"I guess I do. It's going to be more difficult from here on out."

A glint of understanding appeared in his eyes. "No doubt about that. But I hope you don't get completely cynical."

"Like you?" she challenged.

"Like me," he conceded.

"It makes sense to me now where some of your cynicism comes from. You were hurt by your parents, and it was a deep hurt, the kind that doesn't ever really go away."

"I'm not harboring some deep resentment toward my parents, Sophie. I'm over it."

"I don't believe that."

"Well, it doesn't really matter if you believe it," he said with annoyance. "I know what's true. Stop trying to psychoanalyze me."

"I'm not doing that. I'm just trying to understand you."

"I'm not that complicated."

"Oh, come on, Damon. That's not true."

"It is true. I keep things simple. That's my strategy in life."

"And that's how you ended up here with me?" she challenged. "By keeping things simple?" His frown told her she'd struck gold with her words.

"Good point," he admitted. "I knew from the first second I saw you that you were going to complicate my life, and I wasn't wrong."

"Hey, I did nothing to get you to come after me. I never contacted you after the night we spent together. I didn't show up at any FBI functions where you might be there."

"Was that on purpose?" he asked curiously.

"Well, mostly I wasn't around, but my point is that I let you go. You're the one who came to find me."

"I blame your father for that."

"That would make it simpler."

He smiled. "It definitely would."

"But we both know that isn't the whole story."

His eyes flared with blue sparks that immediately sent a rush of desire through her.

"We should watch TV," he said. "Where did the remote go?"

She picked it up off the table. "I have it."

"Well, turn up the sound, find us something with noise."

"Something distracting?"

"God, yes."

The desperation in his eyes made her put the remote behind her. "I don't want to watch television; I want us to finish the kiss you started in the garage."

His lips tightened. "That was a mistake."

"It reminded me of how good we are together. Aren't you curious how it would feel now?"

"It would complicate things, and we don't need that."

"Because you wouldn't be able to leave in the morning?"

"I don't want to have this conversation, Sophie."

"Fine. I don't want to talk anyway. I want to kiss you. And then I want you to take me upstairs to bed." He started to shake his head, but she leaned over and put her hands on either side of his face. "Don't say no, Damon. Not when it's what we both want."

She could see the war going on in his eyes: the need to do the right thing, the desire to feel what they'd felt once before.

"I don't want to hurt you," he said huskily.

"You won't hurt me."

"You said that the last time, but I hurt you then, and I don't want to do it again."

"That was different. We know each other better now."

"That might be true, but there's something else that's also true—I don't do love, Sophie. I'm not good at it, and it doesn't work out. I might be exactly what you want in the night, but I will never be what you want in the morning."

"In the morning?" she echoed. "We don't even know if we're going to have a morning, Damon. I could have died at least twice in the last three days. You told me that I need to stay in the moment. This is the moment I need."

"I said that about surviving."

"I don't want to just survive; I want to live. I want you. I think you want me, too. So, stop fighting. Please, stop fighting."

He sucked in his breath and she could see him trying to hang on to the last bit of control. "You're not playing fair."

"I'm not playing at all," she said, recklessness driving her forward. She pressed her mouth against his, and took what she wanted. It was a heady, glorious, freeing feeling.

Damon let her have her way for a minute, but then he pushed her back and stood up.

She stared at him in shock, unable to believe he was really saying no.

Then he grabbed her hands and pulled her to her feet.

"If we're going to do this, we're going to do it right," he said.

She shivered at the promise in his words.

He led her up the stairs, and into Jamie's room.

She had a second thought as she saw her old friend's things. "Uh, Damon, I don't know about this room…"

"One second," Damon said, going into Jamie's bathroom. He flicked the light on, then off, and came back with a condom. "I saw this earlier. Only one. We better make it good."

"Not here," she said.

"No," he agreed, as she led him out of the room and across the hall into a guest bedroom. She didn't want any memories besides the ones they would make tonight.

With moonlight streaming through a skylight, throwing the room in dark shadows, she went into Damon's arms.

His kiss showed none of the reluctance he'd expressed earlier. It was hungry, impatient, demanding, and she matched him in every single emotion. There was nothing but now…no worries for tomorrow, no regrets for yesterday—just this moment, *this man.*

Damon set her senses on fire. He was the flame and she was the moth, and she didn't care if she got burned. She was all in.

His mouth left her lips and slid along her jaw down the side of her neck. Her nerves tingled with the sensuous trail of delight. His hands crept under her top, his rough-edged fingers drawing goose bumps from every patch of skin he touched.

"I want to see you," Damon whispered, as he pulled her top over her head. Then his fingers were on the front clasp of her bra. He pulled the edges apart, baring her breasts to his hungry gaze. She shrugged the bra off her shoulders while his mouth closed over one nipple. She threw back her head in delight, as he teased and tormented first one breast, then the next.

His mouth moved lower, his hands now working on getting her out of her leggings and panties, and she was more than willing to help him; she wanted him naked, too.

"You need to catch up," she said, feeling a little shy in her nakedness with Damon still fully dressed.

"I'm there," he said with a smile, pulling off his shirt and kicking off his jeans.

She wished she had more light to see him, but what she did see made her swallow hard. He was a beautifully made man: broad shoulders, lean torso, ripped abs, just the right amount of sexy, dark hair, and a body that was made for hers.

They pulled each other down on the bed, kissing, tasting, touching...

The memories of the one night they'd shared together came rushing back, but this time was even better—more passionate, more reckless, more adventurous, more loving…

She didn't want to say the L word, much less think it, but as she and Damon came together, she felt the deepest kind of emotional connection, built not just on passion but also on trust. This man was in her heart, in her soul. She could feel him everywhere. She didn't try to fight the feelings. She reveled in them.

Because who knew what tomorrow would bring?

They had tonight, and she would make the most of it.

He'd definitely complicated what was already a bad situation. He'd done everything he shouldn't have done. He'd given in to feelings instead of sticking with logic.

But as Damon gazed at the beautiful, naked woman snuggled up next to him in bed, strands of her blonde, silky hair covering his chest, he didn't have one single regret.

It might be the wrong time, wrong place, but Sophie was absolutely right.

He'd never felt so in sync with a woman, so desperate to know each sweet inch of her, to please her in every possible way. And it seemed as if Sophie had felt exactly the same way.

They'd been reckless the first time they'd met. They'd come together out of sadness.

But this time, the recklessness had come with a better knowledge of each other, a more complex desire, a deeper caring. It was unsettling, a little terrifying, and it wasn't because he couldn't leave her in the morning; it was because *he didn't want to.*

Sophie had gotten into his head, under his skin. She was

in every breath he took. She'd become his first waking thought and also his last. He wanted to tell himself that the danger of the situation was heightening the feelings, but he knew that wasn't the whole truth. He might not have called Sophie in four years, but that didn't mean he'd stopped thinking about her. She'd always been there; he'd just put her out of reach, kept his eye on the ball in front of him. But now *she* was in front of him and behind him and next to him—everywhere he was. And it still didn't seem close enough.

He was overwhelmed again with a compelling need to have her. It wasn't just her face and body that were beautiful; it was her. It was her spirit, her courage, her curiosity, her loyalty in the face of all odds.

If he did do love, she'd be his first choice.

But he quickly reminded himself that love was a one-way street, a one-way ticket to eventual pain. Maybe a few couples made it, but not many, and usually not without a lot of compromise.

As her body shifted against his, he couldn't help wondering if the journey might be worth it, even if the eventual outcome was bad.

But that wasn't very logical. Why set himself up for a fall when he could avoid one altogether?

Because it was Sophie...Because if there was ever a time to break one of his rules, it might be now.

"It's going to be okay," Sophie said, her voice cutting through his turbulent thoughts. She lifted her head off his chest to look at him, and he could see the gleam of understanding in her eyes. "I can feel the tension coming back. You're thinking too much, Damon. Not a very good role model for staying in the moment," she teased.

He couldn't help but smile at the reminder. "Do what I say, not what I do."

"It's not morning yet," she added. "We still have the night shadows to play around in, before we have to face reality."

"As tempting as that is, I don't have any more condoms."

"So, let's do some other stuff," she said with a wicked

smile. "I have a few ideas."

"You do, huh?"

"I do," she said, meeting his gaze. "We still have a little time before the sun comes up, and I feel like we should use the time well. Because...well, because we don't know what's coming next."

He brushed a strand of hair off her face—her beautiful face. She was an angel and no angel should have to deal with the hell they were running from. Unfortunately, her father had sold his soul to the devil and now Sophie was fighting for her life.

"I know what's coming next. It's this," he said, pulling her face down so he could kiss her again.

She gave him a look of pure happiness, and the defenses he'd built up over many, many years began to crumble.

Love had almost broken him as a child, and years of losing military friends in war and his best friend to an FBI mission had continued the shredding of his heart. He truly did not think he had much left to give her, and she deserved more, so much more.

But denying her what she wanted...what he wanted seemed impossible.

"Damon, stop worrying," she said, giving him a hard look. "That's supposed to be my job. We already agreed that tonight is just about you and me—no past, no future, just now. That's all I want."

Unfortunately, he wanted a whole lot more, and that's what he was really worried about. But he wasn't stupid enough to say no to Sophie's offer. He'd deal with the fallout later. In the meantime, he'd do his best to make her as happy as he could.

Seventeen

He was gone—again.

Sophie sighed as she rolled over on her side and stared at the very empty other side of the bed. She could still see the imprint of Damon's head on the pillow. She could smell the musky scent of his skin on the sheets. But he wasn't there, and she really shouldn't have expected that he would be.

She'd told him no promises, no regrets, and she'd meant it, but she still wished she could have woken up in his arms. But she was alone, and the house felt really quiet.

Sitting up in bed, she told herself this was not like before. There was no way Damon would leave her alone in the house. He wouldn't abandon her—at least not while she was in danger.

After this was over…well, everything would change then. But whether or not she and Damon would ever get together again was probably the last thing she should be worrying about.

She got up, gathered her clothes together, and then walked across the hall to the guest bathroom. She wanted to look for Damon, but she needed to get her head together first.

During a long, hot shower, she gave herself the luxury of reliving a few of the night's best moments. She knew Damon liked her, that the attraction between them was off the charts, but she also knew that he was afraid of love, of needing someone, of thinking about a relationship in terms of forever.

His parents had done a number on his head, and she could understand why he'd be gun-shy. But she would never hurt him. How could she? *She was in love with him.*

The realization shocked her as well as the knowledge that she'd probably been in love with him the past four years; she just hadn't wanted to admit she'd been stupid enough to fall for a one-night stand.

But her love would scare Damon, so she wasn't about to share her feelings with him. He wouldn't want the burden of her emotions, and things would get awkward, and now wasn't the time for any of that.

She turned down the heat on the water, letting the cool spray tamp down her heated emotions.

Damon would no doubt have his guard walls back in place by the time she got downstairs, and she needed to put on her own armor.

By the time she had blow-dried her hair and scoured through Cassie's closet for a pair of jeans and a knit top, she was feeling ready to take on the day.

She found Damon in the kitchen. He had also apparently found different clothes in Jamie's room, putting on a light blue T-shirt and a pair of jeans that, of course, made him look sexy as hell. And just like that, all her resolve went out the window.

Why did he have to look so good? Why did she have to want him so much? Shouldn't last night have kept her going for a while? But being with him hadn't diminished her need; it had increased it.

Damon looked up from whatever he was making on the stove. He started to smile, but there must have been something in her expression to put him off. He turned down the burner and then crossed the room, hauling her into his arms for a hot, scorching kiss that made a mockery of all her plans to just move on and let the night fade into the back of her mind.

"Good morning," he said, finally stepping away from her.

"It is now," she said a little breathlessly. "But I thought we weren't going to take the night into today."

"That was the plan, but when I look at you, plans seem to go out the window."

She liked that she had that effect on him, liked it even more that he'd admitted it.

"Come and sit down," he said. "Breakfast is ready."

"It smells good. What is it?"

"Oatmeal with extra cinnamon."

"That's perfect."

"I don't know about perfect, but it will keep us going for a while."

"I need to call Cassie and Vincent." She glanced at the clock. It was only seven a.m., but it was afternoon in Paris. "Maybe I'll do that after I eat."

"Good idea. We can talk about what you want to say." Damon pulled two bowls out of the cabinet and filled each one up with oatmeal.

She grabbed spoons out of the drawer, and they sat down at the table together to eat. "This is delicious. You really are a wizard in the kitchen. You're not so bad in the bedroom, either," she added lightly.

He gave her a wicked grin. "I'm good in a few other rooms as well."

She appreciated the comeback, happy that there wasn't awkward tension between them. "So, we're okay?" she asked tentatively.

"I'm good. You?"

"I'm good, too," she said, meeting his gaze.

"We don't need to talk about anything?"

"Only what we're going to do to evade capture and find out what happened to my dad. I do have an idea."

"Well, don't keep it to yourself."

She got up and walked over to the suitcase that was still on the floor. She opened it, inwardly wincing once again at the sight of all the money, and then pulled out the fake IDs and returned to the table. "I noticed yesterday that both sets of IDs have the same address. It's in Brooklyn. I wonder if it means anything."

Damon took the IDs out of her hand and perused them. "Interesting. Could be an empty lot or just a fake address."

"It could be, but it doesn't feel like my dad would have just pulled something out of a hat. He obviously had some plan in mind."

Damon pulled out his phone. "Let me look up the address on the map."

She sat down and finished the last of her oatmeal as he did that.

"I've got a satellite image. It looks like an apartment building." He lifted his gaze from the phone. "We could check it out. But it means going back to New York."

"I don't feel like New York is any more dangerous than any other place right now."

"Good point. It might actually be safer. No one would expect you to come back to the city. I like it." He paused, giving her an approving look. "I didn't even pay attention to the address on the IDs. I should have. Nice job, Sophie."

She smiled under his praise. "I was looking at them yesterday while you were hiding out in the house waiting for the cleaners to leave, but then I forgot when I got caught up in the snake tattoo."

"We wouldn't have wanted to go yesterday anyway. Things were too hot." He paused. "This could be your dad's safe house in the city."

A chill ran through her. "I kind of hope it isn't, because so far my dad's secret places have not worked out too well for us. Maybe we shouldn't go."

"Or," he said, a glint in his eyes…"Maybe we shouldn't go alone."

She read his mind. "You want to ask your friends to help?"

"I do. But it's up to you. We're in this together."

The thought of bringing more people into the situation was both tempting and worrisome. She didn't know Bree and Wyatt, but Damon did. If she trusted him, she had to trust them. "If you think it's a good idea, I won't say no."

"I'll send a message. Then you can call Cassie."

She nodded, feeling a nervous tingle run through her. *Was calling Cassie and Vincent still a good idea? What information could they possibly have that might help?* And even though Vincent had been retired for years, he was still former FBI. *Would he have some allegiance to Peter Hunt?* She didn't think Karen Leigh had been there when Vincent worked for the Bureau, but she had no idea if Vincent had kept in touch with anyone.

Still, it was possible Vincent could shed some light on her father's actions. They had remained friends after Vincent retired. He might be able to give her a lead.

Damon slid the phone across the table to her. "Your turn."

"Is calling them too big of a risk? Do you think Vincent will have information we can use?"

He shrugged. "I have no idea. The call could be valuable, worthless, or could create more problems for us."

She frowned. "That's not very helpful."

He thought for a moment. "If you keep it short, say as little as possible, ask more questions than you answer, it's probably worth hearing what Vincent has to say, if he's been in touch with Peter or anyone else."

She nodded. "Okay, that makes sense. I must admit that it feels strange to be worried about calling people I've known since I was a little girl."

"It's good to be worried. Right now, we can't afford to let down our guard for a second."

She nodded, then punched in Cassie's number and put the speaker on.

Her friend answered a moment later. "Hello?"

"It's Sophie," she said, feeling a little less tense at the sound of Cassie's voice. "Are you with your dad?"

"We're in the car. I'm going to put you on speaker, okay?"

"Is there anyone else with you?"

"Just me and my dad," Cassie said. "We're driving to the Loire Valley to drink some wine. Are you okay? Are you safe?"

"I'm hanging in there," she replied, feeling wistful for father-daughter trips like the one Cassie was on.

"Hello, Sophie," Vincent said in his deep baritone voice. "I'm very glad that you're all right. I've been extremely worried about you."

"Well, I'm in quite a bit of trouble."

"How can I help you?"

"What do you know about my dad's death? Have you spoken to anyone at the FBI?"

"Yes. I've spoken to Peter several times."

She shot Damon a quick look, then said, "What did Peter tell you?"

"That your apartment was broken into and that you ran up to the lake, where someone took a shot at you. He said you're with Damon Wolfe—Jamie's friend. Are you still with him?"

She swallowed a knot in her throat as Damon shook his head. "No, I'm not," she lied. "I got scared, and I ran from him, too. I don't know who to trust."

"Let me arrange to get you out of town."

"I'm all right where I am at the moment. What I really need to know is what you think happened to my dad. Did my father tell you he was in trouble?"

There was a short pause on the other end of the line.

"A few weeks ago," Vincent said, "Alan told me that he had some significant financial problems. I asked if I could help, and he said he had it under control, but I could see that he was quite worried. Unfortunately, he didn't go into further detail. After talking to Peter, I suspect Alan may have borrowed money from the wrong person, possibly someone in one of the criminal organizations he was involved bringing to justice."

Her heart sank at Vincent's words. "Do you really believe he would break the law because he was in debt?"

"I don't want to believe it, Sophie, but Peter told me he thought there was a leak at the Bureau, and Alan was at the top of his list. It didn't make sense to me. Alan was the straightest shooter I've ever known. And I would have given him the last dollar I had; all he had to do was ask," Vincent said, his voice laced with sadness.

"When's the last time you spoke to him?" she asked.

"Probably two or three weeks ago. I meant to get back in touch, but I've been traveling."

She frowned as Damon jotted something down on the notepad and then pushed it over to her: *Did he tell anyone about lake cabin?*

"Did you mention the lake house to Peter?" she asked. "Because I don't know how anyone knew I would be there. The cabin was supposed to be a safe place." Her words reminded her that Vincent could have been the person who sent someone to kill her.

Damon sent her a warning look, obviously reading something on her face.

He wrote down on the paper: *Relax. Don't give anything away.*

"No, I didn't mention the cabin to Peter," Vincent replied. "On our first call on Wednesday night, he told me about Alan, and he asked me if I knew any of your friends or if you were in touch with Cassie. I told him that I didn't know who you spent time with and that Cassie was in London. He got in touch with me on Thursday to tell me about the shooting at the cabin and to ask me why I hadn't told him about it. I didn't actually think about the cabin when he first spoke to me. I haven't been there in a long time, and, to be honest, I was so shocked by the news about your father, everything else went out of my mind. I couldn't believe that Alan was dead. I'm very sorry, Sophie. I know how close the two of you were, and I cannot believe that someone killed him or that anyone is after you."

He sounded sincere, upset about her dad, worried about her. A week ago, she never would have doubted him; now, she just didn't know.

"Can you tell me why you're not talking to Peter?" Vincent asked.

"My dad left me a message telling me not to trust anyone."

"I don't understand. Did he say why or who?"

"Unfortunately, no. He sounded panicked, like he was in danger, and obviously he was. He didn't tell you why he was in financial trouble?"

"No, I'm sorry he didn't. I did ask. He just said it was trouble that had been building for a while. That's all he would say. Look, Sophie, we need to get you somewhere safe. I want you to come to Paris," Vincent continued. "Cassie and I will take care of you. I know your father would want me to do that."

"I'd only put you in danger."

"I can handle that."

"But Cassie can't. And I'm not sure I could get on a plane. My photo is everywhere. Everyone is looking for me."

"We could arrange for a private plane. I can make that happen. I have money and connections. Come to Paris. Let everything else cool down. We can figure out this problem together."

She hesitated, somewhat tempted to take him up on his offer, but it didn't really seem realistic.

Damon wrote down: *Say maybe...play along.*

"Possibly," she said, not sure why Damon wanted her to play along, but she would do what he asked. "I need to call you back. I can't stay in any one place for long."

"I can have a plane ready to go in two hours. Can you get to Teterboro, New Jersey?"

She licked her lips as Damon shook his head.

"No, not that fast," she said.

"How long would you need?"

Damon gave another warning shake of his head.

"I'm not sure. I have to go. Please don't say anything about this call to anyone."

"Of course not," Vincent said. "But I'm very worried about you trying to do this alone. If someone at the FBI is involved in your father's death, you're going to need help."

"I'll be all right."

"Sophie, wait," Cassie cut in. "Please don't say no to my dad's offer. I really want you to be safe, and I'm scared for you."

"I know you're scared; I am, too, but I have to do this my way. I'll be in touch. I just can't talk right now. Someone is coming." She hung up the phone before they could say anything more and let out a breath. "What do you think? Do you believe Vincent didn't rat me out about the cabin?"

"His answer was definitely plausible. He could have been shocked as he said about your father's death, and the cabin wasn't in his mind at that moment."

"But?" she asked, seeing doubt in Damon's eyes.

"FBI agents don't usually forget things like safe houses. At any rate, I didn't want you to give him any indication of where you were. Just saying how long it would take to get to Teterboro could have pinpointed our location."

"I'm sure he'd be stunned to know I'm in his house."

"We won't be for long. We need to move and get another phone."

"Again?"

"Vincent could easily have the FBI ping this number."

She pushed the phone across the table as if it were a snake about to bite. "I don't think he'll do that. He knows now that my dad warned me not to trust anyone. He'll be careful who he talks to. At least, he said he would."

"I hope that's true." Damon turned the phone off and removed the battery. "We'll toss this somewhere on the way to Brooklyn."

"Do you think I should have taken Vincent up on his offer to get out of the country?"

"I think you should keep it in mind. But not until we know for sure we can trust him."

She picked up the IDs from the table and returned them to the suitcase. As she was slipping them into the interior pocket, something shiny caught her eye. It was buried deep in the netting in the pocket where the IDs had been. "I found something."

"What is it?"

She freed the metal from the net and pulled out a key. "Where do you think this goes? Another storage unit?"

He looked at the key, then at her. "Maybe an apartment in Brooklyn?"

Her heart sped up. "Do you think so?"

"It's as good a bet as any. It was with the passports. Let's straighten up this place and then go."

She put the key into her pocket but left the IDs and the cash in the suitcase. Then she zipped it up while Damon started washing their dishes.

They spent the next several minutes making sure there was no evidence that they'd ever been in the house. She didn't have time to strip sheets or throw towels into the laundry, so she made the bed, trying hard not to think about the night she'd spent there with Damon, which wasn't an easy feat. But they were back to business, and the night seemed like a lifetime ago now.

After taking care of the bed, she straightened the towels they'd used in two of the bathrooms, wiped down the sinks and counters and then returned to the kitchen.

"Now we just have to hope your gadget will start Jamie's car," she told him, as they prepared to go out the back door.

Damon held up a car key. "We won't have to. I found this in the study."

"We're doing good on keys today. Our luck might be changing."

"That would be nice."

She followed him into the garage, and they stashed the suitcase in the trunk, and then got into Jamie's car. They used the garage opener that was still in the vehicle to exit and then closed the doors behind them as they pulled into the drive.

Within minutes, they were on their way back to New York City. It felt both strange and oddly reassuring to be in Jamie's car.

"I'm glad we're in this car," she said. "It makes me think Jamie is watching out for us."

"I hope so. We can use all the help we can get."

Eighteen

The drive from Greenwich, Connecticut to Brooklyn, New York took almost two hours with heavy traffic and dodging maneuvers on surface streets to throw off potential tails.

Damon felt confident that no one had picked them up anywhere on the way into Brooklyn, but now that they were getting closer, his senses were on hyper alert.

Sophie had chatted a bit on the first part of the ride, mostly about Cassie and Jamie and her relationship with the Rowlands. He could tell she was worried she'd made a mistake in contacting Cassie and Vincent, but he thought it had gone well.

Vincent had shared information regarding Alan's financial problems, which could explain why Alan had crossed a line—if that's what had happened. But why Alan had had money problems was another question. If he hadn't been willing to tell Vincent, one of his good friends, maybe it was gambling or drugs or blackmail, something Alan would have been embarrassed to share.

He certainly didn't believe it was Sophie's schooling that had put Alan over the edge. It was bigger than that. But it didn't appear that too many people were actually that close to Alan. Even Sophie had admitted to seeing her father only a few times a month and knowing little about his private life.

That wasn't unusual. Sophie was an adult with a busy life of her own, and Alan probably wouldn't have spoken to his daughter about other women in his life, unless there was someone serious.

No woman had come forward in the wake of Alan's death, at least not immediately, not that first night. That might have changed by now. He'd been out of touch for a while. But Bree hadn't mentioned it, either, and he would have thought finding Alan's girlfriend, if there was one, to be noteworthy.

So, who was Alan Parker? It was clear he'd had secrets, he'd worn a mask, he'd shown people what he wanted them to see. He was afraid that Sophie's battle to save her father's reputation might be a futile one, but no words would convince her of that. She would take it to the end, because she had to know, and he had to know, too.

He understood why Alan might have felt the need to keep some things in his life private, to have a public persona that might be different from his private one. He was certainly guilty of that. He rarely let people into his life.

But he'd let Sophie in...all the way in...

He took a quick glance at her. She was looking out the window, tapping her fingers nervously on her legs. She was on edge, and she had every reason to be. He wished he could take her back to the place they'd been last night when passion and pleasure had dominated their thoughts, when problems and fears had vanished with a kiss.

When he was with her, he was a thousand percent with her. She took up all the space, all the oxygen in the room. She became everything—a rather terrifying thought.

He needed to stop thinking about the night. It was gone. And they were no longer hiding out in a safe place. He would need his wits about him to keep them both safe. Caring about Sophie too much in this situation could make them both vulnerable. He had to be objective, analytical, anticipatory…he couldn't let emotions cloud his judgment.

He needed to go back to thinking of Sophie as a job.

He just didn't quite know how he was going to make that happen.

Sophie shifted in her seat, then looked down at the phone where she had the list of directions. "We're getting close. A few more blocks now."

"Just let me know when to turn."

"It's a left on Kent Street. It's a mile from here."

"Got it. My realtor mentioned I should look at Brooklyn when I first moved here. She said it was the up-and-coming place to live, but I wanted to be closer to the office. Now I'm thinking I should have taken a look."

"It's definitely trending," Sophie said. "I have two friends who live around here. One is an artist but works at a museum in Manhattan for her day job. The other runs a dance studio. They both love it. They have a view of the Manhattan skyline and are close enough to get to work, but they also have more space, which is nice. My apartment is teeny tiny." She sighed. "I wonder if I'll ever see any of my friends again."

"I'm sure you will."

"I'm not sure at all."

He couldn't blame her for her doubts. Her life now was as far from her previous one as it could possibly get. Would she return to her normal life? That would depend on who was after them and how powerful they were. One thing he knew for sure—taking out the two shooters at the New Haven storage center was not going to be the end of it.

Someone else would be coming after them; They had to be ready.

"Next one is Kent," she said.

He took the turn and drove past several spectacular wall murals, which added to the eclectic and artistic feel of the neighborhood.

"Turn left at Hickerson, and we're there," Sophie said.

"Got it." He found the address they were looking for and drove past the building and around the block, wanting to get a lay of the land before parking. He doubted anyone would be looking for Jamie's car, but he couldn't be too careful. He ended up in a spot about fifty yards away from the building and across the street. "Maybe I should check it out first."

"No way. I don't like waiting in the car. I think we need to stick together."

"We don't know if someone lives in that apartment."

"If the key fits, then I'm guessing no one does. And I've got the key."

He smiled at her proud expression, thinking back to the first time they'd seen each other at the cabin—when she'd held a gun to his head. "You still don't think I can take things from you, do you?"

"I don't think it will come to that. I really don't want to stay here alone, Damon. I got freaked out yesterday when you went into the store to get the phone."

He could understand that, and he couldn't deny that he preferred keeping her close. "Then let's go."

As they got out of the car, he grabbed the suitcase, and they walked quickly down the block. The street was filled with modest apartment buildings, most of which appeared to be well-kept. There were probably better parts of town, but also areas that were far worse. It was the kind of neighborhood where anyone could blend in, and he suspected that Alan had picked it for that reason.

There was no security on the front door to the building, and there appeared to be four units inside: two on the first floor, two on the second.

"Now what?" Sophie asked. "How are we going to know which apartment it is?"

He perused the names on the mailbox. "What's the name on the passport?"

"One of them was Framingham, the name we used at the lake house, and the other was Bennett."

"I've got a Bennett in Unit #3. I'd say that’s us." He led the way upstairs, stopping at the first apartment door. He put the suitcase down, then took the key from her hand and pulled his gun out. "Stay behind me," he told her. Then he inserted the key into the lock and turned the handle.

The door swung open. He raised his gun and took a step inside, glancing in every direction, then moving farther into the room. "Hello, anyone here?" he called out.

The only answer was silence, and it didn't feel like anyone was there. It was quiet, and the place smelled musty, as if no one had opened a window or a door in a while. The living room had a couch, a chair, and a television. There was a round wooden table by a narrow kitchen galley. He moved into the bedroom and saw a queen-sized bed that was unmade and an adjoining bathroom. He checked both rooms. There was no one there, but he did notice male shirts and slacks hanging in the closet.

"Those could belong to my dad," Sophie said. "The maroon shirt looks familiar." Her gaze moved from the closet to the bed. "Why would my father sleep here? He has a lovely townhouse in Chelsea. It has two bedrooms, and it's much nicer than this."

He tucked his gun back under his shirt. "Maybe he was here late at night, or hiding out when things started heating up."

"Heating up?" she asked in bemusement. "Only a week ago, he called me and asked me to come to his house and watch a ballgame with him this weekend. It sure didn't sound like he was on the run or in hiding."

"Then things changed fast."

He strode over to the dresser and pulled out the drawers. Underwear and T-shirts were in one drawer; the rest were empty. He shoved the last one closed and then stepped back to look around the room. His gut told him that there was something in this apartment, something beyond clothes...There was a window seat by the window. He strode across the room and pulled off the cushion, which had been attached with Velcro straps to the wooden bench. There was a large horizontal cut-out in the wood and a gold latch. He pulled the latch up and found himself staring at a safe with a coded lock.

"A safe?" Sophie said in amazement.

"We need to get inside. Do you know any of your father's PINs? It looks like a four-number lock."

She frowned as she mulled over his question. "He used my mom's birthday sometimes—1012."

He tried that. It didn't work. "What else would he use?"

"I don't know."

"What about his anniversary, date of graduation, an old address, a memorable holiday?" he asked.

She stared back at him. "My bike lock was 1492 to rhyme with when *Columbus sailed the ocean blue*, a question I missed on my history test."

He punched in 1492 and the lock clicked. He opened the safe and found himself staring down at a box of papers, folders, photos…

His pulse leapt. He pulled out several loose photos lying on the top and put them on the bench.

"Oh my God," Sophie muttered, as she picked up the first photo. "This is me. I'm—I'm leaving my office building at NYU."

He glanced at the other photos, all shots of Sophie going about her daily life, at work, at home, out with friends. Anger ran through him as he thought about someone following her, watching her.

"I don't understand," she said in confusion. "Why was my dad taking photos of me?"

"Your dad wasn't taking pictures. Someone else was," he said grimly. He turned one of the pictures over and saw the words scrawled on the back: *Any time we want*. His stomach turned over.

"What does that say?" she asked.

He really didn't want to tell her, but she had a right to know. He handed her the photo. "Someone wanted to let your father know they could get to you—they knew where you lived, where you worked, where you spent your time."

Her face turned white. "Why didn't my dad tell me? Why wouldn't he warn me to be careful? Why didn't he go to the police if he couldn't trust the FBI?"

Sophie's voice rose with each word, and he saw the hysteria building in her gaze. He stood up, grabbed the picture out of her hand and tossed it back on the bench. Then he took her hands in his.

"Look at me, Sophie."

Her wild gaze couldn't seem to find a place to settle, but finally it swung back to him.

"We don't know everything yet," he said forcefully. "You can't jump ahead. We have to take this one step at a time."

"Every step I take makes me more afraid. How can I keep going? God! What else are we going to find?"

"I don't know, but you're going to keep moving forward because you have to," he said simply. "You need to know the truth. These photos are another clue. Your father was being blackmailed. Someone was using you as leverage. We still have to figure out who that was and what they wanted him to do."

"I wonder when he got the photos." Her gaze went back to the top picture. "I think I wore that top last week. Or maybe this was going on for a while. I'm sure I've worn that outfit to work a dozen times in the past year. I can't believe someone was following me, and I had no idea. It's creepy. What if he was looking through my windows at home? What if I left the curtains open one night? How could my father not tell me about any of this? How could he act like nothing was wrong? He wanted to barbecue ribs and watch the baseball game with me. That's the last thing he said to me before his crazy voicemails on Wednesday."

He squeezed her fingers, seeing pain, anger and frustration in her eyes. He wished he could say that Alan had had a good reason for everything he'd done. He'd never been one to make false promises or offer reassurances that couldn't possibly come true, but right now he really wanted to do that—to do anything that would help ease the fear racing through her.

"Look, you have to hang on to what you know is true. Your dad adored you. I'm sure that in his mind he was doing everything he could to make sure you were safe."

"Not everything. He might have made me fake IDs, but he didn't talk to me, he didn't tell me his problems. He didn't trust me, Damon. That's what it comes down to."

"More likely he didn't want to disappoint you or put you in more danger by giving you information someone might try to get out of you."

"Keeping me in the dark only put me in more danger," she argued.

He couldn't disagree. "We need to go through every item in this safe and see if there is anything else in this apartment of note. Hopefully, we'll find more clues." He pulled the box out of the safe and put it on the bench. He could see file folders and more loose papers as well as bank statements. They might have just struck gold. "I'm going to take the box to the kitchen table. You can start going through it while I send Bree and Wyatt a message in the forum as to what apartment we're in. I asked them to meet us at noon, and that's about twenty minutes from now."

He carried the box into the other room and set it down on the table.

"I just hope that…" Sophie gave him one last troubled look as her voice fell away.

"Hope what?"

"That your friends—especially Bree—is not a part of this. She does still work in the FBI."

"But not in your father's department. She was never under his direction. Besides that, Bree wouldn't betray me; I'd bet my life on it."

"You're betting mine, too."

His lips tightened. "I know that, Sophie. But I think it's the best play." As she nodded and turned away, he really hoped he was right.

Sophie put the photos of herself in one pile on a chair.

She turned them face down, so she wouldn't have to look at herself, wouldn't have to think about the fact that someone had been watching her go about her life. It made her feel sick to her stomach.

Aside from the photographs, there were five file folders in the box, marked with names, only one of which she recognized—Venturi. Of the other four, one was labeled Scusa Restaurant Fire, the second was tagged Express Package Hijacking, the third read Maximillian Steelworks, and the fourth just had a name—Donald Carter.

She had no idea what any of the cases were about, but she'd leave that to Damon to figure out.

As she put the files aside for him, Damon was pulling board games out of the living room closet.

"I don't think we have time to play a game," she said.

"Your father replaced the games inside with electronic equipment." He brought one of the boxes over to the table and showed her the array of devices inside. "He has listening devices, micro-cameras, flash drives, even a cell phone reader," he added, picking up something that looked like a radar gun. "It can capture the phone number of a person using their mobile device a hundred yards away."

"There really is no personal privacy anymore, is there?"

"These devices help catch criminals; don't forget that." He picked up one of the two flash drives. "I'd like to know what's on this. We're going to need to get a computer at some point." He set the box on the ground. "What have you found so far?"

"Case files that don't mean anything to me, but maybe will be significance to you." She turned back to the box she'd been going through. "There is a stack of bank statements for someone named Justin Lawrence. They show a couple of large deposits and a couple of large withdrawals. It looks like the bank is in Belize."

His expression turned grim. "Your father has an offshore bank account."

"Justin Lawrence does—not my father."

"I think they're the same person, Sophie."

"Really?"

"What's the last statement you have?"

She grabbed the one on top. "This is from May, probably last month's statement. There's a little over four hundred thousand dollars in the account." She blew out a breath, unable to believe her father had been hiding that kind of money in an offshore account. "I can't believe he had that much."

"It might match the amount in the suitcase," Damon suggested.

She hadn't thought about that, but he was probably right.

Damon took the statement out of her hand. "We need to follow the money. Figure out where it came from and where it went when it was withdrawn, and, of course, determine who Justin Lawrence is."

While Damon was looking at the bank statements, she looked through the rest of the items in the box. She found an envelope with her father's first name—Alan—scrawled across the front. There was no address, no return sender, and no stamp. The envelope had at one time been sealed and then ripped open. There was still a piece of paper inside.

"What's that?" Damon asked, as she picked up the envelope.

"I don't have a good feeling about this. It was sealed before being opened. There's no address; it looks personal."

"Do you want me to read it?"

"No. I have to do it. I just…have to do it." She pulled out the piece of white paper that had obviously come out of a printer. There were two types sentences: *One last chance or someone dies. You know what to do.*

She stared at those words until they blurred and then handed the paper to Damon. She walked over to the window and looked out unseeingly at the street below. Her father had been blackmailed. He'd had to cross a line, and because of the photos she'd seen of herself, she had to believe that she'd been the bargaining chip, the person who was going to die if her father didn't do what they wanted.

Damon came up behind her, putting his arms around her, pulling her back against his chest as he rested his chin lightly on her head. The chills running through her were instantly warmed by his presence. She felt safe and protected in his arms, and a part of her wanted to stay there forever, but she couldn't.

Nothing was over. The case wasn't solved. She had a few more clues, but she still didn't know the whole story. There was a lot left to do if she was going to get the answers she needed. She had to know what had happened to her father, because he was never going to be able to explain it to her. If she was going to find some peace, some closure, some understanding, it would be through the clues he'd left behind. It was almost impossible to believe that these random things were all she had left of him.

The finality of her dad's death hit her hard again—a sharp, breath-catching body blow. Because she hadn't seen his body, hadn't said good-bye, hadn't gone through the formality of a funeral or a service, his passing had felt surreal, as if maybe it wasn't even real. The bullets at the cabin, the gunmen at the storage unit, the voicemails should have convinced her of what was real and what was not, but for some reason, it was this apartment that had finally pushed her into painful reality.

Her dad was dead. He was never coming back.

He'd lived a double life. He'd had aliases and safe houses and an offshore bank account. He'd been able to put together fake IDs for her. He'd had an exit plan, at least for her, if not for himself, too. And then there was the cash—blood money, she was sure. She just didn't know whose blood.

"You okay?" Damon asked.

"Not really," she said with a sigh. She pulled slightly away from him, turning in his embrace, so she was looking at him and not at the street. She saw compassion in his eyes as well as what looked like regret. He was probably dealing with the loss of some of his own illusions about her dad. Not that he'd admit to that. But she suspected her father's actions were going to feel like betrayal to Damon. Her dad was going to be one more person to disappoint him.

"I'm sorry," she said suddenly.

He raised an eyebrow. "What are you apologizing for?"

"For whatever we're going to find out. It's not going to be good. It might hurt you, change the way you think about my dad."

"Don't worry about me. I can take whatever is coming."

"I wish I felt that strong. I'm trying to hold it together."

"You're doing well."

"I think someone was threatening my dad with my life."

"Based on the photos and that note, it seems likely."

"I understand that he didn't want to worry me, but why didn't he tell any of his friends? Surely, there was someone at the Bureau he could trust." She paused, realizing the one person her father had trusted was standing right in front of her. "Why didn't he tell you, Damon? I know he had the utmost respect for you. I didn't let him say much about you if I could help it, but I couldn't always stop the conversation when he started raving about how good you were. He was very proud of you."

A shadow ran through his expression. "I have been wondering if the trouble he was in was behind his calling me to come to New York, if that's why he wanted me to work in his department, if that's why he didn't have Karen Leigh assign me to anything but instead told me he wanted to give me a special assignment."

"It could have been," she said. "That makes a lot of sense."

"Does it?" He let out a breath. "I don't know why he didn't confide in Peter, which certainly puts Peter under suspicion. And what about his old friend, Vincent? He told him about his financial problems. Vincent was FBI, he would have known how to help Alan? Why not tell him?"

"We could ask the same questions about every person who was friends with my dad and works at the FBI. Next on the list would be Karen. She worked extremely closely with him. What does she know?"

He glanced toward the table. "Those files might be able to tell us something. We need to start reading, Sophie."

Before they could move, three sharp raps came at the door.

Her heart leapt into her throat.

Damon pulled out his gun as he stalked to the door and looked through the peephole. She saw his shoulders relax as he said, "It's okay, it's Bree." Then he opened the door.

A very pretty brunette of medium height entered the room. She wore white jeans and a loose-fitting soft blue sweater that brought out the blue in her eyes. Her long hair was pulled back in a ponytail, and dangling earrings hung from her ears. She had a bag over one shoulder, looking more like a woman out for some Saturday shopping than an FBI agent.

"I am so glad to see you," Bree told Damon, giving him a hug.

An odd wave of jealousy ran through Sophie, as she saw Damon give Bree a smile, the kind of smile that he gave her.

"You must be Sophie. I'm Bree Adams," she said.

Bree's words made her stand a little straighter as Bree came across the room to shake her hand. "It's nice to finally meet you."

"You, too."

"Thanks for coming to help us."

"I hope I can help," Bree returned.

"What about Wyatt?" Damon asked. "Have you heard from him?"

"Not since last night. He came by my apartment for a few minutes, but he didn't think it was safe to stay. I don't know where he is now. I tried the phone I gave him, but he didn't answer."

"Is he better?" Damon asked.

"He is," Bree said with a nod. "The first night I met up with him I was really worried, but he's getting his head together, his bruises are fading, and he got at least a few hours of sleep at my place on Thursday night. He's very focused on finding out who tried to kill him. He's quite sure it's connected to Alan's death." She gave Sophie an apologetic smile. "I'm truly sorry about your father. I respected him a great deal. He encouraged me to work in New York. He helped me get the job I have now. I'm very grateful to him."

Her dad had certainly made a positive impression on the agents he'd taught at the academy. It made her feel a little better to hear good things about him, to know that others had thought highly of him. It made her feel less oblivious and stupid for not seeing signs of his secret life.

"So, where are we?" Bree asked. "Is this apartment significant in some way?"

"This appears to be Alan's safe house," Damon said. "We found a safe in the bedroom. We're just starting to go through the box of information he had hidden away."

"That's good news."

"I hope it is," Damon said. "So far, we've found photos of Sophie. It looks like someone was tailing her for several days."

"Using Sophie for leverage against Alan," Bree said.

Sophie was impressed with the speed at which Bree had gotten to that conclusion.

"Yes," Damon said. "We need to find out who wanted leverage."

"How did you find this place?" Bree asked curiously.

"Alan left Sophie a fake passport with this address on it. We weren't sure it meant something until we came here."

"He left you a fake passport?" Bree queried, giving her a measuring look. "Is that why you ran to the lake?"

"Actually, no. I ran to the cabin to get a key that my father had left for me. The key to the storage unit where the passports were located. You know what happened there."

"Yes, but what I don't know is what's in the case," Bree said, her gaze drifting across the room to the silver suitcase that was resting on the floor by the couch. "I'm assuming it contains more than passports."

"It doesn't matter," Damon cut in. "We need to focus on what's on this table."

"All right," Bree said. "It's your show. You call the shots."

At Bree's acquiescence, Sophie felt a wave of guilt. The woman was risking her job and maybe her life to help them. At this point, she needed all the information they had.

"It's money," she said abruptly, drawing Bree's gaze back to hers. "A lot of money. I don't know where my father got it, but it probably wasn't legal."

"I understand," Bree said, her expression showing little surprise. "Thanks for telling me."

"It is possible he emptied an offshore bank account," Damon added. "We found statements under the name of Justin Lawrence, but we don't know who that is."

"That's Alan," Bree said. "That's the name that was listed on the storage unit rental contract."

"Well, that solves that," Damon said, gazing at her.

"Another alias," she murmured, wondering how many more there were.

Three more raps at the door sent her heart racing again. Damon and Bree both pulled out their guns.

Damon moved toward the door, while Bree took a step closer to her, as if to protect her.

"It's Wyatt," Damon said, opening the door once again.

The man who entered the apartment wore faded jeans, a navy-blue T-shirt and a Yankees cap on his head. His brown hair was longer than Damon's and peeked out from under the baseball cap. He had a rough beard on his face, and tattoos ran down both muscular arms. He also had a gun in his hand, and his jumpy gaze moved from Damon to Bree to her.

She felt more than a little unsettled by his stare. While all three of the people facing her were FBI agents, Wyatt felt the darkest, the one who made her the most nervous.

"Okay, I think we can all put down our weapons," Bree suggested, returning her gun to the back of her white jeans.

Now Sophie knew why she'd worn a loose, thin sweater on a day that was already heading into the eighties.

Wyatt and Damon tucked their guns under their shirts as well.

"Sophie Parker—Wyatt Tanner," Damon said, making the introductions.

"Hi," she said tentatively, the hard, distrustful look in Wyatt's eyes not particularly welcoming.

Wyatt gave her a nod, then turned to Damon. "Glad to see you're still alive."

"Right back at you," Damon said. "You look better than the last time I saw you. Next time, don't take off."

"I wasn't thinking straight that day," Wyatt admitted. "What's the plan?"

"We're formulating one," Damon replied. "This apartment was rented by Alan. We found information in a safe in the bedroom. So far, we've determined that someone was following Sophie and using her to threaten Alan. We've also determined that Alan had access to an offshore bank account under an alias."

"I knew he was double-dealing," Wyatt muttered.

Unlike Bree and Damon, who seemed willing to give her father multiple chances to not be a bad guy, Wyatt seemed confident in his assessment. And that made her feel worse, because Wyatt had been the closest to her father this past year. Wyatt been the one undercover, the one working with the Venturi family, the one her father had been using to allegedly build a case against the crime family. But maybe he hadn't been doing that. Maybe he'd actually been working for the Venturis and against Wyatt. Maybe her father was the reason Wyatt had been almost killed.

A wave of nausea ran through her. She really hated to think her father had been working for the mob, that he could be a criminal. It went against everything she'd always thought he believed in.

Wyatt moved to the table. He picked up one of the file folders.

"Do you know what those relate to?" she asked. "The labels didn't mean anything to me and Damon."

"Donald Carter is a construction worker on a Venturi-run construction project in Jersey City. He was injured when a section of flooring collapsed. He's suing the Venturis, and his trial is starting in two weeks," Wyatt said. He put down that folder and picked up another one. "Maximillian Steelworks supplied the steel for that construction project, but they didn't use the steel they were supposed to use; they bought cheaper steel out of China and swapped it in. The steel was not just used in this one building but also on six others that have already been completed. A few weeks ago, I discovered that the Venturis had paid off a city inspector to look the other way so they could save on building costs, but those buildings could all be potentially dangerous. They could all collapse. I gave Alan this information three months ago."

Her heart sank again. "What did my dad say?"

"That he'd look into it; that's what he always said."

"What about the other files?" Damon asked.

Wyatt cleared his throat. "An Express Package Delivery truck was robbed last month. The trucking system is responsible for moving drugs and guns throughout the northeast, but someone hijacked that load. I gave Alan that lead, too. Apparently, he wasn't just keeping the information out of his office; he wasn't doing anything with it. He and his team weren't building a case against the Venturis. He was just throwing what I gave him in a box."

"Maybe they were working on it," she suggested, unable to not defend her father. "There's a very thick file on the Venturi family. Perhaps my dad was putting it all together here, because he knew there was a mole at the FBI."

Three pairs of eyes came to rest on her. She saw compassion in Damon's gaze, thoughtfulness in Bree's and complete skepticism in Wyatt's.

"If he wasn't the mole, he would have warned me not to keep the meet that almost killed me," Wyatt said.

"He might not have known about the meet if the

information was intercepted. Look, I know it doesn't look good. I'm not stupid. But my dad is dead. He obviously didn't do everything someone wanted him to do."

"Let's keep talking about what's here," Damon said. "We can get into the blame game later." He looked at Wyatt. "Why don't you tell us what else you know?"

"I know a lot. The Venturis have their hand in everything. Extortion—that was the Scusa restaurant fire," he added, pointing to the other file. "Antonia Scusa didn't want to pay off the Venturis the way her late husband had been doing. Now her restaurant is no more. She's just lucky they didn't kill her. But they did take away the Scusa family business. They sent a message to anyone else who might be having doubts about paying for protection."

"I can't believe people still do that," she muttered.

"They do it a lot more than you would think," Wyatt returned. "But protection was a side game. The family's biggest money came from drugs, in particular opioids, as well as weapons. They laundered the illegal money in a variety of ways, through casinos, the real estate deals, and the basic bank drop where I and other hired hands would make cash deposits just under $10,000 at banks around town."

"That's what you did for them?" she asked.

"I also worked construction and gambled with Lorenzo until he ended up in the river. I occasionally drove a van, the contents of which I was not allowed to look at. Because I had a partner, I was never able to confirm the cargo I was transporting, but I was working on that. I've fed Alan a ton of information over the last year. This is barely a tenth of it."

"There might be more on the flash drives," Damon said. "We found two in another box. But before we get to those. You told me everything changed recently, Wyatt. You mentioned something about a third party."

"Yes, a few months ago, I heard that there was a turf war brewing. Stefan was interested in partnering with this new player instead of taking them out as the Venturi family usually did. Lorenzo was opposed to the idea of a partnership.

As you know, he ended up dead."

"Do you think his brother killed him?" she asked.

"It's quite possible. Or the new player who saw him as an obstacle."

"Did you tell my dad about the new player?"

"I did," Wyatt replied. "He was concerned. Said he'd heard similar rumors." Wyatt paused. "I never thought Alan would burn me. I thought he was taking too long to build the case I was handing him on a silver platter, but until recently I didn't have reason to doubt his motivations."

"What changed?" Damon asked.

"There was desperation in Alan's eyes. He kept telling me to get more, that we didn't have enough to bring a case. That it had to be rock solid before he could move. But I think I misread his desperation. He was probably being blackmailed and he was trying to juggle me and the blackmailer. When I started pushing him too hard, he had to get rid of me. He either burned my cover or he sent someone to take me out, but one way or the other, I'm certain he was involved."

She was shocked at his harsh, unyielding words. "There's no way my father would turn on a fellow agent. Maybe I can believe that he buried information to protect me, but to take someone else's life—an agent he was handling? No, he wouldn't do that."

She could see doubt in Wyatt's eyes and Bree also didn't appear convinced. She turned to Damon. "You don't believe my dad would have tried to get Wyatt killed, do you?"

"I don't want to, Sophie."

"That's not an answer."

"Look, we just don't know," he said. "We have to work with what we have, and right now we don't have that piece of the puzzle."

"Alan might have been killed because I survived," Wyatt said. "Because he didn't get the job done."

She pressed a hand to her temple, her head suddenly pounding. Her dad's voice message rang through her head: *"I thought I could stay out of the mud, but it turns out I'm covered in it."* Did that confirm what Wyatt had just said?

But she still didn't believe her father would let a fellow agent get killed.

"I have another question," she said. "My dad is dead. So, he's done. Why isn't that the end of it? Why are they coming after me? What do they want?"

"Maybe the cash," Bree put in.

"And you're a loose end," Wyatt said. "The Venturis don't like loose ends. They don't know what you know. That makes you dangerous."

It was hard to hear herself described that way, but she couldn't deny it.

"Getting back to the new player," Damon said. "Do you have the feeling it's an already established group wanting to expand territory or a completely new organization?"

"Already established. I heard Lorenzo and Stefan arguing one night. Stefan said something like: *'They can take us global. We own the East Coast. They own Eastern Europe. Together we will run the world.'"*

"Then it's an Eastern European operation," Damon said.

Wyatt nodded. "That would be my guess, but it doesn't narrow it down much." He paused. "The last few days I've had time to do nothing but think. If Alan didn't order the hit on me, then someone else did, someone in the Bureau. If Alan was getting cold feet, and I'm not saying that's what happened," he added, his gaze directed at her, "but if it did, then the Venturis needed another mole. Someone they could leverage—perhaps the same way they leveraged Alan. One of Stefan's strengths is finding someone's weakness and using it. Alan's weak spot was his daughter."

Damon frowned. "I don't know about that. Alan has always been a father. He's always had a family. It feels like whatever sent him down the wrong road was more complicated than threats against Sophie's life. He could have hired bodyguards for her. He could have sent her out of the country. He could have done any number of things to keep her safe. I think there's something else he was hiding, something that made him vulnerable." He glanced over at her. "Sorry, Sophie."

She sighed. "You're all just trying to get to the truth. And that's where I want to get to as well. Vincent Rowland told me that my dad had financial problems. Maybe it goes back to that. Maybe he was gambling. I never knew him to be a gambler, but obviously I didn't know him as well as I thought I did. The gambling debts could have put him in the position of having to do some favors."

"Let's move on from your dad," Bree said. "Alan is gone, but the hits on Sophie and Damon keep coming. Are the Venturis trying to get whatever info they thought Alan had on them? Or is someone from the FBI on the Venturi's payroll trying to destroy the evidence and cover their tracks? The Venturi organization will be harder to crack, because there are so many of them with criminal intent, but our New York field office…Who else could be leveraged?" Bree asked. "I don't see Peter Hunt having a weak spot. I did a little research on him. He's divorced. He has no children. He's very high up in the department, so he wouldn't need the mob to boost his career trajectory. He doesn't appear to have any vices or any appearance of wealth. But he does have a lot of powerful friends from his Yale days."

"The fact that Alan didn't tell Sophie to trust Peter still makes him suspicious in my mind," Damon said. "Why did Alan give Sophie a blanket order to avoid everyone from the FBI?"

"Is that what he did?" Bree asked.

She nodded. "Yes, he told me to trust no one."

"Then maybe he knew the mob had pulled someone else in, but he didn't know who," Wyatt speculated. "I'm putting my money on Agent Leigh. In fact, I staked out her apartment last night after I left Bree's place. I thought Karen was in for the night, but around ten, she left in a taxi. I followed her to a bar in the Bronx, a Venturi-supported bar, I might add. She met with Paul Candilari, Stefan Venturi's number-two man. I took some photos." He handed the phone to Damon. "A younger woman joined them halfway through drinks. I never got a good look at her, beyond the fact that she had dark hair. She might have been Candilari's daughter. Or she could be connected to the new player."

"It's difficult to see her," Damon said. "But she doesn't appear to be very old."

"Well, I doubt she's in charge, but she could be related to whoever is in charge."

Damon passed the phone to Bree, who took a look and said, "This picture is certainly damning for Karen. Meeting with a known crime boss outside the office? Although, she could play it that she called the meeting to get info on Alan, that she was using Candilari and it wasn't the other way around."

"May I see the phone?" she asked, feeling a little left out of their crime-solving club.

"Sorry," Bree said, passing her the phone.

She looked at the photo for a long moment. Karen and the older man seemed to be having an intense conversation, while the younger woman appeared to be looking at her phone and not all that engaged in the discussion. In fact, she looked bored…and a little familiar. "I feel like I might know her," she murmured.

"The woman?" Damon asked in surprise. "From where?"

She shook her head, trying to think. "I'm not sure. She's in her twenties, I'd bet. Maybe she was in one of my classes or just a student at NYU?" She frowned. "There's something about her...I wish I could see her face better."

"It's the best shot I could get," Wyatt said. "You can look through the other photos if you want."

She scrolled through the four other pictures, but none of them captured the young woman any more clearly. She gave Wyatt back his phone. "Did they all leave together?" she asked.

"No, Karen left first. I was on her tail, so I went when she did. Unfortunately, she went straight home. I was hoping she might meet up with someone else, but she didn't."

"So, what are we going to do?" she asked. "Are we going to confront Karen?"

"Yes," Damon said with a nod. "That's exactly what we're going to do. We need to set up a meet. I think we should send Karen the photo. She'll want to protect herself, so she'll come alone."

"But how are we going to get in touch with her?" she asked.

"I can make it happen," Wyatt said. "I'll use the emergency protocol we set up for my cover. I'll send her the photo and a time and place to meet."

"Why would Karen come at all?" Sophie asked. "Why wouldn't she just run?"

"If she's guilty, she'll want to know what I know," Wyatt said. "I'll offer her additional enticement. Instead of a threat, I'll tell her I want in on the action. That the Venturis trust me more than they trust her, so we need to partner up. I think she'll come. She'll be too afraid not to."

"She might not come alone," Bree put in. "And you're assuming she is guilty. What if she's innocent? How does that change the scenario?"

"I don't think it does change it," Damon said. "She'll want to know why Wyatt thinks she's double-dealing. She'll still want to protect herself from whatever he thinks he has against her. But I'm with Wyatt, I think the only reason Karen went to talk to Candilari is because she's involved in some way with the family."

"But it seems kind of stupid on her part to go to such a public meeting," she couldn't help putting in. "Why do it?"

"Sophie makes a good point," Bree said.

"She has a cover," Wyatt said. "She's looking for info on Lorenzo's murder, so she took a meeting. That photo alone isn't enough to bring her down. We just want her to think we have more."

"Okay," she said with a nod. "How are we going to do it?"

"I'll send the message," Wyatt said.

"You will," Damon agreed. "But I'm going to take the meet. You and Bree are going to back me up."

Wyatt frowned. "No way. I've got more skin in this game than you."

"Doesn't matter," Damon said. "If Karen brings Venturi backup, they won't know what to make of me. You'll still be my ace in the hole. If they take me out, you can still take them down. I can use you as leverage against Karen, Wyatt. If she doesn't come clean with me, you'll take it to the Bureau, and she'll be ruined"

She could see Wyatt starting to cave as Damon made his case. As much as she didn't want Damon to be in the hot seat, it made sense.

"He's right," Bree said. "Damon should take the meet. Let's keep Karen in the dark about where you are and what you have. Where will you meet her?"

"Central Park. It's where I used to meet Alan," Wyatt said. "She'll feel confident that it's me she's talking to if we go with that location. Of course, once she sees Damon, all bets are off. But there are lots of trees and plenty of people around for cover."

"I don't think Karen is calling the shots," Damon said. "When I meet with her, I'm going to make sure she's as scared of me as she's scared of whoever is running her. If we can turn her, then we'll be one step closer to taking this whole thing down."

Sophie listened to the three of them as they continued to plan their strategy. She wanted to go, too. She wanted to face Karen and ask her if she was the one who set her father up, if she was the one who'd sent gunmen after her, not just once but twice.

She could still remember how kind Karen had pretended to be when she'd first told her that her father was dead. Her questions hadn't been about helping to find her father's killer; Karen had wanted to know what she knew. She was really glad that she'd run that first night.

"I'd like to be a part of this," she said, interjecting herself into the conversation.

"It's too dangerous," Damon said quickly, immediately shaking his head.

"I'm not going to stay here by myself," she said. "Someone could figure out this apartment is tied to my dad. You said yourself we can't stay too long in one place, especially not a place rented by my father."

Damon frowned. "Then maybe Bree—" he began.

"No," she interrupted. "You are not going to ask Bree to babysit me. You need her to protect you and to take down Karen. Just let me go with you. I don't have to do anything. I'll just be nearby."

The three of them exchanged a look. Then Damon said, "You can come as far as the park, then I'll reassess the situation."

"Where in the park are you going?" she asked Wyatt. "It's a big place."

"The Alice in Wonderland statue near 5th and East 74th," he replied.

Her heart thudded against her chest at that piece of information. "My dad used to take me there when I was a kid. He used to say that his job sometimes made him feel like Alice going down the rabbit hole." She paused, an unexpected rush of tears coming into her eyes.

The irony of Damon, Wyatt, and Bree possibly taking down her father's killer at a place that had once held happy memories filled her with emotion.

"I'm sorry he let you all down—that he let me down," she said. "But I want to know the truth—the whole truth. Get Karen to that park and make her talk."

Nineteen

A little before three Damon drove back over the Brooklyn Bridge into Manhattan. As he maneuvered through the busy city streets, he felt like it had been a year since he'd been in the city. So much had happened since he'd impulsively decided to drive up to the Adirondacks to find Sophie. He was very glad he'd followed his instincts; he just hoped his gut was steering him in the right direction today.

Wyatt had come up with a bold plan to draw Karen out, and while he was happy to move from a defensive position to an offensive one, he was worried about Sophie. He was torn between taking her into the park and making her a potential target and leaving her alone in the car where anything could happen. He liked when she was right next to him, when he could see her, touch her, know she was okay.

He glanced over at her. She was looking toward the park, probably thinking about the statue where she used to go with her father. They hadn't had any time to talk just the two of them since Bree and Wyatt had arrived, and he suspected she'd felt a little left out of their strategy session, but she hadn't complained, and he hadn't had time to include her.

After Wyatt had initiated the emergency protocol with the photo of Karen at the bar in the Bronx, Karen had responded almost immediately. They'd only had ninety minutes to study a plan of the park, pick up four phones with earpieces that they could use for an emergency communications system, and then get into Manhattan.

Now, he would have to waste more valuable minutes, finding a parking spot. "It's not going to be easy to park around here," he muttered, hoping Bree wouldn't have trouble finding a spot, too. She was driving Wyatt to the park in her car. They'd decided to split up to make the group less of a target.

"Try one of the side streets," Sophie suggested, her voice tense. "Wait, I think someone is leaving," she said, pointing down the block.

He let out a breath of relief. The spot was about twenty-five yards from the park entrance nearest the statue and across the street, which would keep Sophie close but not too close. There was a busy intersection nearby, so there would be plenty of people around. He knew she wouldn't be happy to wait in the car, but he had to persuade her that it was the best option.

He parked and removed the key from the ignition. "Sophie, we need to talk."

"I know what you're going to say." She gave him an unhappy look. "I'd rather go with you, Damon."

"I know you would. Here's the thing, Sophie. If you're there, my focus is going to be on you. That's just the way it would be. And that won't work. I have to concentrate on Karen. I have to be alert to any possible danger she might be bringing with her. This meeting is crucial. It might be the one opportunity we have to turn Karen to our side. If I can make her understand that giving up her boss will ultimately put her in a far better position than taking the fall, we might be able to unravel this whole tangled ball of yarn."

"She's not going to get immunity, is she? If she's complicit in my father's death, then I want her to go to jail."

"She won't go unpunished; I promise you that. But we don't believe she's running the show, and, ultimately, we want the head guy, the one giving the orders."

"Maybe that's Peter. Bree doesn't think he has motivation or that he's vulnerable, but I'm guessing most people wouldn't have thought my father was, either."

"I haven't eliminated Peter or anyone else for that matter, but right now Karen is the play." He paused. "I wouldn't leave you if I thought this wasn't the safer, better choice. When I get out, take the wheel, and if you see anything you don't like, just drive away."

"Okay. I'll stay here. I get it. I don't like it, but I understand. You and Bree and Wyatt operate with a kind of shorthand. You're well-trained, you know what you're doing, and you trust each other."

"Bree and Wyatt are two of the best," he agreed.

"Wyatt is a little unapproachable."

"He's been living in the shadows for a long time; it's isolating to be undercover that long. Sometimes you can forget who you are."

"That makes sense. I feel like my old life is a million miles away, and it's been less than a week. I know when this is over, I'm going to need to actually deal with my dad's death."

"You will, and I'll help you any way I can."

"Thanks," she said softly, her gaze meeting his. "Damon, be careful. Promise me you'll come back."

"I promise," he said, knowing he would do absolutely anything to keep that promise.

He leaned over and kissed her hard on the mouth. Then he got out of the car and closed the door. He saw her crawl over the console and get behind the wheel. Then she flipped the locks.

He took a look around, then walked up to the intersection to cross the street. As he moved through the entrance to the park, he hoped that in a few minutes they would have at least some of the answers they were looking for.

After being off the grid the past few days, it felt strange to be walking in the open air. There were security cameras around the park, and he'd already noted where they were, so he could keep away from them. He didn't need the police getting in his way.

Pulling out his phone, he initiated the four-way call, knowing Sophie would feel better if she could listen in. "I see the statue," he said. "I'm almost there."

"I'm on the west side, in the trees," Bree said. "I have eyes on the statue. No sign of Karen."

"I'm to the east," Wyatt returned. "All good on my end."

"Sophie, you okay?" he asked, feeling like he needed to hear her voice, too.

"I'm here," she said. "I don't want to interrupt, so I'm just going to listen."

"If you need anything, speak up," he said.

"I will. Hey, Bree," Sophie added. "Did the FBI ever figure out that tattoo on the shooter at the storage unit?"

"Not that I'm aware," Bree said. "It wasn't in the update we got last night."

"Maybe I'll research that while you're all doing this."

Damon was happy Sophie was going to keep herself busy; that would make the time go faster.

He moved toward the statue, a bronze art piece about ten-feet tall, depicting Alice in Wonderland and some of her friends, including the Mad Hatter and the White Rabbit. It was quite a work of art, he thought, beautiful and whimsical. He could see why Sophie had liked it, and why there were lots of kids crowding around it now with their parents.

He moved away from the statue to a drinking fountain and a bench tucked behind a small building with two family restrooms. Wyatt said he and Alan had had most of their conversations there, away from the crush of tourists.

He glanced at his watch. Five minutes to go.

He really hoped Karen was going to show up, because there was no Plan B.

No one had spoken in a couple of minutes, and Sophie's pulse began to beat faster. To distract herself, she opened up the Internet on her phone and started looking for more information on snake tattoos from Eastern Europe since Wyatt had mentioned that he thought the Venturis' new partner might be from that part of the world. That encompassed several countries, but at least she could narrow her search a bit.

As she read more about the snakes, she wondered if she was going in the wrong direction. Maybe it wasn't the snake or the vines that were meaningful; perhaps it was the symbol.

She opened her bag and pulled out her sketch. As she stared at it, she felt increasingly unsettled, uneasy. She really felt like she'd seen it before. But where?

An old memory covered with cobwebs began to shake loose in her head.

There was a party.

Her mother had wanted to go. She was feeling better after her chemo treatments, and she'd wanted to wish her friend a happy birthday.

She was fifteen, and bored with the adult conversation. The only kid at the party that she knew was Elena, and she'd disappeared. A housekeeper told her the teenagers were in the pool house. She'd gone down there and found a wild party scene. There were drugs everywhere. She couldn't believe this party was going on so close to the main house.

She felt awkward, uncomfortable, scared. She was way out of her element. She went toward the bathroom. She thought she'd seen Elena go in there. She knocked. She thought she heard someone say something. The door was unlocked, so she opened it. Then she gasped, seeing Elena with a boy, her breasts hanging out of her shirt, the guy's hands under her skirt.

"Get out," Elena ordered, fury in her eyes.

She turned and ran out of the bathroom, bumping into a tall guy on her way through the pool house, her hair catching in the sharp edges of his ring.

She could almost feel the tug, the sting against her scalp.

She stopped as the guy swore and tried to disentangle her hair from the ring. It was a thick, male ring, with a red stone in the middle that looked like an eye.

Her heart beat faster as she tried to hold on to the memory. *Who was the guy?*

He'd had brown hair. He was tall. She had to look up at him. He wasn't smiling.

Suddenly, she saw his brown eyes, and it clicked in. It was Michael Brennan's son, David. He was five years older than her and very intimidating.

"Just hold still," he said, yanking her hair out of his ring. "What are you doing here anyway? You and Elena were supposed to stay in the house. Go back there now."

She didn't tell him Elena was in the bathroom. She scurried out of the pool house and ran to find her parents.

She wanted to tell them what was happening in the pool house, but her mom wasn't feeling well, and her dad was worried about her. So, she'd said nothing, and they'd gone home.

They'd never gone back to the Brennans' house after that.

Her mom had died several months later.

As the memory ran around in her head, she felt like she was on the verge of something big.

David Brennan had had a ring with the exact same design as the one she'd seen on the gunman's neck.

Had David been the gunman? Had Damon shot David Brennan in the storage unit?

No. That wasn't possible. Bree had reported that the FBI had no identity on that shooter. It hadn't been David.

Maybe the design was popular. Maybe it was just a coincidence that David had a ring with the same image.

She looked back at her phone and typed *Michael Brennan hedge fund investor and family* into the search box. An image popped up of Michael, his wife Katya and their two children, David and Elena. In this photo, the kids were teenagers, about the same age as they'd been in her memories.

David had his arm around his mother's shoulder, and she could see the ring she remembered on his hand. The image was too grainy to see the details, but she felt sure it was the same design.

She scrolled through more search results, wondering if there was a clearer picture of the ring.

In the next photo, everyone was older—mid-twenties, probably. And Michael was with another woman, a young, pretty blonde. She clicked on the article, which talked about Michael Brennan's new girlfriend, who was an actress. She remembered her father mentioning that Michael had gotten a divorce, but she hadn't paid much attention. They hadn't spent time with the Brennans after her mother died, and she'd certainly never been interested in hanging out with Elena or her brother after that strange party.

She looked up from the phone and stared out the front window, thinking about the importance of Michael Brennan's son, David, having a ring with the very same design as the gunman's tattoo.

If the design was Eastern European in nature, David's mother's name suddenly stood out in her head—*Katya.* Where had Katya been from? *Czechoslovakia? Ukraine, Croatia?*

She felt like she'd been told at some point, but now she couldn't remember. All she remembered about Katya was a sweet, quiet woman, who liked to bake but always seemed a little sad.

She needed to talk to Michael…or maybe Katya. Who would be more likely to tell her the truth? Her father's friend…or his ex-wife? Somehow, she thought it might be the ex-wife, especially since she knew Michael had been meeting with Peter over the past few days. Anything she said to Michael could be immediately passed on to Peter, and she couldn't risk that.

A woman heading toward the intersection suddenly caught her eye. She had long brown hair almost down to her waist, straight and sleek. She looked ballerina thin—and exactly like Elena Brennan.

Sophie sat up straighter. *Was her mind playing tricks on her?*

The woman wore tight, white jeans and bootie sandals, a clingy, cropped top barely covering her midriff. She was talking on the phone and as the light changed, she walked with pace and purpose, going in the same direction Damon had.

Her breath stuck in her chest as she remembered the photo Wyatt had shown her. Was Elena the woman from last night's meeting with Karen and the Venturi boss? Were the Brennans involved with the Venturis?

Her earpiece suddenly crackled.

"I see Karen Leigh," Damon said. "It looks like she's alone."

As Wyatt and Bree confirmed his message, Sophie felt an overwhelming rush of fear.

Why was Elena in the park? If she was there, were other mob soldiers there as well? Had Damon just walked into the middle of a set-up?

"I don't think Karen is alone," she said into the phone, but Damon didn't answer, and she could hear him speaking to someone.

Karen was there.

She couldn't interrupt him now.

If she kept yelling in his ear, or rushed into the park to find him, she might distract him, and put him in more danger. She had to have faith in him and also in his friends.

Maybe it hadn't been Elena at all. She hadn't seen Elena since that horrible party. She could be wrong…but she didn't think she was.

"Please be safe, Damon," she silently prayed. She could not lose another person that she loved.

Damon heard Sophie's rushed words, but he couldn't respond, not with Karen a foot away. His gaze swept the area, but he didn't see anyone out of place. If Karen had brought someone, they weren't visible. Hopefully, they were just there as protection for her and not to take him out.

"What are you doing here, Damon?" Karen asked.

She was dressed in jeans and a baggy top, and he wouldn't be surprised if she had a weapon on her. She wore a baseball cap, her hair pulled back in a ponytail, sunglasses covering her eyes.

"We need to talk," he said.

"Where's Wyatt?"

"He's safe. He's putting together a very detailed case about you and Alan."

She didn't flinch, but her tongue came out and swiped her lips. "I don't know what you're talking about. Wyatt needs to come into the office. He's in danger. So are you, for that matter. And where the hell is Sophie Parker?"

"You're not here to ask questions. You're here to answer them. You saw the photo Wyatt sent you."

"That was a business meeting. I was looking for information on Wyatt, as a matter of fact. I've been extremely worried about him."

"Cut the crap, Karen." He purposefully used her first name, deliberately not acknowledging her status as an agent above him.

"I don't think you're going to last on our team, Damon," she said, snapping back at him. "But then you might be spending some time in jail for murder."

"You know one of the people I shot was working for the Venturi family, maybe both of them, the same family you're working for." He paused. "What do you think Wyatt has been doing for the last year, Karen? He's been collecting evidence against their organization, and you're right in the middle of it."

"I'm not. I haven't done anything."

"Stop lying. It's over."

"If it was over, you wouldn't be here alone. What do you want?"

Good. She was ready to negotiate. "I want to know who's calling the shots."

"If you don't know that, you don't know anything."

"I know enough to get you into a hell of a lot of trouble. But, hey, if you want to be the fall girl, that works for me. One less player off the game board."

"You don't have anything on me but a picture that I can explain. You're bluffing."

"I know you're dirty, Karen. And I don't just know it; I can prove it—with Wyatt's help, of course. He's not too happy about almost being killed the other day."

"I don't know what happened to Wyatt, but if anyone set him up, it was Alan. I've had my suspicions about him for a long time."

"Suspicions, huh? Yet you did nothing but cozy up to Alan. I'm not buying it. Try again."

Karen took a quick look around, as if debating her next move. He honestly wasn't sure what she was going to do. Then he saw her eyes widen in shock as she fell to her knees, putting a hand to her chest, to the blood suddenly spreading across her shirt. She crumpled awkwardly onto the ground.

"Karen," he yelled, stunned that she'd been shot right in front of him.

He dropped down next to her. She was writhing on the ground.

"Help me," she said.

He heard a woman scream, "She's been shot."

A man shouted "Gun!"

People went running.

He put his hands on Karen's chest, trying to stop the flow of blood from the gushing wound. She was gasping for breath, her eyes wide and terrified.

"Who did this, Karen? Tell me."

"I—I can't. Help me," she pleaded.

"I'm going to help you." He could see her gaze losing focus. "But you have to stay with me." He pressed harder on the wound. "This is your last chance to come clean—to tell your story."

"I didn't want to be a part of it," she said breathlessly. "I didn't have a choice."

"Why not?"

"He had pictures of me and Alan—together. They told me Alan wasn't keeping up his end of the bargain. If I didn't take over, they'd release the pictures. They'd let everyone know I was sleeping with the boss, and that's why…" She struggled to breathe. "That's why I got promoted. My career is all I have. Alan didn't really want me. He was just lonely. He said it was a mistake. Oh, God, it was such a mistake. Now it's going to end like this. I don't want to die."

"You're not going to die. Help is coming. Who's in charge, Karen? Stefan Venturi? Peter Hunt? Who?"

Her eyes closed.

"Dammit, wake up," he yelled.

Bree appeared at his side. "Damon, get out of here," she said. "I called 911. Ambulance, police, and FBI are on the way. I've got my badge. I can talk my way out of this. You can't be here when they get here."

"She was just about to tell me—"

"I heard," Bree interrupted. "I recorded everything she said on the phone. Get out of here, Damon."

He jumped to his feet, looking around the now deserted area. "Who shot her? Who the hell shot her?"

"I didn't see."

"Where's Wyatt?"

Her silence spoke volumes.

"Dammit! Did he shoot her? Why? Because she was going to talk?"

"Maybe," Bree said, her eyes tormented. "I don't know, but you have to leave now. Get Sophie and go."

Sophie!

A new terror ran through him. "Sophie?" he said, hoping she could hear him through her earpiece. "Are you all right?"

There was no answer.

He sped through the trees as the sirens got closer,

stopping for a second to wipe his bloody hands on the grass. He slowed his pace as he reached the sidewalk. He didn't want to draw attention to himself as someone fleeing from the scene.

Finally, he was able to get through the crowd, and he ran across the street.

Fear squeezed his chest so hard he could barely breathe. "I'm coming, Sophie," he said. "Please be there. Please be there."

Twenty

Sophie was in the back of a van.

When she'd heard screams coming over her headset, she'd known something had gone terribly wrong. Damon and Karen had been having a tense conversation when all hell had broken loose.

It had sounded like someone had shot Karen.

Damon had been yelling at Karen to stay with him. Someone in the background had been screaming about a gun.

She'd yelled into the phone, but no one had heard her. Or they were too busy to answer.

So, she'd grabbed the key from the ignition and jumped out of the car. To hell with staying behind locked doors. She was not going to sit there and do nothing.

Unfortunately, she'd barely taken two steps when she'd been shoved from behind. The phone and the car key had gone flying out of her hand as she hit the side of the car and fell to her knees.

A man had hauled her to her feet. A van had come up next to her. She'd been thrown inside. Her head had bounced off the inside wall, and stars had exploded in front of her eyes. She thought she might have passed out for a minute.

But now she was wide awake, and she needed to get her bearings, figure a way out of this mess.

She looked around the van. There were no seats. It was obviously a work van. There were some paint cans, rollers and tins in one corner next to some tarps. She wondered if she could use the paint to her advantage. *Paint was explosive. Maybe she could start a fire*. But she didn't have a lighter or a match.

Fear coursed through her as the van picked up speed. She couldn't see who was driving. She thought there were at least two people, and at least one of them was male.

Was the other one Elena?

It didn't seem likely. She'd gone into the park.

Had Elena shot Karen?

That seemed like a ridiculous thought.

Elena was a preppy, private-school educated, wealthy young woman with the world at her fingertips. *Why would she be involved in this dirty business?*

She wasn't even sure the woman she'd seen was Elena. Still, her brother had had a ring with the same tattoo.

She pressed a hand to her throbbing head, not sure if she was on the right track or the wrong one. She had to remember that the people most likely responsible for grabbing her were the Venturis. They were at the center of everything—or their new partner was.

Had someone followed Karen to the park and shot her before she could spill any information?

That might make sense.

But why hadn't Wyatt and Bree seen the shooter? Why hadn't they stopped him?

At least, Damon hadn't gone down. She could still hear his voice in her head.

He was alive. She had to hang on to that.

She just didn't know how long they were both going to stay alive…

The car key was on the ground, the door was unlocked, and Sophie's phone was lying next to the front wheel.

Damon picked up her phone and scoured the street. Police cars and an ambulance were pulling up down the block, near the entrance to the park. Help was on the way for Karen. He hoped she'd survive because she could provide valuable information, but right now his main concern was Sophie. If only she'd been able to keep the phone with her, he could have pinged her location.

Had she gotten out of the car when she'd heard the screams?

He remembered her voice in his ear, but he didn't think he'd answered her.

He should have said something. He should have told her to run.

It was too late now.

A car pulled up next to him; he was shocked to see Wyatt behind the wheel.

"Get in," Wyatt said.

For a split second, he hesitated. *Had Wyatt shot Karen? Was he the double agent?*

"Damon," Wyatt said sharply. "I know where they're taking Sophie."

Oh, hell. If Wyatt was the double agent, then he'd just said the one thing guaranteed to make him get in the car.

He opened the door and jumped in.

"Where's Bree?" Wyatt asked, as he sped down the street.

"She's with Karen—handling the scene. Did you shoot Karen?"

"Hell, no, I didn't shoot Karen." Wyatt gave him a dark look. "You think I'm the dirty agent?"

"If you didn't do it, did you see who did?"

"I saw a woman with dark hair running through the trees right after Karen went down. She looked like the woman I saw in the bar last night. I ran after her. When I got to the street, I saw a guy throwing Sophie in the back of a van. The woman jumped into a black SUV with tinted windows. The vehicles took off in different directions. I don't know where the woman is going, but I've seen the van before. It's used by Venturi Construction. There's a warehouse not far from here that they use."

"You think that's where they're taking her?"

Wyatt's jaw tightened. "Yeah. It's private. I've seen people brought there before," he said harshly.

Damon sucked in a breath, the reality of Wyatt's words making him sick. He knew exactly what Wyatt meant when he said he'd seen people brought there before. And he was betting not all of those *people* had left the building alive or in the same shape in which they'd entered.

The thought of anyone hurting Sophie was torturous. He couldn't bear the thought. He wished to hell he could trade places with her, that he could take whatever pain was coming her way.

He'd let her down. He should have taken her into the park. He should have stayed with her. She hadn't wanted to be alone. She'd been terrified to be on her own, and he'd left her. He'd chosen the mission over her.

"Keep it together," Wyatt ordered, giving him another hard look.

"This is my fault."

"We'll get her back."

"We have to."

"We will. I heard Karen's confession—is she going to make it?"

"I don't know; doubtful. She didn't give me the name I wanted."

"That's why they took her out. They must have been watching her. They must have believed she was vulnerable."

"I don't think she realized they thought she was weak. She wasn't giving me anything until she was shot. Then the truth hit her—she was going to die for them. That's why she started talking." He let out a breath. "Dammit. I can't believe how badly we blew this. Where was the shooter? Why didn't either you or Bree see them?"

"I've been asking myself that, too. I thought we had the area covered."

He wondered again if he was smart to trust Wyatt, especially when Wyatt turned down an alley, heading toward the water.

Trust had never come easy for him, not after the number his parents had done on his head. But he'd trusted the men and women he'd served with in the Army, and he'd trusted Wyatt and Bree more than once. He could trust them again. At this point, he had to.

As his hand tightened around Sophie's phone, he felt as if he could still feel the warmth of her hand. She must be so scared. He silently willed her strength and prayed that Wyatt was taking him to the right place.

It suddenly occurred to him that maybe Sophie hadn't dropped the phone by accident. Maybe she'd left him a clue.

He turned on the phone. An Internet page came up. Sophie had been looking at a picture of her father's friend, Michael Brennan, standing with a girlfriend and his adult children—David and Elena.

His pulse sped up at the sight of the beautiful brunette with the long, brown hair. "Is this the woman you saw?" he asked, enlarging the photo so it was just the woman in the frame.

"That's her," Wyatt said, surprise in his voice. "Who is she?"

"Elena Brennan, the daughter of Michael Brennan."

"One of the Yale guys who met with Peter Hunt last night?"

"Yes. Maybe Brennan is the new player in the Venturi operation, and that's why his daughter was at the bar. I wonder why Sophie was looking her up." He got out of the image and went back a page, seeing Sophie's search for a ring with a snake and an eye in the middle of a circle. Somehow, she must have connected the tattoo with the Brennans; he wasn't sure how she'd done that, but maybe it would help them later when they had to connect all the dots.

But first he had to save her life.

The people who had grabbed her probably wanted to know what she knew, which was why they'd taken her alive. But she wasn't going to stay that way long.

"There's the car," Wyatt said suddenly, coming to an abrupt stop behind a Dumpster in a back alley between two large warehouses.

The dark SUV was parked in front of a warehouse door. There was no sign of the van, but it could be inside.

"Looks like the players are here," Wyatt said, a light of battle coming into his eyes. "Ready to kick some ass, Damon?"

"More than ready."

"So, you trust me again?"

Wyatt had always been skilled at reading people. "I do," he said, pulling out his gun.

Wyatt nodded approvingly. "Then let's go get your girl back."

He almost said Sophie wasn't his girl. *But wasn't she? Hadn't she been for the last four years?*

Sophie struggled against the plastic ties that held her hands together behind the back of a chair. She was sitting in the middle of a large room in a dark, cavernous warehouse. They'd come in through a loading dock, and she hadn't seen any light when they'd taken her out of the van, so they'd obviously parked in a garage of some sort. A man had brought her into this room, tied her up and left. She hadn't recognized his face. And he hadn't said one word to her despite her begging him to let her go.

Now, she was waiting. If she could somehow get her hands free and off the chair, maybe she could find a way to escape. They hadn't tied her feet, so she could at least kick out, perhaps injure someone that way. But despite the optimistic thought, she knew her odds of getting out of this room were slim.

Someone had been after her for days, and they'd finally caught up to her.

Hopefully, she'd at least get some answers before they killed her.

A chill ran through her. She really wasn't ready to die. She had so many things she wanted to do. She couldn't help wondering if her father had had the same thought as someone rammed his car from behind, running him off the road. But unlike her father, she couldn't leave anyone a voicemail. She couldn't apologize or tell someone—Damon—that she loved him.

Perhaps it was better that way. Her father's messages hadn't really eased her mind; they'd only given her more to worry about.

A side door opened, and she caught her breath. A man came through first. He was short and stocky, built like a linebacker, like a man who knew how to fight.

Behind him came a woman—a woman wearing white jeans and a short top, a woman with long, brown hair and familiar brown eyes.

"Well, well, well," Elena said, a mocking expression on her beautiful, cold face. "Little Sophie Parker. You always end up in the wrong place at the wrong time, don't you? Just like that party when we were in high school. Only this time, you won't be able to run away."

"What are you doing, Elena? Why are you involved in this business?"

"Involved in what? Making money? It's not just business—it's the *family* business," she said. "We thought your father understood loyalty to family, but he didn't."

Anger ran through her. "He was not a part of your family."

"My father treated him like a brother. My mother took care of yours when she was sick. But how quickly you both forgot.

"Are you saying that you killed my father?" she asked in disbelief.

"He drove off the road. Sometimes that happens when you speed."

"It wasn't an accident. Someone was chasing him. Was it you?"

"Does it matter?"

"Yes, it matters. Why? Why did you do it? Why did you drag my father into your business?"

"Drag him?" Elena challenged. "Your father asked my father for help, and he gave it. But when it came to collect on that favor, your father was not very helpful."

She hated Elena's mocking, condescending tone, but right now she wanted answers, and playing along seemed to be the only way to get them. "Why did my father need help? He didn't care about money."

"He did when your mom was dying—when she needed experimental treatment that insurance wouldn't cover. When she wanted to go to that clinic in Switzerland—do you remember that?"

"Of course, I remember."

"How do you think he paid for all that?"

"I don't know. He never said. I assumed he took out a loan on the house or something."

"Or something. My father gave him money, everything he needed to save your mother. And then when it was our turn, your father wasn't so generous."

"Your turn? What did you need? I don't recall anyone getting sick and dying."

"We needed someone at the FBI to take care of a few things for us—small things, nothing too difficult. He managed the first few, but then he started to balk."

"What did you do?"

"We made sure he knew that he was in too deep to get out. He got a little more cooperative. He even left Quantico and came to New York when we needed him to. We thought for a time he understood his role. But that changed. We realized he was starting to work against us. He was betraying our friendship. So, we had to make it clear that it was no longer just about paying back his debt to us; it was about keeping his daughter alive."

"That's not friendship; that's blackmail."

"Call it what you like, it worked. You provided excellent incentive, but then there was one line Alan just didn't want to cross."

"What was that?"

"We needed him to take out an undercover in the Venturi organization, someone that Alan neglected to tell us was feeding him information."

"He wouldn't do it," she said, feeling remarkably thankful that her father had drawn the line there.

"No."

"You're the new partner. Your family business is joining forces with the Venturis, aren't they?"

"So, you've learned a little while hiding out with your hot FBI agent," she drawled. "It's too bad he's not here. But then he left you alone. He was more interested in getting information from that stupid FBI bitch than in protecting you. I probably should have killed him, too, but there's always time for that."

She could see the evil swirling in Elena's eyes, and she was reminded of the snake tattoo with the sinister red eye. "You shot Agent Leigh? How do you even know how to do that?" she asked in bewilderment. "I thought you were a fashion designer."

"You were supposed to think that."

"Is your whole family involved? Your mother was so nice to me when my mom died." She couldn't believe Katya was part of a criminal enterprise.

"My mother is nice, but she's also a Belenko. Her brothers have been running a very profitable business in the Ukraine for the last few years, but they wanted to expand. They asked me to help them."

"And your father's hedge fund?"

"It's an excellent place to make money."

"And launder dirty money?"

"Don't be ridiculous," she said with a laugh. "My father is as clean as the purest snow. That's why he can meet with senators and FBI directors and get useful information."

"But he knows what you do with the information. Is your brother involved?"

"David was involved for a short time, but he was too erratic, and he wanted too big of a cut. He's been on a world tour for some time now. No one knows when he'll be back—*if* he'll be back."

Bile rose in her throat. She'd never seen pure evil before; she was looking at it now.

"Why are you doing this? You're wealthy. You have everything you've ever wanted, Elena."

"I don't just want money; I want power—total and absolute power. I'm tired of being Daddy's little girl, David's little sister, the Belenkos' niece. My uncles don't hold women in particularly high regard, but soon they'll realize I'm in charge. I'm not just bringing in a partnership with the Venturis as they asked me to do—I'm taking over their operation. I've already gotten rid of one of them—Lorenzo Venturi. Stefan will soon be charged with his brother's murder; that information has already been passed on to Peter Hunt. You see, Sophie, we don't always need an FBI agent to do something wrong to get our way. Sometimes we just have to help them do something right by pointing them in the direction we want them to go."

Elena's brain was a terrifying thing. "So, Peter Hunt has no idea you and your father and your whole family are running a criminal operation? How is that possible? Surely, he must know about your mother's family ties to organized crime in Ukraine."

"He has no idea. No one does. My mother changed her name when she came to this country. She didn't want to be part of the Belenko family anymore. She wanted to marry a rich American and live a different life. And that's exactly what she did. But as she got older, she missed her family. She was lonely. She was unhappy with my father. He didn't treat her well. So, she reached out to her brothers. They accepted her apology. And they invited David and me to visit when we graduated from high school. It quickly became clear to us that we were Belenkos not Brennans."

She shook her head in disbelief. "I don't remember your mother ever talking about being from somewhere else. But I guess I wasn't around her that much. Your dad never told Peter?"

"My father never told anyone. As I said before, his business is squeaky clean. Unfortunately, he made some mistakes in judgment that my uncles took advantage of. He probably wouldn't have made your father do anything if he hadn't felt pressure from them. But when you make mistakes, sometimes you have to pay."

"What kind of mistakes?"

"Like I said, he didn't treat my mother well," she said, her lips drawing into a hard line.

"You're not going to get away with this, Elena."

"Of course, we will. Recently, Peter Hunt discovered that your father was abetting the Venturis. Everything he did for us has been turned over to Peter. Peter believes that the Venturi brothers were paying your father to help them. And soon Agent Leigh's misdeeds will also be known."

"And then what?" she asked.

"With Alan and Karen dead, Peter Hunt will announce that all of the FBI leaks have been sealed. The Venturis' operation has been shut down. He'll send Stefan to jail for his brother's murder with the proof that we'll make sure he gets. It will be a big day for him. And then in a few months, or a year, we'll use him as we need to, because once Peter realizes he's been played, he won't be able to escape the trap he was so happy to get into."

"If only you would use your brain for good things," she murmured.

Elena smiled. "Believe me, I have very good things in

my life, Sophie. When I see something I want, I go and get it."

"One day you're going to pay for all of this."

"Well, you won't live to see that day." Elena pulled out her gun. "I thought you might know more than you do, that your father might have shared information with you. That's why we let you live until now. But I no longer have any use for you."

Elena was going to kill her. She could see the intent in her cold, dark eyes. And there wasn't a damn thing she could do about it. She just hoped the truth wouldn't die with her, that Damon would figure it all out, that he'd find a way to bring Elena and her family to justice.

She wished she could say good-bye to him, tell him she loved him, tell him that he had to find a way to allow himself to love someone back, because he wasn't meant for the lonely existence he'd chosen. He could find a woman who would stand by him, who wouldn't betray him, who would love him for the rest of his life. He just had to be open to it.

A crash came from somewhere in the warehouse, followed by the smell of smoke.

She stiffened, hope rushing through her veins.

Elena exchanged a look with the man behind her. "Find out what's going on," she ordered.

As the man moved toward the hallway, she caught a glimpse of someone moving along a raised platform behind Elena. She didn't want Elena to see him.

"Please, let me go," she told Elena, drawing the woman's attention back to her. She didn't want to beg, but she wanted to keep Elena focused on her. "I'm not involved in any of this. I'm not going to talk. I don't care what you do. I'll move away. You'll never see me again. No one will be looking for me; my parents are both dead."

"You're stalling, Sophie."

"What about the money? Don't you want that? My dad left me a suitcase filled with cash. I have it stashed somewhere. I could get it for you."

Elena looked marginally interested. "I'm sure I can find it after you're dead." She tilted her head, giving her a thoughtful look. "Oh, I see. You think he's coming for you, don't you? He won't get here in time." Elena lifted her gun.

Sophie fought hard to keep her eyes open and not cower in her chair. She was going to fight to the last breath. She had to. She turned her head to the right, seeing nothing and no one coming to rescue her, but pretending like she was. "Thank God," she murmured. "You're here."

It was enough of a ruse to make Elena look.

In that split second of distraction, a shot rang out, and Elena went down.

She fell onto her back right in front of Sophie, a hole in the middle of her forehead, her eyes opened in shock and disbelief.

She had died in an instant.

Sophie found herself wishing Elena had suffered a little longer.

Pounding footsteps made her fear what was coming next.

And then she saw Damon, coming down a ladder. He dropped to his feet and ran toward her, his gun in his hand, relief flashing through his eyes. He stopped for a quick minute to make sure Elena was dead and then he came to her.

"Sophie!" he said in a voice choked with emotion.

"I'm all right. But there are other men here. I don't know where they are."

"Wyatt and I took care of everyone else. She was the last one."

"I thought I smelled smoke."

"Wyatt started a small fire to lure out Elena's bodyguard. Then he took him out." Damon pulled out his keys and used the small penknife to slice through the plastic ties. Then he kissed her on the lips and put his arms around her, pressing her into the tightest and most welcome embrace of her life. "Thank God you're all right."

She wrapped her arms around his neck, overwhelmed with gratitude that he was alive, too, that they were both safe. But then she heard sirens and the fear returned. "We need to get out of here. The police are coming, and I'm sure the FBI won't be far behind."

"No," he said, shaking his head. "We're not running anymore."

"We aren't?" she asked in confusion.

"I recorded your conversation with Elena," he said, reaching into his pocket to pull out his phone. "Wyatt called Peter once Elena confirmed that Peter is innocent. He's on his way. It's over, Sophie."

"I want to believe that, but what about Michael Brennan, and the Venturis, and—"

He put his fingers against her mouth. "We're going to take them all down."

"Do we have enough evidence?"

"If we don't, we'll get it."

"What about Karen? Is she dead? Elena said she was."

"She was alive when I left, but I don't know if she'll make it." He paused. "Did you hear what Karen said?"

"About sleeping with my father and being blackmailed? Yeah, I heard that. I wonder if she even cared about him at all or if she was just using him."

"I think a lot of things will become clear as we dig into this."

"I just don't understand why my dad didn't tell me that Michael and Elena were blackmailing him. At least I would have had that information."

"The more you knew, the more danger you would be in. He was trying to protect you. And I think, in some ways, he was trying to prevent you from knowing what he'd done. That's why he made plans for you to leave."

She stood up as Wyatt entered the room, followed by Peter Hunt and a half-dozen agents and cops.

Peter came toward her, apology in his eyes. "My God,

Sophie. I am so sorry."

His words seemed bitterly ironic. "That's exactly what you said to me last Wednesday when you came to tell me that my father was dead."

"I meant it then, too," he said heavily.

"Why didn't you tell me that you knew my father was a double agent? Elena said that they fed you that information a few weeks ago."

"I was still reviewing it. I'm always skeptical of evidence that comes my way too easily. There's usually an agenda behind it."

Maybe Peter wasn't as dumb as Elena had made him out to be. "Did you know about Karen Leigh, too?"

He shook his head, as anger filled his eyes. "No, I didn't. Not until today. Agent Adams read me in at the hospital."

"Is Karen dead?" Damon asked.

"She's still in surgery," Peter replied. "There's a slim chance she'll make it. Agent Adams turned over the recording she made of your conversation at the park. Even if Karen doesn't recover, we have her last words." He paused. "You should have come to me, Damon. That first night when I asked you into my office, you should have told me you were going after Sophie."

"I hadn't decided at that point," Damon replied. "I wasn't sure she was at the cabin; it was a hunch."

"One you should have shared."

"I'm not going to apologize when God knows how many people in the field office you oversee are compromised," he returned.

Sophie sucked in a breath as anger flared in Peter's eyes.

"I do not believe that anyone else is compromised," Peter said.

"You don't know that for sure," she said. "Elena told me her in-laws are part of a powerful crime family. How did you not know that Michael's ex-wife was tied to organized crime?"

"I never had any reason to look into Katya's background. And they've been divorced for almost ten years now. As for Michael, his business has always been clean. I know that hedge funds can be used to launder money; I checked him out a long time ago. I wanted to be sure our friendship could never be questioned."

"Well you didn't dig deep enough," she said.

"That's going to change. Wyatt played me the recording of your conversation with Elena. I'm on my way to see Michael now. If we get him to cooperate, and I think he will considering his daughter is dead, we'll be able to nail the Belenkos and the Venturis to the wall."

"I want to come with you," she said. "Don't tell me I can't, Peter, because I have to see the man who lent my father money to save my mother's life, knowing that the Belenkos would then force him into becoming a traitor. Did you know that the Belenkos threatened my life? That they sent my father pictures of me, telling him that they could get to me at any time?"

"I didn't," Peter said.

"My father was trapped. He could do what they wanted him to do, or he could watch me die. But he couldn't kill Wyatt. That was the one thing he couldn't do. So, the Belenkos killed my dad, and Michael Brennan knew about it. He's going to tell me how he could do that to his friend. He owes me that. And, so, do you."

"Then let's go," Peter said grimly.

Twenty-One

Despite her forceful plea to Peter, Sophie was a little surprised that he'd agreed to let her come along, but they were now driving to Michael Brennan's house in a bullet-proof, black Escalade. Wyatt and Peter sat in the middle row, discussing various aspects of the case, while she and Damon sat in the back row, their fingers intertwined.

She couldn't seem to let go of Damon, and he couldn't seem to let go of her. That would probably change when the shock wore off, but for now she was happy to hang on to him.

"Thanks for saving me again," she said quietly. "I was afraid it was going to be three strikes and you're out."

He gave her a smile. "You're channeling Jamie with the baseball metaphor."

"I am," she admitted. "By the way, how did you know where to find me?"

"Wyatt saw them grab you. He was chasing Elena out of the park after she shot Karen. When he saw the Venturi van, he guessed where they'd be taking you. He knew the way things worked there, the layout inside, where the guards would be. We took out the two guys by the front door, then got inside. We would have moved in earlier, but you were getting some good information out of Elena. We thought we should let her talk."

"She was talking to me, because she wanted to brag, and she didn't plan on me living to tell anyone about our conversation. When I saw a shadow on a ledge behind her, I was hoping it was you, but I wasn't sure."

"I was getting into position. Thanks for distracting her by the way."

"It was all I could think to do. You made a tremendously good shot—one bullet right in the center of her forehead." A chill ran through her as she saw Elena's image again in her head. "I think she was stunned that she'd been caught. It was in her eyes when she fell to the ground. I'm glad she knew. She was so full of herself. She thought she could rule the world."

"Not with us in it," Damon said.

She smiled. "At least not with you in it."

"You did your part. I probably should have shot her in the arm, but I couldn't risk her taking a shot at you. Keeping her alive might have given us more evidence."

"I'm glad she's dead. I know that I probably shouldn't admit to that, but it's true. She was a bad person. I knew she was wild when I was a kid, but I didn't know how horrible she was. She had no heart, no soul. It was terrifying to see nothing in her eyes. I think she killed her brother, too. The family believes he's traveling around the world, but she made it sound like he's never coming back."

"I heard that. She didn't want to share her power."

"He was also bad." She paused, remember what had made her look up the Brennans again. "Her brother had a ring with the same design as the tattoo. I knew I'd seen it before. When I was waiting in the car, I was thinking about the tattoo so I wouldn't worry about you taking on Karen, and I remembered being at a party when I was a teenager. I bumped into a guy, my hair got caught in his ring, and I shivered when I saw this red eye looking back at me. I think now the symbol is probably from Ukrainian culture and tied to the Belenkos."

"The man in the storage unit was probably tied to them, too; that's why there was no record of him in this country." Damon paused. "I found your phone and I saw the photos of the Brennans. I showed Wyatt the picture of Elena, and he confirmed she was the woman he'd seen last night at the meeting with Karen."

"I thought I saw Elena going into the park, but it seemed like such a ridiculous idea that I couldn't quite believe it. I tried to say something to you, but you were already talking to Karen."

A light came into his eyes. "You did say something about someone else being there."

"I guess I should have said it louder." She took a breath. "I'm glad you took out Elena, but I'm worried the rest of the rats are going to scatter."

"More likely they're going to talk. When the boss is dead, the first people to talk usually get the best deal."

"But only one boss is dead. Stefan Venturi is still alive and so are Elena's uncles."

"We'll get them all," he promised. "I'm not stopping until that happens."

"The one I want the most is Michael. Maybe he runs a clean business, but when it comes to my father, his hands have blood on them."

"I know."

"I hope he's home," she said, as the car stopped in front of Michael Brennan's home on the Upper East Side of Manhattan. The luxury home came with two security guards out front, but Peter's badge forced the men to step aside.

They found Michael Brennan on the second floor in his study, standing in front of his floor- to-ceiling windows with a spectacular view of the Hudson River, sipping what appeared to be a whiskey. He didn't look surprised to see them when he turned around. He looked resigned…

"Is my daughter alive?" he asked.

She couldn't believe the lack of emotion in his question. Maybe all the Brennans were devoid of heart.

"No," she said, taking the lead from the three men behind her. She took a step forward. "She's as dead as my father is. And you stand here, having your drink, as if nothing in the world has changed? What is wrong with you?"

"I'm very aware that everything has changed, Sophie," he said, meeting her gaze. "I never wanted your father in the middle of any of this, but he was desperate for my money. So, I helped him."

"You didn't help him. You made him your pawn."

"Not *my* pawn. I didn't force him to do anything."

"No, you let your family do that. Do you think that makes you innocent?"

"You don't understand. It didn't start out that way, but the more money he needed, the more interest he drew from my in-laws. I was under pressure to utilize his connections. I—I had my own problems to deal with—a wife who couldn't get through a day without a drink, a son who was willing to waste his life snorting coke and getting involved with under-aged girls, and a daughter who was, sadly, as evil as her uncles. She told them about my relationship with Alan, the money he owed me, owed the family, really, because Katya funded my business in the beginning. It was her money that she'd brought with her and the Belenkos made sure I knew that. I wasn't just lending my money; I was lending theirs. That's why I told your father no at first. But he begged me. He said he had to do everything he could to save Maggie."

"Did he pay you back?"

"He couldn't. He got too far in debt. You have no idea how much it all cost, and he spared no expense. So he did a few favors, small things, nothing that raised suspicion. But a few years ago, the family wanted more from him. They wanted to expand their operations in New York. They needed an agent in the New York office. Alan had to be that agent. I made sure he knew that more might be required of him. I urged him to retire, to leave the FBI, to make himself unimportant."

She was shocked to hear that. "Why didn't he do that?"

"He said he needed the money."

Her heart twisted. "For my schooling?"

"He didn't say. I knew he was going to be in trouble. Elena was making a play for power. She wanted to impress her uncles and also the Venturis. She was angry with me for leaving her mother. I didn't want her to hate me. I tried to get her to lay off of Alan, but she wouldn't."

"So, you gave her what she wanted—my father on a silver platter," she said bitterly.

"I didn't know how to stop her. I didn't see a way to contain her ambition. Your father was willing to do anything to save his family. I was willing to do anything to make my daughter love me again."

"Make her love you?" Sophie echoed in bewilderment. "She was incapable of love. Do you know where your son is?"

He paled. "He's traveling."

She could see the truth in his eyes. "You don't believe that."

He finished off his drink. "I've called my lawyer. He'll be here soon."

"A lawyer isn't going to help you," Damon said, stepping up next to her. "You're going to go down for multiple murders and a whole list of other crimes. If you turn evidence on the Belenkos and the Venturis, you may be able to shorten your sentence."

"He's right," Peter put in. "You should have told me, Michael. If you wanted to get out, you should have told me."

"He never wanted to get out," she said. "He just wants to pretend that he did now, so he can make himself feel better. If he has regrets, it makes it all okay."

"That's not true," Michael said. "It's not okay, and I know it. I never thought things would go this far. I never imagined that Alan would die. I'm sorry, Sophie."

"And I'm really tired of people apologizing to me for things they should have done differently."

Michael's gaze moved from her to Peter. "They're

coming after you next, Peter."

"I know," Peter said. "Who else at the Bureau is involved? I need names, Michael, every single one."

"As far as I know—only the woman who was shot in the park today."

"You know about that?" Sophie asked.

"I was recently informed," he admitted.

"I'm surprised you didn't run," she said.

He gave her a tired smile. "The world is a very small place, and even if the FBI couldn't find me, the Belenkos could. There's only one way for me to be free. It's almost a relief," Michael added, his voice getting thick, his words slurring. "I don't know why I fought it for so long. I had so much in my life, but not the most important things—love and family. Maybe I'll find Elena again in another life, and she'll be the girl I remember, not the woman she grew up to be."

Sophie's gaze narrowed. "What's wrong with you?" she asked.

"He took something," Damon said, striding forward as Michael fell to the ground.

Peter rushed to Michael's side, putting his hand on Michael's neck. "There's no pulse." He pushed Michael onto his back and started CPR.

Damon called 911, requesting an ambulance.

For long minutes, Peter, Wyatt and Damon took turns working on Michael, trying to bring him back to life. But it was to no avail. By the time the paramedics arrived, he'd been dead for several minutes.

As the medics put Michael on a stretcher and carried him out, Sophie went over to Peter. He looked shell-shocked. It seemed as if he'd aged ten years in the last few minutes. "You did everything you could," she said.

"I didn't do nearly enough." He looked at her through strained, exhausted eyes. "And I'm not talking about Michael; I should have known your dad was in trouble. I should have asked more questions about why he left Quantico. He loved the academy. I didn't understand why he wanted to leave there to come to New York, but now I do. He still had a debt to pay."

"He should have asked for help," she said. "He should have told me about the money. I could have dropped out of school. I could have helped him. And if he didn't want to tell me because he was ashamed, he should have asked for help from one of his friends. I don't understand why he couldn't find a way out."

Peter stared back at her. "I think Alan was working on a way out. He was trying to play both sides without getting caught by either."

"He said something like that in his voicemail. He said he was trying to put things right, that there still might be a way out. Maybe he was using Wyatt to build a case against them all, but they figured it out." She turned to Wyatt. "Elena told me that my dad wouldn't take you out. That's why they killed him. I know he was using you, and you probably can't forgive him, but I'm glad he didn't cross that line."

"I am, too," Wyatt said. "But he must have found out that someone else at the FBI stepped in and tried to make it happen without him. That's why he ran."

"And why he told you not to trust anyone, Sophie," Damon interjected. "He wasn't sure who else at the FBI was involved. He might have thought they'd already gotten to Peter and to Karen."

"I did tell him that I'd found some discrepancies in his cases," Peter said. "I asked him to sit down with me. I don't know if he believed I was going to pressure him to do what the Belenkos wanted, or if I was going to turn him in. But we never had that meeting."

"We'll probably never know everything," she said with a tired sigh. "But I have a pretty good idea now of what happened."

"You just need to remember that your dad loved you, Sophie," Damon said, as Peter and Wyatt moved away.

"I know that," she said, looking into his compassionate eyes. "And my dad loved my mom, too. He was willing to do anything to save her life. It doesn't negate what he did, but it makes it easier for me to understand." She let out a breath. "I am surprised Michael killed himself instead of running away. On the other hand, he was able to take his secrets to his grave. He protected his family, his daughter, his son, even in his death. We can't get evidence out of him now. He won't have to turn against them."

"Actually, I don't think Michael was trying to protect anyone," Wyatt interrupted, waving them over to the desk. "Looks like Brennan left us everything we need to take down the Belenkos. He couldn't do it himself, but with all this, we can."

"Really?" she asked, walking over to the desk.

"Michael wrote the whole story down—everything," Wyatt said in amazement, skimming through a handwritten letter. "It's all here. Names, contact information, bank accounts…and not just on the Belenkos, the Venturis, too. We're going to be able to take down both families." He handed Peter the letter.

"Damn," Peter said, shaking his head in disbelief. "Maybe he was a coward to take his life, but at least he left something good behind. I need to get a team in here as soon as possible."

"I'll help," Wyatt told Peter. "I'm going to personally make sure that no leads get dropped. There's likely still a hit on my head. I want all the players in jail."

"I'm in, too," Damon said. "Whatever I can do."

"No," Peter said, shaking his head. "Take Sophie home, Damon. Get some food, some rest, and then when you're ready, you can dive in." He paused, glancing at Wyatt. "You should do the same."

"No way, I'm good," Wyatt said, already reading through papers. "I think this information, combined with what we found at Alan's safe house in Brooklyn, will be a good start to making some arrests, and I'd like those to happen as soon as possible."

"Will tonight be soon enough?" Peter asked, as he pulled

out his phone.

"That will be perfect," Wyatt said.

Damon turned to her. "Ready to go home?"

"If you want to stay—"

"Actually, I could use a break," he said. "I think we can leave this to Peter and Wyatt for tonight."

She was happy to hear that. As much as she wanted to know everything, her brain was already spinning from information overload, and a time-out was much needed. "Then let's go."

Taking Sophie home had been his first thought, but Damon got a better one a few miles down the road. "Change in plans," he said to the driver. "Take us to The Plaza."

Sophie raised a brow. "I thought we were going to my apartment."

"Your apartment was ransacked. I'm not sure what it looks like."

"Oh, I forgot about that," she said with a sigh.

"I don't think you need to deal with that tonight. I'd take you to my place, but the air conditioning isn't working, and you know how I feel about heat."

She smiled. "I do. So, it's The Plaza? Kind of fancy."

"We'll get the best room they have—my treat."

"It should be my treat. I still have a few hundred dollars in cash."

"And I have a credit card."

"Well, I have one of those, too. It's going to be weird to be able to use it again. Is this really over, Damon? I know Elena and Michael are dead, and Karen is in the hospital, but there are still other dangerous players out there."

"They'll be busy covering their asses. They won't be looking for us anymore." He paused. "It's going to take a little time for you to feel back to normal. Re-entry is never easy."

She cocked her head to the right, giving him a thoughtful

look. "You've done it before?"

"Twice, but I was never undercover that long. One job was four days, another was two months, but it still felt strange to be operating under my own name again."

"It will be nice not to have to look over my shoulder every second, but I'm not there yet."

He nodded, seeing the tense lines around her eyes. "You'll get there." He wrapped his fingers around her hand and gave it a squeeze. "You were amazing today—in every possible way."

"I was terrified for most of it."

"You have so much courage, Sophie. Your father would be more than proud." He almost regretted bringing up Alan's name when he saw the shadows enter her eyes. "Sorry, maybe we should put a moratorium on discussing your father and his actions for a few hours."

"It's fine. Even if we don't talk about it, it's there. I just have to work through it all."

"You will."

He looked out the window as they made their way through the city. He couldn't believe he'd only arrived a few weeks ago. So much had happened. And there was still so much up in the air.

"You're thinking about what's next, aren't you?" she asked. "You came to New York to work for my dad, to be part of his team, but I'm sure the team is going to undergo some massive scrutiny and reorganization."

"To say the least. I'm sure I'll be going through many interrogations myself."

"Do you think we're going to get in trouble for stealing that car?"

He smiled at the question. "That's probably the last thing we'll get in trouble for. But, no, it's going to be fine. The Bureau will take care of all that now that they understand we were operating on the right side of the law."

"I hope so. I am glad that Peter wasn't guilty, too. I thought he was a good guy, and it's nice to know I wasn't wrong about him. Not that I was right about much else."

Sophie had definitely lost some of her innocence this week, but she would bounce back. Deep inside, she just couldn't help wanting to believe in the good in people. It might take her a while to recover from the evil she'd witnessed this week, but she would find a way.

"Do you think you'll stay in New York?" she asked.

"I haven't thought that far ahead." Right now, he couldn't imagine leaving Sophie's side, much less the city she lived in. "We'll see how things go, what arrests are made, what kind of indictments go down, how Peter wants to reorganize the team, whether I'll be a good fit there."

"You already have friends there—Wyatt and Bree. I assume Wyatt won't go back undercover."

"No, not in this city at any rate. I have no idea what his plan will be. Bree seems to like her job. She doesn't work on organized crime. She finds missing kids. That's her passion. She only got involved in this to help me and Wyatt."

"She finds missing kids? That's a wonderful endeavor."

"She's good at it, too. But it can be heartbreaking."

"I can't even imagine."

"Don't even try. You've dealt with enough evil for one day."

"I really have. And I feel so amped up. I'm tired and wired. I don't know if I should sleep or run five miles."

"How about something in between?" he asked, as he put his arm around her, and she rested her head on his shoulder.

"This feels nice," she murmured.

"It really does."

She raised her head. "Do you think we should have gone back to Brooklyn? We did leave some things there," she said cryptically, obviously not wanting to mention the money in front of their driver.

"Wyatt told me as we were leaving that he'd go back there and collect everything of importance."

"Who will take charge of the suitcase and its contents?"

"I have no idea. I'm sure it will be locked away as

evidence for a good long time, but you might be able to make a pitch for it."

"I don't want what's in that suitcase," she said with a shake of her head. "If anything, I'd give it away to someone who really needs it, maybe someone with a serious illness, whose insurance doesn't cover everything."

He saw the moisture gather in her eyes and realized her adrenaline rush was probably starting to crash. "That's a good idea."

The cab pulled up in front of The Plaza. He paid the driver and led Sophie into the hotel. They were able to get a luxury suite on the top floor for an outrageous amount of money, but he didn't care. He wanted to take care of Sophie tonight. He wanted her to feel the beauty in the world instead of all the ugliness.

When they got into their room, her look of amazement filled him with pleasure.

"This is spectacular, Damon," she said, wandering around the suite, examining the plush sofas and chairs, the view of the city from their twenty-second floor windows, the fully-stocked kitchen with a bowl of fruit on the counter and a refrigerator filled with drinks.

He followed her into the bedroom, the sight of the king-sized bed also making him happy.

Sophie wandered into the bathroom and then came out again with an even bigger smile on her face. "There's an enormous tub and a shower for two, all the luxuries you could ask for. This must be costing you a freaking fortune, Damon."

He laughed. "I don't even care. We deserve it."

She threw her arms around him. "We so deserve it," she said, as pressed her mouth to his.

Everything else in the world fell away. It felt like forever since he'd last kissed her.

He pulled her tight against him, wanting to feel every inch of her body—from her silky hair, to her soft skin, sensitive breasts, curvy hips, hot center, and her smooth, sexy legs that wrapped around his in the most perfect way.

He wanted to take her to bed and never let her up. But it wasn't just sex he wanted, it was everything else. He wanted to spend the rest of his life talking to her, laughing with her, sharing their lives.

He'd told himself and her that he didn't do love…but this sure felt a lot like it.

He'd put steel bars around his heart a long time ago, wanting to protect himself from more pain. But Sophie was his kryptonite—in a good way. He didn't want to live in a cold, lonely fortress; he wanted to live with her.

She pulled away, and disappointment ran through him. He missed her already.

But then she smiled and grabbed the hem of her shirt and pulled it over her head.

His mouth watered at the sight of her luscious breasts peeking out of her lacy bra. His body hardened. "Did you say they have *everything* in the bathroom?"

"Yes. Second drawer on the left."

He raised a brow. "You checked?"

"After I saw this room—absolutely." She took off her bra. "Don't be long."

He made it into the bathroom and back in record time, stripping off his clothes along the way, more than happy to join a beautiful, naked Sophie in the king-sized bed.

"This bed is huge. I hope I don't lose you," she teased.

"Not a chance," he said, pulling her into his arms. "I don't intend to let go of you all night."

"I'm counting on that," she said, as he made good on his promise.

They'd made love three times, reaching for each other every time they woke up. Now, the sun was pricking at her eyelids, and she was almost afraid to open her eyes. The night had been amazing, but every night with Damon was like that.

It was the mornings that weren't so great. She didn't want

to turn onto her side and see that he was gone, that his side of the bed was empty. She didn't want the night to be over yet.

He'd told her he was good in the dark, but not so great in the day.

That wasn't true. He was wonderful everywhere—the best man she'd ever known.

And now there were tears pricking at her eyelids. *She was not going to cry. She was not going to ruin whatever time they had left.*

"Sophie?"

His husky voice made her heart squeeze tight. "Yes?" she asked, her eyes still closed.

"Are you awake?"

"Maybe."

"How come your eyes are still closed?" he asked, trailing a finger down her bare arm.

"I'm not sure I'm ready to get up yet." His lips found hers, and she felt an overwhelming rush of love for him. Opening her eyes, she found his face just inches away. "Hi."

He gave her an intimate smile. "Good morning."

She licked her lips. "You're still here."

A gleam of understanding darkened his blue gaze. "So, that was the problem—why you didn't want to open your eyes."

"You'd think I'd be used to you getting up first, moving on with your day—your life. I know that's where we're headed, Damon. You don't have to tell me differently. It's okay. I get it. You have your life, and I have mine. The danger is over. You don't have to feel badly about leaving. It's all going to be fine."

"Are you done?" he asked. "Can I talk now?"

"If you want to."

"I told you I wasn't good at love, wasn't interested in relationships, didn't believe in soul mates or happily ever after."

"You did tell me all that," she agreed.

"Well, I was wrong."

"You were?" she asked, her heart beating faster.

"Yes. I am interested in a relationship with you, a long-term, happily-ever-after kind of thing, because you have definitely taken over my heart and my soul."

Happy shivers ran down her spine. "Really? It's not just the afterglow of amazing sex?"

He laughed. "I can say it again later if you want, but since I'm planning on having more sex with you, I don't know when there won't be an amazing afterglow." He paused, his gaze turning serious. "But the part about me not being the greatest at love might still be true. I'm going to make mistakes, Sophie. I'm not going to share my feelings enough. I'm probably going to piss you off on a daily basis. But I will try to make you happy, too—that is, if you're interested in giving things a shot."

"Well, even with that glowing reference, I'm definitely interested." She drew in a breath and let it out. "I don't need you to change, Damon. I just want to love you. I fell for you the first second I saw you. But we weren't ready then. I think we are now."

"I do, too," he said in a husky voice. "And I don't want to change you, either, Sophie. I want you to have everything you want—your job at NYU, your digs around the world, whatever makes you smile."

"You make me smile. We can work it out. I love New York, but I could leave if you needed to be somewhere else. It's all negotiable."

He grinned. "I think I'm going to like negotiating with you." He kissed her again. "But we need to get one thing straight."

"What's that?"

"I don't want you to ever be afraid to open your eyes again, Sophie. I might get up before you. I might run out to pick up pancakes, but I will always come back. I will never leave you."

She nodded. "You're stuck with me, too."

"And there's another thing…"

She frowned, sensing a change in his mood as his gaze darkened. "What else?"

"I'm feeling a little guilty for rushing you into this big talk when you're in a vulnerable place. You still have a lot to deal with emotionally. We can have this conversation again. I just wanted you to know that I'm here, and I'm not going anywhere."

"I appreciate that. I do have a lot of emotions that I need to work through. But you and me—we're solid. We're good."

Relief flooded his eyes, and she felt a wave of protectiveness toward him.

Damon put himself on the line every day, but he never put his heart there. She felt incredibly touched that he'd done that for her.

"How about some breakfast?" he asked. "I'll order you anything you want."

"Well, that will be easy, because I want you. We'll get food later."

"Much later," he agreed, as he slid his mouth down her neck and sent her senses spinning again.

Epilogue

One month later...

Sophie taped up the last box in her father's house and pushed it against the wall with the other four boxes that were ready to be moved. The furniture had already been picked up to be sold at consignment. Only the boxes of personal items were left.

She'd given most of her father's things to charity, but she'd saved photo albums and some family treasures for herself. As a lover of history, she just couldn't bring herself to get rid of everything. Someday, she would tell her children about her mother and her father, and she would pass along a few of their favorite things to the next generation.

As she looked around the empty room, she felt more relief than sadness. In the past four weeks, she'd finally had time to grieve. She'd even allowed herself a few more tears as she went through her dad's things and read the big book of instructions that she'd always tried to avoid.

She'd even held a small memorial dinner with a few of her father's closest friends, which had included Harrison Delano, Peter Hunt, Diane Lewis and Senator Raleigh. They'd all claimed complete shock over Michael Brennan's part in everything, and while she didn't know if she completely believed all of them, she was happy that they had come out to pay their respects to her dad. Her father's reputation had been ripped apart in the press, but his longtime friends didn't care about that and neither did she. She'd made her peace with what her father had done. And she still loved him for being a good father, because he'd certainly done his best to be there for her in every way possible.

"Are the boxes ready to go?" Damon asked, entering the room, wearing jeans and a T-shirt, looking as sexy and appealing as ever. She wondered if she'd ever get tired of seeing him come through the door. She doubted it.

Damon had rented a truck for the day so they could not only move her father's things out of this house, but they could also move her stuff out of her apartment and his stuff out of his apartment. They had rented a new place together by the university. It was a perfect one-bedroom ground floor apartment with a small patio—an incredible find in the city. But more importantly, it had excellent air conditioning.

"What are you smiling about?" Damon asked curiously.

"You," she said. "I was thinking about our place, and how cool it will be on hot summer nights."

He grinned. "I like the AC, I must admit. But with you around, it's going to be hard to stay cool."

He was right about that. They'd had a lot of trouble keeping their hands off each other the past month. For a man who had always liked his own space, Damon had definitely grown comfortable sharing whatever space he was in with her.

"So, where's our manpower?" she asked.

"Did someone say manpower?" Wyatt asked, coming through the door, with Bree on his heels.

"I think she meant womanpower," Bree said dryly.

"I mean all power," she said with a laugh. "I really appreciate you guys helping us with all the moves. I'm sure you have better things to do on a Saturday."

"I'm just happy to not be taking another polygraph test,"

Wyatt said. "How many lie detectors do I need to beat?"

"I didn't realize that was still going on," she said with a frown.

Wyatt certainly looked a lot better than he had the first time she'd met him. He'd added a few pounds to his frame, and his face didn't look so hollow or his skin so pale. She knew he'd spent the past few weeks in grueling, long interviews helping the Bureau build their cases against the Venturis and the Belenkos, as well as Karen Leigh, who had miraculously managed to survive her injuries. In exchange for her help, Karen would probably receive a lesser sentence than the other players, but she would serve time for what she had done, and Sophie was extremely happy about that.

"Hopefully, it's almost over," Wyatt replied. "By the way, while it appears that the Belenkos will be impossible to bring to justice in this country, we're sharing some of our intel with our friends in Eastern Europe, and it looks like they may do time over there."

"That's excellent news." She'd worried that while the Belenko's US operation had been shut down, Elena's uncles were still conducting business somewhere in the Ukraine. Now, it appeared that might end as well.

"So, what are you doing, Damon?" Wyatt asked. "I hear rumors you're leaving, then you're staying, but no one seems to know for sure."

"I'm curious, too," Bree put in. "And if you want my help on moving day, I think I should get some answers. Are you going to take over the organized crime unit?"

"No, definitely not," Damon replied with a shake of his head. "I was only interested in that area because Alan asked me to work for him. I think I'd like to do something else."

"Like what?" Wyatt asked curiously.

"Not sure. I'm thinking about it. I told Peter that I haven't had a vacation in about thirteen years, so I'm going to take some time off. If he's still interested in having me on staff in September in a position we both agree on, then I'm there."

"What are you going to do until September?" Bree asked

with a grin. "Or am I getting too personal?"

Damon grinned. "Besides *that*," he said pointedly, "Sophie and I are heading to Egypt for an archaeological dig."

"Seriously?" Bree asked in surprise. "You're taking time off to dig in the dirt?"

"Real dirt for a change," he said with a happy smile. "I can't wait."

Bree shook her head in bemusement. "I don't know what you did, Sophie, but I like the new Damon."

"I didn't do a thing," she said, as Damon came over and put his arm around her. "But just for the record, I liked the old Damon, too."

Wyatt cleared his throat. "Okay, enough of the hearts and flowers, people. Are we moving boxes or what?"

"We're moving boxes," she said. "But first, what are you going to do next, Wyatt?" she asked the man, who still remained a bit of a mystery to her. "Are you going to stay in New York?"

"Nope. I'm going to London," Wyatt returned.

"What's in London?" Damon asked.

"Need to know," Wyatt said with a grin.

"Try to stay out of trouble," Damon said.

"What fun is there in that?" Wyatt retorted.

"Will you be undercover?" she asked curiously.

"Nope, not doing that for a while. What you see is what you get."

She wondered if that was true. With Wyatt, she didn't think anyone saw what he didn't want them to see.

She turned to Bree. "I hope you're staying in New York."

"I am. I love my work here. I hope to see a lot of you and Damon when you get back from your summer vacation."

"Definitely," she said. "I guess we should start taking boxes to the truck."

As Bree and Wyatt grabbed a box each and headed outside, Damon turned to her with a quizzical look in his eyes. "Everything okay, Sophie? Feeling any pangs of sadness with all of this?"

"A few," she admitted. "But not too many. This house doesn't really hold my memories. Our family home—the one we lived in when my mom was alive—was much harder to give up. But I've learned that love isn't in what we have; it's who we're with. I'm just glad I'm with you."

"Me, too." He gazed into her eyes with a tender expression. "We're going to be happy, Sophie. That might be hard to believe now—"

"It's not hard to believe at all," she interrupted. "I love you, Damon. And that's never going to change. We're good together—in the night and in the day."

He smiled. "I like mornings a lot better now when I wake up with you."

"So do I."

"I love you, too, Sophie." He kissed her and then grabbed a box. "Let's get started on the rest of our lives."

"I can't wait."

THE END

Want more
OFF THE GRID: FBI Series?

Available in 2018

Reckless Whisper (#2)
Desperate Play (#3)

Read on for an excerpt from

BEAUTIFUL STORM

the first book in Barbara's
Lightning Strikes Trilogy

Excerpt from
BEAUTIFUL STORM

Lightning Strikes Trilogy #1

© Copyright 2015 Barbara Freethy
All Rights Reserved

From #1 NY Times Bestselling Author Barbara Freethy comes the first book in a new romantic suspense trilogy: Lightning Strikes. In these connected novels, lightning leads to love, danger, and the unraveling of long-buried secrets that will change not only the past but also the future...

When her father's plane mysteriously disappeared in the middle of an electrical storm, Alicia Monroe became obsessed with lightning. Now a news photographer in Miami, Alicia covers local stories by day and chases storms at night. In a flash of lightning, she sees what appears to be a murder, but when she gets to the scene, there is no body, only a military tag belonging to Liliana Valdez, a woman who has been missing for two months.

While the police use the tag to jump-start their stalled investigation, Alicia sets off on her own to find the missing woman. Her search takes her into the heart of Miami's Cuban-American community, where she meets the attractive but brooding Michael Cordero, who has his own demons to vanquish.

Soon Alicia and Michael are not just trying to save Liliana's life but also their own, as someone will do anything to protect a dark secret...

One

The clouds had been blowing in off the ocean for the last hour, an ominous foreboding of the late September storm moving up the Miami coast. It was just past five o'clock in the afternoon, but the sky was dark as night.

Alicia Monroe drove across Florida's Rickenbacker Causeway toward Virginia Key Park, located on the island of Key Biscayne. Most of the traffic moved in the opposite direction as the island had a tendency to flood during fierce storms. According to the National Weather Service, the storm would bring at least six inches of rain plus high winds, thunder and lightning.

Alicia pressed her foot down harder on the gas. As her tires skidded on the already damp pavement, a voice inside her head told her to slow down, that a picture wasn't worth her life, but the adrenaline charging through her body made slowing down impossible.

She'd been obsessed with electrical storms all her life. She'd grown up hearing her Mayan great-grandmother speak of lightning gods. Her father had also told her tales about the incredible blue balls of fire and red flaming sprites he'd witnessed while flying for the Navy and later as a civilian pilot.

Their stories had enthralled her, but they'd been an embarrassment to the rest of the family, especially when her father had begun to tell his stories outside the family. Neither her mother nor her siblings had appreciated the fact that a former Navy hero was now being referred to as *Lightning Man.*

A wave of pain ran through her at the memories of her father and the foolish nickname that had foreshadowed her dad's tragic death years later in a fierce electrical storm.

She'd been sixteen years old when he'd taken his last flight. It was supposed to be a typical charter run to drop a hunting party in the mountains and then return home, but after dropping the men at their destination, her father's plane had run into a massive storm. When the rain stopped and the sun came back out, there was no sign of her father or his plane. He'd quite simply disappeared somewhere over the Gulf of Mexico.

Everyone assumed he'd crashed. They'd sent out search parties to find him or at least pieces of the plane, but those searches had returned absolutely nothing. How a man and a small plane could completely vanish seemed impossible to accept, and she'd spent years trying to find an answer, but so far that hadn't happened.

What had happened was her increasingly obsessive fascination with storm photography.

Her sister Danielle thought she was looking for her dad in every flash of lightning. Her brother Jake thought she was crazy, and her mother Joanna just wanted her to stop challenging Mother Nature by running headlong into dangerous storms. But like her dad, Alicia didn't run away from storms; she ran toward them.

While she worked as a photojournalist for the *Miami Chronicle* to pay the rent, her true passion was taking photographs of lightning storms and displaying them on her website and in a local art gallery.

It was possible that she was looking for the truth about her dad's disappearance in the lightning, or that she just had a screw loose. It was also possible that she was tempting fate by her constant pursuit of dangerous storms, but even if that was all true, she couldn't stop, not yet, not until she knew...something. She just wasn't sure what that *something* was.

Her cell phone rang through her car, yanking her mind back to reality. "Hello?"

"Where are you?" Jeff Barkley asked.

"Almost to the park." Jeff was the weather reporter at the local television station and had become her best resource for storm chasing.

"Turn around, Alicia. The National Weather Service is predicting the possibility of a ten-to-fifteen-foot storm surge, which would make the causeway impassable, and you'll be stranded on the island."

"I'll get the lightning shots before that happens. How's the storm shaping up?"

"Severe thunderstorms predicted."

"Great."

"It's not great, Alicia."

"You know what I mean," she grumbled. She didn't wish ill on anyone. But the more magnificent the storm, the better her pictures would be.

"You keep pushing the limits. One of these days, you'll go too far," Jeff warned.

"That won't be today. It's barely drizzling yet. The island is the perfect place to capture the storm in two places—over the ocean and then as it passes over Miami. Don't worry, I'll be fine."

"You always say that."

"And it's always true."

"So far. Text me when you get back."

"I will."

Ending the call, she drove into the parking lot. The attendant booth was closed, and a sign said the park was closed, but there was no barrier to prevent her from entering the lot.

She parked as close as she could to the trail leading into the park. She'd no sooner shut down the engine and turned off her headlights when lightning lit up the sky. She rolled down her window and took a few quick shots with her digital camera. She didn't have a great angle, so she would definitely have to find a higher point in the park to get a better picture.

Putting her digital camera on the console, she grabbed her waterproof backpack that held her more expensive film camera and got out of the car.

The force of the wind whipped her long, brown ponytail around her face. She pulled the hood of her raincoat over her head. It was just misting at the moment, but the sky would be opening up very soon. With tall rain boots and a long coat to protect her jeans and knit shirt, she was protected from the elements, not that she worried much about getting wet. She was more concerned with keeping her equipment dry until she needed to use it.

This was her second trip to the island, so she knew exactly which path to take, and she headed quickly in that direction. While the trails were popular with walkers, hikers, and bikers on most days, there wasn't another soul in sight. Anyone with any sense had left the park to seek shelter.

She was used to shooting storms in dark, shadowy places, but for some reason her nerves were tighter than usual today. The air was thick, almost crackling, and the atmosphere was dark and eerie. She felt a little spooked, as if someone were watching her.

A crash in the trees behind her brought her head around, and her heart skipped a beat at the dancing shadows behind her.

A second later, she saw two raccoons scurry into the woods, and she blew out a breath of relief. The animals were just looking for shelter. Everything was fine.

Ten minutes of a rapid jog had her heart pounding and her breath coming fast as she traversed the hilly section of the park, finally reaching the clearing at the top of the trail. Instead of thick brush and trees, she was now looking at the churning waves of the Atlantic Ocean. But it wasn't the sea that sent a nervous shiver down her spine; it was the towering, tall clouds that the meteorologists called cumulonimbus clouds. These clouds were associated with thunder and lightning storms and atmospheric instability. Alicia felt both terrified and entranced by the potential fury of the stormy sky.

She pulled out her film camera. While she used digital more often these days, there was still nothing like capturing a storm on film.

She took several quick consecutive shots as lightning cracked over the ocean. She checked her watch, noting the lapse of fifteen seconds before the thunder boomed. That meant the lightning was about three miles away.

Eight seconds later, lightning split apart the clouds, jagged bolts heading toward the beach. The storm was moving in fast—the lightning less than a mile away now.

She had a feeling she knew where it would strike next.

Dashing down the adjacent trail, she headed toward the old carousel with the shiny gold decorative rods that would more than likely attract the lightning.

As she moved through the thick brush, the rain began to come down harder, but she didn't slow her pace. She just wiped the water from her eyes and kept going.

When lightning lit up the park in front of her, she raised her camera and snapped two more photos before venturing farther down the trail. The carousel was just ahead.

The thunder was so loud it almost knocked her off of her feet.

She stopped abruptly as another jagged streak of lightning hit the carousel, illuminating the area around it.

Captured in the glaringly bright light were a man and a woman engaged in a struggle.

The man raised his hand, something metal glinting between his fingers. A knife?

The woman screamed.

Alicia took a step forward, but the light disappeared and everything was dark again. She juggled her phone, trying to turn on the flashlight so she could see where to go.

Another boom of thunder.

Another flash of lightning.

She saw more dancing shadows. Then heard a long, penetrating scream. Closer now. The woman seemed to be running toward her.

She needed to help her. She moved down the path, stumbling over some rocks, and then the lightning came again. The tree next to her exploded from the strike. A heavy branch flew through the air, knocking her flat on the ground. She hit her head on a rock, feeling a flash of pain that threatened to take her under.

She battled against the feeling, knowing she had to get away from the fire that was crackling around her.

Where the hell was the rain now?

It was still coming down but not enough to smother the fire.

She got to her feet, ruthlessly fighting her way through the flaming branches.

Finally, the skies opened up, and the rain poured down, putting out the fire and allowing her to get free.

She grabbed her backpack from under a branch and moved down the trail.

Using her flashlight again, she walked toward the carousel, her tension increasing with each step, but there was no one around. No man, no woman, no knife, no struggle. What the hell had happened? Where had they gone?

She looked around in bewilderment. It had only been a few minutes since she'd seen them—hadn't it? Or had she lost consciousness when the tree had knocked her down?

She didn't think so, but her mind felt hazy and her head ached.

Despite the fuzzy feeling, she couldn't forget the image of the tall man towering over the smaller woman. She could still hear the woman's scream of terror in her head.

She turned slowly around, seeing nothing of significance in the shadowy surroundings. Then something in the dirt brought her gaze to the ground. She squatted down and picked up a shiny, rectangular military ID tag.

Her stomach turned over. She had a tag just like this in her jewelry box at home, the tag that had belonged to her father.

But it wasn't her father's name on this tag; it was a woman's name: Liliana Valdez, United States Navy, blood type O positive, religion Catholic. Her birth date indicated that she was twenty-eight.

The name didn’t mean anything to Alicia, but she still felt an odd connection to the woman who'd lost it. Had it been the woman she'd seen fighting for her life? Had that woman been wearing a uniform?

She couldn't remember. She had the sense that the woman had worn a long, dark coat, but the details escaped her. Maybe she'd caught them on film. That thought took her to her feet.

She needed to get home and develop the photographs. She walked quickly back to the parking lot, pausing for just a moment to get a few more shots of the lightning now streaking across the Miami skyline.

Then she got into her car and sped toward the causeway, hoping she hadn't waited too long to cross before the storm surge made the bridge impassable.

When she reached the bridge, water was splashing over the rail, but she made it back to Miami without incident. She felt relieved to be in the city, but the pain in her temple reminded her of what she'd seen by the carousel. Who were those people? Had something terrible happened? Had she been a witness to…what?

Alicia's gaze dropped to the ID tag sitting on her console—to the name Liliana Valdez. She needed to find Liliana; not just to return her tag but also to make sure she was all right, that she was still alive.

Alicia lived in the Wynwood Art District, a neighborhood just north of downtown Miami and known for its art galleries, boutiques and charming cafés. She lived on the second floor of a two-story building, and the bottom floor housed the art gallery where she displayed her storm photographs.

The owner of Peterman Art Gallery, Eileen Peterman, had leased her the apartment a year earlier, and Alicia was happy to be close to the gallery and in a neighborhood filled with artists and designers. She'd always been more comfortable among creative people who thought outside of the box, colored beyond the lines, and who put their emotions on display, whether it be in a sculpture or a painting or a photograph. She'd never been able to trust anyone who hid their emotions. It always made her wonder what else they were hiding.

After entering her apartment, Alicia dropped her backpack on the floor, set her keys and the ID tag on the side table, and then took off her wet raincoat and hung it on a hook by the door. She kicked off her boots and walked into the bathroom to grab a towel.

After drying her face, she pulled out the band from her hair and ran the blow-dryer through the damp dark tangles of her unruly mass of dark brown waves. Her hair was thick and long, drifting past her shoulder blades, and it was a constant battle to straighten the rebellious curls, which had gotten more out of hand in the wind and the rain.

As she stared at her face in the mirror, she was a little

surprised at the size of the bump on her throbbing forehead. It was turning a lovely shade of purple and black and definitely stood out against her unusually pale skin. A dark-eyed brunette with olive skin, she usually had a vibrant, exotic look about her, but today was not one of those days. What little makeup she'd put on earlier that day had washed away in the rain, and the pain of her aching head injury had put strained lines around her eyes.

She set down the dryer, grabbed some ibuprofen from the medicine cabinet, took two capsules, and told herself she'd feel a lot better in about thirty minutes. Then she walked back to the living room.

She picked up Liliana's ID tag and took it over to the kitchen table. Opening her laptop computer, she typed in Liliana's name, age, and birth date. The Valdez surname would be common in Miami, a city made up of thousands of Cuban and Puerto Rican immigrants, so she was expecting her search to be complicated and long.

Surprisingly, it was neither.

The headline of the first article jumped off the page: *JAG attorney missing in Miami.*

As she read through the news story, she discovered that Liliana Valdez, a Navy lieutenant and attorney with the Judge Advocate General, had gone missing while visiting Miami in late July for the wedding of her sister. She'd last been seen in the parking lot outside of Paladar, a popular Cuban restaurant in Little Havana. The vehicle she'd been driving had been recovered from the parking lot, but there was no sign of a struggle or any other clues to her whereabouts.

Alicia let out a breath and sat back on the couch, staring out the window where rain now streamed against the panes.

Liliana Valdez had disappeared two months ago, and no one had seen her since.

Alicia picked up the ID tag, still a little damp and gritty with dirt, and ran her fingers over Liliana's name, feeling the same sense of connection she'd felt earlier.

She had a clue to a missing woman. She needed to take it to the police.

Jumping to her feet, she paused, struck by the thought that she might have more than one clue. Retrieving her camera, she took it into the walk-in closet off her bedroom that she'd turned into her personal darkroom.

Unfortunately, as the pictures developed, Alicia's enthusiasm began to fade.

The couple she'd seen by the carousel did not appear in any of the shots. The lightning was spectacular, but it was so close, so bright, it was impossible to see anything but shadows beyond the light, certainly nothing that clearly defined a person, which meant she had no other clue besides the military tag. Still, it was something. Hopefully, it would be enough to help find the missing woman.

END OF EXCERPT

Get the complete trilogy:

Beautiful Storm (#1)

Lightning Lingers (#2)

Summer Rain (#3)

About The Author

Barbara Freethy is a #1 New York Times Bestselling Author of 65 novels ranging from contemporary romance to romantic suspense and women's fiction. Traditionally published for many years, Barbara opened her own publishing company in 2011 and has since sold over 7 million books! Twenty of her titles have appeared on the New York Times and USA Today Bestseller Lists.

Known for her emotional and compelling stories of love, family, mystery and romance, Barbara enjoys writing about ordinary people caught up in extraordinary adventures. Barbara's books have won numerous awards. She is a six-time finalist for the RITA for best contemporary romance from Romance Writers of America and a two-time winner for DANIEL'S GIFT and THE WAY BACK HOME.

Barbara has lived all over the state of California and currently resides in Northern California where she draws much of her inspiration from the beautiful bay area.

For a complete listing of books, as well as excerpts and contests, and to connect with Barbara:

Visit Barbara's Website:
www.barbarafreethy.com

Join Barbara on Facebook:
www.facebook.com/barbarafreethybooks

Follow Barbara on Twitter:
www.twitter.com/barbarafreethy

CPSIA information can be obtained
at www.ICGtesting.com
Printed in the USA
LVOW03s0117150917
548554LV00002B/8/P